UNDER
THE
FADING
SKY

CYNTHIA KADOHATA

UNDER THE FADING SKY

A CAITLYN DLOUHY BOOK

atheneum

NEW YORK · AMSTERDAM/ANTWERP
LONDON · TORONTO
SYDNEY/MELBOURNE · NEW DELHI

atheneum

An imprint of Simon & Schuster Children's Publishing Division
1230 Avenue of the Americas, New York, New York 10020

For information about special discounts for bulk purchases, please contact Simon & Schuster
Special Sales at 1-866-506-1949 or business@simonandschuster.com.
Simon & Schuster strongly believes in freedom of expression and stands against censorship in all
its forms. For more information, visit BooksBelong.com.
The Simon & Schuster Speakers Bureau can bring authors to your live event. For more information
or to book an event, contact the Simon & Schuster Speakers Bureau at 1-866-248-3049 or visit our
website at www.simonspeakers.com.
The text for this book was set in Sabon Next LT.
Manufactured in the United States of America
First Edition
2 4 6 8 10 9 7 5 3 1
Library of Congress Cataloging-in-Publication Data
Names: Kadohata, Cynthia, author.
Title: Under the fading sky / Cynthia Kadohata.
Description: First edition. | New York : Atheneum Books for Young Readers, 2025. | Audience
term: Teenagers | Audience: Ages 14 up. | Audience: Grades 10–12. | Summary: "Sixteen-year-old
Elijah thinks his vaping habit is harmless until it becomes a crippling addiction of nightmarish
dimensions"—Provided by publisher.
Identifiers: LCCN 2024033509 (print) | LCCN 2024033510 (ebook) | ISBN 9781534482395
(hardcover) | ISBN 9781534482418 (ebook)
Subjects: CYAC: Vaping—Fiction. | Substance abuse—Fiction. | Friendship—Fiction. | Family life—
Fiction. | Japanese Americans—Fiction. | California—Fiction.
Classification: LCC PZ7.K1166 Un 2025 (print) | LCC PZ7.K1166 (ebook) | DDC [Fic]—dc23
LC record available at https://lccn.loc.gov/2024033509
LC ebook record available at https://lccn.loc.gov/2024033510

FOR SAMUEL FINLAY

UNDER THE THE FADING SKY

ONE

So the difference between humans and demons is not as big as you might think. Sometimes you can't really tell which is which just by looking. In fact, sometimes I even walk into a random store and wonder exactly what kind of person, like, the salesclerk is. Good or evil? I know this sounds crazy, but let me explain. The first time I realized I wasn't sure who or what I was talking to, it was like I felt out of balance. "Discombobulated" was the word me and Lee Fang decided on. It was when him, me, Banker, and Davis were buying drugs at some dude's house, which was in this normal neighborhood in Playa del Sol, about forty minutes from downtown Los Angeles. You know, nice lawn, with an olive tree out front like you see all over—those trees with complicated, twisting trunks. They're really cool, the way they always look so old even when they're small. I'm kinda obsessed with old stuff and history, because I legit was born in the wrong era.

Anyway, the neighborhood was so normal that it could've been a set in *The Truman Show*—which I never watched but I know the story. The movie's about a guy who's living in a reality show but doesn't know it. There's a big set that he lives in, and he thinks it's the real world. One day Lee and I were high and talking about how even though Truman lived in a set, it was still *his* reality, right? Otherwise, you could make a case that just about everybody is living in a set. What I mean to say is, once you've met a demon, you realize just about nobody you know truly lives in reality—they have *no idea* of the really bad stuff that's out there.

So, this house we were at looked hypernormal. As in, the kind of house a richer Truman might live in. White with a few stone steps and a big plant on either side of the door. I paused. It was January, drizzling a little, and I looked up and let the cool mist hit my face. A bunch of crows did that thing they do, when they all cry out at once, some landing on electric cables, some swirling around. The other guys were now a few steps ahead of me, so I sped up. I decided to make sure we were at the right place. "Banker, dude . . . you sure this is the right house?"

"Dude, it's the address I have."

"You've never been here before?" I asked.

"Nah."

Lee and I looked at each other. Then Banker rang the bell, and a few seconds later a little girl answered the door. Lee and I looked at each other again.

The girl said, "Daddy's peeing," then giggled like she knew she wasn't supposed to tell us that.

Then a man came out, a big guy with a big face and big hands. "Thanks, sweetie," he said to the little girl. He looked at her with that expression I'd seen my parents give me: unconditional love. He was a total dad. *Total.* Which was weird since we were there to buy drugs from him. He led us into an office, indicated for us to sit down. The couch wasn't that big, so I sat on an arm. He rummaged in a drawer, placed a baggie of pills—Banker had said they would be Percocets—on his desk, and looked at us. And I kid you not, when he looked at us, I thought I was gonna puke. It was like he'd just turned into something else, which I realized later was a demon.

"I didn't expect you boys to be Asian," he said. He was messing with something below the desk where we couldn't see.

I thought he meant because we were the model minority or some stuff like that, so he was surprised we did drugs. Plus, I had my glasses on that day instead of contacts, so maybe I was looking studious. Then he stood up, and his, uh, *thing* was hanging out, and he said, "I never got head from an Asian kid before."

I heard a kind of snort, I think from Davis. It was one of those moments, like right before you crash on your skateboard or bike, where you're thinking *Oh, shit*, but there's nothing you can do. Nobody moved, because I guess we all knew we should be cool—the last thing I wanted was to get this big guy alarmed. I mean, didn't drug dealers have guns? Then I glanced at Banker; Lee and Davis were also looking at him. Because this was Banker's deal.

Banker quickly said, "We have money."

The guy looked genuinely surprised. "Oh, money!" he said pleasantly. He zipped up his pants. "That's good too. I take money as well—sorry for the misunderstanding."

And just like that, he seemed like a totally normal guy again. He seemed like a *dad*.

Do you ever ask yourself, *Wait, what just happened*? That's what I was asking myself as I replayed the last two minutes in my head.

"All good," Banker said calmly. He gave the guy two hundred dollars from the money we'd stolen earlier. The guy handed Banker the baggie and said, "This is guaranteed straight from the medical clinic." We started to leave.

"By the way," the man said, so we stopped. He took three long strides to where I was and laid his right middle finger on my forearm. "Study hard," he said.

It was like I could feel heat coming out of his finger, not regular heat, but dry-ice kind of heat, if you've ever accidentally touched dry ice. Blank face for me, though; I kept myself totally blank inside and out. "Uh, yeah," I said. "See ya." Then as I moved through the doorway, I added, "Or not." I made a mental note not to wear glasses next time I bought drugs, which you can say wasn't an entirely rational mental note to make at that moment. But if you haven't been there, all I can tell you is that you react the way you react.

On the way to the car I gave Lee my best WTF look. But blank face from Lee. Davis was looking curiously at me for some reason. I felt anger rising up. "Banker, you coulda warned us."

He glared at me, turned away. "It was a misunderstanding, okay? Stop acting like a kid."

"Well, I am a kid," I shot back.

Lee frowned at me. But he took a couple of long breaths, and I could see he was shook like I was.

Lee and I walked around the car to the passenger side. "I know, I'm discombobulated too," he said quietly. "Because do you think the high-class dealers are two people in the same person?"

"That's what I was thinking!" I said urgently to him. "He's a dad AND a demon."

Banker liked Lee to ride with him in front, so I sat in back with Davis, who was a quiet kid from a different school. All four of us were different ages: Banker oldest at eighteen, Lee next at seventeen, me sixteen, and Davis fifteen. I didn't know how Davis knew Banker, but then, who cared?

As Banker hopped onto the freeway, I tried to wash that guy out of my thoughts. I searched my mind for something to make sense of our lives. All I could come up with was the words of another big man with big hands, a celebrity chef guy named Anthony Bourdain who I'd never heard of until he killed himself in a hotel room. To be honest, I didn't even know what a "celebrity chef" was exactly. But anyway, in his last interview this chef guy said, "There are forces out there who are really fucking powerful and scary." The interviewer herself said they'd talked about "the powerful forces of evil arrayed against decent people." That interview, which I'd filed away in my brain, now made something click inside me. All of a sudden, I wondered what was up. Like, in the world.

I thought about that as we drove, and about whether it was possible to be two different people. Or more accurately, a person and an *entity* rolled into one body. I felt like that guy could put his little girl to bed with a kiss and could also put one of those hands on someone's face and stop them from breathing. I felt, in short, that he was a force out there who was really fucking powerful and scary.

So that was my first experience with how weird and at the same time how normal some of these demons are. Which kind of makes them even more demonic. Some of them live in regular houses and all. So if the people who lived next door to that guy didn't know he was a dealer and a perv, weren't they kind of living in a set? Because they didn't even know the reality going on right next door to them. It looked like a "nice" street, as my mom would say. "Good trees," as my dad would say.

I leaned forward toward Lee in the front passenger seat, and what came out of my mouth was, "Do you ever wonder what we're all doing here?"

"Shut the fuck up with that shit," Banker snapped at me.

Lee turned all the way around to look at me. "Doing here right now, or here in general?"

"Both," I said.

"I think guys used to fit in better with the world, and now we don't. Maybe it's technology that changed us," Lee said. "More likely it's the end of time."

Lee was a doomer? That was news to me.

"It is what it is," Banker said. He floored it for a few seconds, for no reason, and we all jerked forward when he slowed down again.

I glanced at Davis. He shrugged. "I guess . . . it is what it is."

I've never understood what people mean by that. Of course it is what it is. It seems like what it really means is: "Don't think, move on." Which is sometimes maybe good advice. The problem was that Lee and I, we liked to think about stuff. That was literally our thing.

Then at a stoplight Banker handed each of us three Percocets. Which wasn't entirely fair since it looked like he had about twenty in the baggie. But I popped one into my mouth and gulped water from my bottle. My mom was texting me that dinner was ready and everybody was waiting. I texted that I would be right there. When I pressed the send arrow, I looked up suddenly: I'd just had the thought, *Well, here I am kind of being two people in the same person—one with these guys, and one with my family.*

The guys dropped me off at my home in Rocosa Beach. It's a town south of Los Angeles, but my family didn't live on the beach. We'd stepped up a lot in the world, but not enough to live too near the water.

When I got inside, everybody was already at the dining room table, all staring at me as I walked over. Not in a bad way, but still, it felt awkward. I went to join my family with my two pills in my pocket. Still feeling discombobulated.

I smiled at everyone. Mom, Dad, Grandma, Grandpa, and Joshie, who was five, all lit up at my smile. Everybody loved me! My dog, Kiiro, had met me at the door and followed me to the dining room. My mom beamed, and as I sat down, she said, "Why don't you say grace, Elijah?"

Which was freaky right there, because we hadn't said grace since Thanksgiving, and I had said it then as well. It was like she somehow knew I needed to be purified or something. On the other hand, it coulda just been that I didn't have a clue what was going on.

I licked my dry lips. "Um. Dear God, thank you for the—" I glanced at the table. Dinner was covered up, but I saw my mom's special lasagna dish, and it smelled like lasagna. "Thank you for the lasagna." Which I meant sincerely—she made awesome lasagna. And suddenly, I was really feeling it! "Dear God, thank you for the lasagna! I mean it! Sometimes I just look at dinner, and I feel like . . . like I just *love* this world, and I'm glad I'm *here* instead of somewhere else, because I *know* there are other places I could be that would be *incredibly crappy* and that there are a whole lotta people in those crappy places, and there's not enough food there. I'm *here*, though. I'm *here*. And I haven't really had hard times yet, thanks to you, and ..." I looked up, and everybody was staring at me with their mouths open. I looked down and quickly mumbled, "Amen."

"What a lovely prayer," Grandma said. Now *she* beamed at me, really proudly, like I'd just given the Nobel Peace Prize speech or something. Which was nice, I guess.

"Help yourself," Mom encouraged us.

And we did what we always did when my grandparents were over for dinner, which was that Grandma scooped out food onto Grandpa's plate and then put food on her own plate and passed the food to her left, which was my mom. We'd been doing this for years in the same order. For reals, I never had a stronger feeling than I did that night that I was living in a set.

Meanwhile I grabbed some salad. As I reached out, I noticed the place on my arm where the dealer had touched me. He'd touched me *for no reason*. He'd just reached out with his big finger and laid it on my skin for about one second. Now it was like I could sense a mark on my skin, only I couldn't actually see anything. But I knew the exact place. It still felt like touching dry ice in that little spot. That seemed strange, so I thought about getting up to scrub that spot with soap. But I didn't. Later I thought I should have. Later I thought if I had washed off my arm, everything would've turned out different. Somehow.

Except for Grandpa, we all waited for everybody to be served before we started eating. But Grandpa plunged his fork into the lasagna as soon as it hit his plate. I think he would feel super bad if he ever noticed that the rest of us always waited until everybody had their food before we started eating. But he never noticed, because he was eighty. I mean, I guess when you're eighty and you're hungry, you're just focusing on your plate and not even thinking about anything else. He was a really nice dude, though. An OG if ever there was one.

Watching his wrinkled, hairy hand raise the fork to his mouth, I suddenly felt kind of tired, not sleepy tired, but tired like I wasn't sure how I was ever gonna be able to make all the effort it took to get to eighty. I used to think it'd be easy. But now I had a sense that it was going to be very, very hard. Only this morning it hadn't felt that way.

I ate a couple of bites and asked, "Does anyone ever think about the past, like how you miss it?"

I was actually asking the grown-ups, but Joshie answered. "Bro! Just this morning I thought about that time we played Uno for an hour, and I won every game. I miss that."

"Bro, that was only a few weeks ago," I answered.

"Bro, I know!"

I had taught him to say "dude" and "bro" and "homie." Mom had taught him kiddie Japanese words, like *shi-shi* and *unko* (pee and poop) and all the numbers up to a hundred—*ichi*, *ni*, *san*, *shi*, *go*, *roku*, and so on. And I'd taught him to say, "I got ya, homie."

I tried to make him say it now, just for fun. "Joshie, you know you should eat some salad, right?"

"I got ya, homie," he said in his squeaky voice, and reached for the salad bowl.

Then Mom said, "As far as missing the past, I think that happens more when you're older."

And Dad said, "There are things I look back on and think I would have done differently."

"Yeah, that too," I said. "I'm starting to feel that way."

"Ohhh?" said my mom, leaning forward to study me more closely. She squinted right at my eyes.

I glanced at my plate and said, "Great lasagna, Mom." Then, for good measure, I stuffed some in my mouth, chewed twice, and added, "Mmm, really great!"

She brightened up and started talking about how she'd found the recipe on a website that sometimes had good recipes with so-so reviews and sometimes had bad recipes with good reviews, and there was another time she found a recipe that had only four stars, but she'd tweaked it a bit and . . .

It was confusing sometimes how parents could be so easy to manipulate—all I had to do was say the word "lasagna" and Mom was onto some whole thing about recipes and websites and reviews. Do you ever wonder how your parents even got as far as they have? Because I think about that all the time. How did we even, like, own a house in Rocosa Beach? Was life just easier back when they were young, and all you had to do was go to school and get decent grades, get married, start a contracting business like my dad did, have kids, and then magically get the money to buy a house? And it all went pretty smooth-like?

I mean, I knew everybody had hard times, and there were probably demon-people all throughout history, but it seemed like life must have been pretty easy for parents, and they never ran into bad people, and even when they were kids, they must have never lied, or else why did they believe *anything you said*? That is, how did they survive if they were so gullible? Later I realized that they just wanted *so bad* to believe good things about you. And they would pretty much do anything in the world if they could make those good things be true.

TWO

Later that night, after meeting the high-class perv, I lay in bed listening to what was now a hard rain. I got up and went to my open window, watched the water pummel our small backyard. I mean, do you ever watch the rain pummel your backyard and kind of just think? Do you think about some bad stuff you might have done, like when you were little and didn't know better, or the year before when you maybe 75 percent knew better, or maybe even that same day when you totally did know better? Because lately I'd been doing that kind of thing a lot. You know, to figure it all out.

I pulled my chair away from my desk, turned off my lights, stared out at the downpour, and went to that place—the "file" in my brain—when Joshie was born, when I was eleven. That seemed to me the time when everything kind of began. Obviously I was alive before that, but it was like nothing had really *begun* yet. My story, I mean. I'm gonna tell it all to you now.

I was at the hospital that night, in the waiting room in an orange chair with a book. I was reading a novel by Philip K.

Dick that some of the guys had gotten into, because it was really trippy sci-fi that made sense and also made no sense. They made movies of some of his books, but the movies made more sense. I liked the books better.

But it was hard to concentrate, because I'd just learned a couple of hours ago that my mom had to "push the baby out." Which seemed kind of crazy. I'd thought a doctor was just going to take it out.

I was alone. I guess nobody else was having a baby at that moment. There was a clock on the wall that said it was two o'clock. As in, a.m. I fell asleep, and when I woke up, my grandpa was leaning over me grinning like he might have lost his mind, in a good way. "Would you like to see your new brother?"

I dropped my book and picked it back up, saying, "Sure! Sure thing! Really, he's here?"

So I followed him, and he held open a door as I walked in. My mom was in bed holding my new brother, Joshua Haruto Jensen. Haruto means "soar" or "fly." It was my great-grandmother's idea to name him that. I gaped: he had so much hair! It was like a black wig on his head. I reached out and touched his face, but he didn't notice, because he was in his own little world.

My dad said, "Crazy hair, huh?"

His hair! I mean, wow. I tugged softly to make sure it was real—I actually had the thought that everybody was pranking me. But nope, it was real. And suddenly, I felt all this responsibility. It was shocking, though, because until this moment all I'd had to do was clean my room and get all A's. I washed the car a couple of times too, but it wasn't a regular job. And now I was a big brother! I mean, I knew my parents were responsible for him. I also knew a lot of kids keep secrets from their parents, but sometimes they'll tell their older brothers or sisters, who then have to give them advice. If my brother needed to tell somebody his secrets, that would be on me. So I touched his face again and thought about what to say and came up with "Don't worry." On account of he was suddenly frowning.

There was another thing: his eyes were kind of far apart. Not a lot, but it was noticeable. "Don't worry," I said again. His eyes fell briefly on me, but he didn't exactly seem to see me. He made a noise almost like a quack. Then he made it again, except louder. He was looking right at me, so I nodded.

Next thing, Grandpa said, "Come on, bud. I guess I'm bunking at your place tonight."

"Really?"

"Yep."

I hugged Mom and Dad goodbye, then leaned over and pecked Joshua on the top of his wild-man hair. He looked like a little Neanderthal.

Grandpa and I walked quietly out of the hospital, me walking double-time to keep up with him. He always did this striding thing almost like he was in a cartoon. The parking lot was dark, cool, nearly empty. "He's a good one," Grandpa said as he started the car.

"Yeah, I like his hair a lot," I said. I thought a moment. "But he was frowning. Do you think he's okay?"

Grandpa chuckled. "Oh, you should've seen yourself. We didn't think you were ever going to stop crying!"

I wanted to think about that, but I suddenly felt exhausted. It was hard work having a baby!

My parents and I lived in an apartment in Lombard back

then. You know, the palm trees, the metal gate for a front door into the complex, the two-feet-wide balconies on each apartment where people put plants.

I have no idea why, but the buzzer system for the building was broken, so if you rang the front doorbell, nobody would let you in because they didn't know you were out front. That woulda been okay on account of, you know, *keys*. Also, cell phones. However, for the last two weeks the lock had been loose, and nobody's keys worked. Where was the landlord? Well, if you ever figure that out, let me know. So if the person you were calling didn't answer their phone, and nobody else in the building was going in or out, you had to go around the building as close as you could to wherever your place was and yell.

Grandma was staying with us that night "getting things ready," so I said to Grandpa, "I'll go." I went around to the side of the building by where our third-floor window was and bellowed, "I'm home! Elijah here! Grandma, home!" Nothing happened, so even though it was the middle of the night, I had to yell again, because otherwise we'd have to spend the night in the car. "Grandma, it's Elijah! Home, Grandma! Home!"

Finally, a light turned on. It wasn't our light, but a neighbor we didn't know stuck his head out and said, "Got ya, bro!"

So I went around front, and the neighbor let us in. We fist-bumped and Grandpa said, "Thank you, young man." Even though the guy looked like he was fifty.

The guy answered, "What's up with the landlord, man? Who's in charge here, anyway?"

I trudged up the stairs and into our apartment and to my room and lay in bed and felt the great and awful responsibility of being a big brother. Actually, it was a good feeling. I was pretty sure I was gonna be at least an A- at it. Maybe even an A+. I was a solid skateboarder, and I was going to get a mountain bike at some point, which I would be really good at by the time Joshua was old enough to ride. Also, I got good grades. In short, I could teach him a lot of stuff.

I had these supposed blackout curtains, but streetlight streamed in through the cracks. I started to drift off, thinking, *Do you ever wonder what would happen if they called products by accurate names? Like, instead of "blackout curtains," they could say "supposed blackout curtains."* Then I fell asleep.

When Joshie came home a couple days later, Grandma stayed on to help my mom out while my dad worked. And just like that, I was no longer the little kid of the family. Dad worked a lot, because his contracting business was doing really well. It was doing super well. In fact, we were about to move into a house in a pretty rich neighborhood. Not the richest, but pretty rich. That is, a neighborhood where for sure everybody's doorbell and keys worked. We'd already bought the house and moved a lot of our stuff. I was stoked, because I was going to get my first dog. I had already picked him out. He was a three-year-old yellow Lab, and he was being fostered by a family in Torrance.

We stayed at our apartment for two more weeks. I gotta say, it started to seem crowded with a new baby, Grandma and Grandpa over a lot, and other friends and family coming to see the baby. Some days when it got too crowded, I went downstairs and sat just inside the metal front door. I wasn't allowed outside, on account of there was a "cocktail lounge" near where we lived, plus a 7-Eleven that had gotten robbed a couple of times. But there was an old chair near the entrance for some reason, and I liked to sit there and look out the metal grating and see some of the people my mom thought were sketchy. I saw a guy getting mugged once, and I yelled out, "Hey!" The mugger glanced at me and ran away. I got scared that he could've seen what I looked like through the grating, so I rushed back upstairs.

Dad worked almost every moment he was awake, and whenever he got home, I'd hear him yell out, "Justin is home! It's Justin! Justin is home!" I think he enjoyed that, because he coulda just called our cell phones. But I loved to run down to let him in, and as we walked up the stairs, he would say things like, "It's one of those clients who look over your shoulder every second." Or, "Two guys called in sick today."

Then one day Dad drove me, my mom, and Joshie to our new house. I'd already seen it and been amazed. We didn't have a pool, and our yard was mostly a sloping hill, but it was *ours*. And it was beautiful. I seriously felt like a rock star living there. And I got my new dog!

He knew right away he was mine too. He followed me everywhere the very first day we brought him home. I named him Kiiro, which means "yellow." So there I was: new brother, new dog, new house. My mom bought two nectarine trees, and she planted them in the backyard. This didn't thrill me, because there wasn't much to our yard, and nectarine trees grow big. On the other hand, the trees made her so happy, you would've thought I'd just gotten a guaranteed spot at Stanford or something. I would peek outside and see her standing there looking and looking at the trees. Even though they were mostly bare branches. Sometimes her lips were moving, so I guess she was talking to them? She loved those trees so much, Dad said he was getting jealous.

I think he was kidding?

THREE

A few weeks later, I was feeling good about things when I walked into sixth-grade homeroom at my new school. New house, new dog, first-rate little brother. I mean, I was nervous because I was new, but then when I walked into the room, I spotted a few Asian guys sitting together. So I headed in that direction. There was an open seat. "This free?" I asked.

"Sure," one of them said.

I sat down, laying my backpack on the desk.

"Cool backpack," the boy said. "I'm Anthony Chin." Anthony's glasses were falling down his nose, so he pushed them up. Then he pushed them up again.

My backpack had waves of green on the bottom. On top it was black with a picture of an alien in the upper-right corner.

"Aliens are real. I'm Logan Ho," another boy said, and we knocked fists. He had hair down to his shoulders and wire-rimmed glasses.

"Elijah Jensen." I paused, then added, "I'm hapa." Hapa is half Asian, half white—at least, that was the way my family used the term.

"My half sister is hapa," another boy said. His hair spiked up like mine. "I'm Ben Matsumoto."

I paused, tried to decide what to say next. "Yeah, I think aliens are real," I said. "But why aren't they either helping us or killing us?" Anthony kept pushing up his glasses, which made me extra aware of my own, so I pushed them up my nose.

Ben stretched his back. "Dude, you're thinking like a human. Maybe they've already conquered us. How would we even know?"

We all looked at him. "Wow," I replied. "That's a good point." I pondered that while the seats filled up. If aliens got all the way to Earth, they were for sure smarter than us. I subscribed to an online newsletter called "The Long Night." It was about how artificial intelligence would be able to study what we did online, and pretty soon it would know exactly what kind of content to show us to shape our thoughts and make us have specific beliefs and opinions. And we wouldn't even know they weren't ours. So like propaganda, except personalized. Maybe the aliens were already doing that, making us believe stuff just for kicks?

The teacher hadn't come in yet, so I told the guys my thoughts about this. "What if I'm not even Elijah? You know?"

They all stared for a minute. Logan put his hair behind his ears. Anthony pushed up his glasses. Ben ruffled his spiked hair. "Maybe we're being farmed. But for what?" Ben asked.

Logan just said, "Cool, Elijah." He high-fived me.

"I see what you mean," Anthony said. "I could be you, and you could be me."

The teacher walked in then. She wrote her name on the board: Ms. Lawrence.

"Good morning, class."

"Good morning, Ms. Lawrence."

She smiled with teeth. People who smile with teeth when there's no reason are phony. My grandpa told me that, and why would he lie? Ms. Lawrence was a middle-aged white lady in blue polka-dot pants and a white blouse. "I treat everybody the same, and I hold everybody to the same high standards. My pronouns are she/her. This will be a class where we all treat one another with compassion, respect, and tolerance." As she spoke, she sometimes lifted her hand in the air and made a little slicing motion with each word. Then she wrote "compassion," "respect," and "tolerance" on the board.

She went around the room and had everybody introduce themselves. Some of the girls gave their pronouns, but only one of the boys did. I guess we didn't see the point, you know?

Ms. Lawrence frowned and wrote on the board: *Boys will be boys, unless you teach them to be something better.* Which, did that even make sense? Also, it was kind of annoying.

But I got over it, because Ms. Lawrence was a teacher, so what were you gonna do? It was like when my dad got pulled over by a cop even though he was only going five miles per hour over the speed limit. I could see he wanted to argue, but he didn't.

She was also our English teacher, so after we went around the room, she gave us a reading exercise with multiple-choice questions at the end, to see where we were each at. It was hard but not too hard. That is, I had to concentrate but not a lot.

Later, on the way out for recess, I walked alongside who I hoped would be my new friends. I thought we might continue the alien conversation, but the recess teacher suggested the two sixth-grade classes play four square together and maybe have a four square tournament later in the week. So me, Ben, Logan, and Anthony started hitting a ball really hard on a set of squares. I already had a posse! Ben began hitting the ball with his fist, so we all hit it with our fists. It was like *bam bam bam bam*!

Then we all had to go to other squares, so everybody played with everybody else. But the girls didn't like us hitting the ball so hard because they said it wasn't "fun" and "accuracy is more important than strength." Which, actually, it was fun, though. Plus, you could be strong and accurate both. Why not? So me and my new posse kept hitting it hard, and we kept winning games against different people.

Then Ms. Lawrence, who was also on recess duty, told us not to hit the ball so hard. Which, why did we have to play the girls' way?

Ben said, "But why can't we play separately from the girls, then? We like to hit it hard."

"Why. Would. You. Want. To," she said, as if we were slow.

"Because we like beating the crap out of people in four square?" I answered.

"Language! Boys, do you remember what I wrote on the blackboard?"

We stood there stewing for a few seconds, refusing to answer. Then Ben crossed his arms and turned his back on the teacher. The rest of us did the same. I mean, I knew there would be no more hard hitting. Because it was one of those times when you knew your teacher was wrong and you were right, but they're the cops at school, so what are you gonna do?

I heard her walk away, announcing, "There will be no more hard hitting going forward!"

Then we started playing again, hitting the ball softer. But

we were super accurate, so we still won every game, and that got the other recess teacher irritated. She said that it "wasn't fun" for the same people to keep winning. Which, actually, it was fun, because I liked winning. Winning was fun! If the kids who were upset would be more accurate, then maybe they would win. Then I would have to try harder. What could be more fun than that?

But anyway, there was no more four square. And we got reported to our parents for turning our backs on the teacher. I didn't get in trouble, though. My parents just said the whole thing was "ridiculous." My dad added, "They're boys, for Chrissakes, let 'em play four square."

After that I didn't like my new school as much as I'd liked my old school, even though the new one was "top-rated," whatever that meant. I mean, we were twelve years old—what did we need a "top-rated" school for?

FOUR

Anyway, to skip ahead, the rest of sixth and seventh grades pretty much went the same way. Mostly the teachers had to stick to the regular stuff, because this was after all a top-rated school. But one time the principal brought in a dude in makeup to dance in our auditorium instead of the usual student achievement awards and performances. It was funny, I guess, and we all cheered, but me and my homies, we just didn't understand what this had to do with school. The teachers, however, got so excited, it was like he was a dude in makeup who'd cured cancer. I mean, I got it, it was the Current Thing in grown-up world, but damn . . . my dad was ready to pull me out of that school. He wasn't down with that stuff.

Eighth was a bit more of a life education. For one thing, the girls started to seem a lot hotter than the year before. Like, a *lot*. I had a girlfriend for a while, but then she moved because of hard times. Her mom and dad got divorced, and they couldn't afford to be there anymore. Eighth grade, you kinda learned on a daily basis that life was not particularly fair. Which your parents really never told you about. The good thing was that Anthony, Logan, Ben, and I were a regular posse.

Ninth was mostly a blur, because all we did was study. The studying got so intense I'm not sure we even knew we were human that year. It was the first year of high school, and we were now officially on the college prep treadmill.

Then, during spring of ninth grade, I told the guys about how I'd always wanted a mountain bike. We got into mowing lawns and washing cars to buy bikes. The other important thing that happened was I took a special writing class where I worked on a history essay. At the end of the class, we all entered our essays in a contest. The reason this was important was that I started thinking I might want to be some kind of historian. This was a little different from my friends, who would for sure do some kind of STEM thing. Ben's parents were even thinking of moving someplace where they had one of those elite STEM high schools. Ben took an entrance exam, got into one of those schools, and then his parents decided it was too disruptive for the family to move.

What we all did that summer was ride our new bikes, which were actually used, *everywhere*. Mine was a used Trek and cost three thousand, but my parents paid for half. We were out riding one day on the trail by the beach, and there was a guy riding there we knew enough to say hi to. His name was Lee Young Fang. Famous for being *the* smartest kid at the high school and a year older than we were. I'd played a little softball with him and a bunch of kids in the neighborhood. I'd heard he was taking a couple AP classes with seniors, and he'd taken summer classes at Caltech.

"YO," Ben called suddenly. "YO, DUDE, that's a pro level bike!"

"Uh, yeah," Lee said shy-like. He was maybe five nine, black glasses, and hair a little past his ears that looked like he maybe ran his fingers through in the morning and never thought about again. He seemed embarrassed. Then he brightened up. "Want to see what it can do?"

"Yeah!" we all said.

He looked around. "Make sure nobody's down the stairs. I don't want to take anybody out." He rode away, then turned around. I checked to make sure that nobody was coming. He pumped hard, made a sharp turn, jumped his bike down a small flight of stairs, plopped on a small landing, then somehow rose up and jumped down the next flight, and landed.

"Holy crap, the suspension on that bike is *sick*!" I yelled.

So we spent the whole rest of the remaining daylight trying to copy Lee, and failing. It was hot, which was bad but also good, because there weren't many people walking around. When we took off our helmets, our hair was soaked. We sat finishing off our water.

"That was a sick jump," Ben said. He and Lee fist-bumped.

And that's how it all started. We biked together all fall whenever we were burned-out from studying, sometimes just random rides and sometimes trying to do tricks. Felt good to get away from the books and the computer.

In September it turned out my essay from ninth grade had won first place. It was a twelve-page piece on America's Great Depression. Usually the kids who won were juniors or seniors, so my mom told all the other Asian moms.

The essay started out because I liked to look at those pictures where half the sky was filled with dark clouds of dust during the drought in the Great Plains in the 1930s. A lot of things were going wrong in America back then, just like now. Different vibe from today, though. The way I wrote essays was I liked to imagine what it would feel like to be back in time. In this case I pretended I was sitting on a porch watching a giant cloud of dust coming. And my grandpa was able to find a man in his nineties in Oklahoma, where Grandpa once lived, and this man was eight years old when his family had to leave Oklahoma in the 1930s because of those dust storms that turned where he lived into a ghost town. I got to call him up and ask a lot of questions.

So I wrote my paper from the perspective of him as a little boy. I wrote that whole paper at the beach, sitting with Kiiro and Joshie. I used a pen and paper, which felt kind of old-fashioned.

I figured some Asian mom—possibly my own—told the assistant principal I'd won this prize. And she decided that during our monthly assembly I should read my essay. My mom *really* wanted me to get a suit, but I refused. I ended up getting a Hawaiian shirt, and that's how I went onstage, right after the assistant principal gave a speech about . . . something. At one point I heard "service to your community," but it was hard to listen on account of I was so nervous. My mouth went dry. I was in the front row next to a kid who was going to be playing the piano onstage later.

The kid elbowed me and hissed, "Ms. Adams just called your name." So I marched up onto the stage, and it turned out she'd only said my name, not really called it. Which meant I had to stand to the side while she kept going, talking about how she believed in the future because she believed so much in us. Pretty sure my face was red. Then she nodded at me, and, yeah, I kinda tripped going to the microphone. Not a face-plant or anything that bad. Still, I wasn't doing great so far.

It's weird how you can talk individually to anybody at your school without getting nervous, but when they're all in front of you at the same time, it makes you want to barf.

At one point as I read, I dropped a piece of paper, and then two times I had to lick my fingers to get some pages separated. Didn't have a lot of saliva in my mouth, though. And I'd left my bottle of water at my seat. Was this really happening?

But when I was almost finished, I looked up, and I got the feeling that everybody was pulling for me. It swept over me like a wave. Anthony shook his fist at me like I was doing great, keep going.

I spoke my last lines looking up, since I knew them by heart: "The man told me, 'My two-year-old sister had died in Oklahoma, and the last thing my mom asked me before she herself died was to please go back one time and clean off my sister's grave. It was fifty years after my sister's death, but I went back to clean up her grave. I ended up staying in Oklahoma because it was in my blood.'" Then I dropped a sheet of paper, picked it up, and said, "That's the end."

Everybody cheered, some of my friends even standing up and chanting, "Eli-JAH! Eli-JAH!" After that everybody was kind of goofing around cheering, like they were at a baseball game. Still, it made me happy.

Pretty much, that was a truly great day. I lived off the fumes from that for a few weeks. I had the thought that I might be president one day. Why not?

FIVE

I had the fever then, and I bugged both my high school English and history teachers about finding me some good contests to enter. The big thing that bothered me about history, though, was why humans did idiotic stuff over and over. This one book I read about Nazi Germany explained that someone doing bad stuff actually can't tell they're doing bad stuff. Like, they don't even consider it, because they feel they know *for a fact* that they're a good person. They have a good job and good manners, and everybody likes them. A writer named Hannah Arendt I was into for a while thought it was because people became ideological, and ideology ruined your relationship with reality—it was using someone else's template to process what you saw in the world. That was pretty heavy stuff, and sometimes Lee and I wondered if that explained all of history. Lee even called it the Theory of Everything.

History became one of my Things to Get into College With. The problem was, this kind of made it less interesting. Why couldn't I just love history, but also not have to *use* it? But everybody was like, "You need some special things to put on your college application." I had my history prizes—I'd also won a state history prize for an essay about the legendary typhoons and tsunamis in Japanese history—but my mom had read that a couple of prizes were not going to impress anyone at a top school. She wanted me to go all try-hard on history. So she encouraged everybody in the extended family to send me anything to do with history. Relatives sent me old newspapers, old photos, and articles they'd read about historians.

I didn't figure out what all this *supportiveness* meant until one time when I went over to Lee's house. His mom let me in. She didn't speak English well, but she nodded at me and said, "Welcome, Elijah." I followed her to a bedroom with an open door. She held her hand toward it, smiled, and waited until I walked in.

Lee was on the floor surrounded by papers.

"'Sup, Lee," I said.

He glanced up. "'Sup."

"What is all that?"

"It's an article I printed out."

I stepped over some clothes on the floor and asked, "About what?" We'd planned to play some PS4 together, but he didn't get up. I glanced at his setup by the window: PS4, two chairs, two controllers. The chairs didn't match. I was kind of OCD about that kind of thing, but Lee was the kind of guy who, if he came to school with mismatched socks, would be like *whatever*. Because that was Lee; he had stuff on his mind. Me, I always kept my floor clean—in fact, I was a little OCD about that as well. So it was interesting to see how a genius like Lee lived.

Lee waved a piece of paper in the air, crinkling it in the process. "You should read this!"

"What's it about?"

"This is me, man. It's an article about how parents with money today try to max it out to create their kids' future good lives. They *design* their kids' lives. They're building the sidewalk you walk on through life. So their kids end up with good, designed lives, but also, they're living in the box."

"Uh . . ." was all I said, because I wasn't quite sure what he was talking about. I mean, what box were we living in? Because we could ride to the Pacific Ocean, or wherever, anytime we wanted.

He held up the paper again. "They talk like they love blue-collar working people, and then they design their kids' lives so that they never become that," Lee explained. "But then you also don't become Einstein, because in order to become Einstein, you have to be willing to jump over the abyss. Your parents can't design that. And you can't get there if they design your life." He paused and thought that over. "So I'm a little worried that my life is overdesigned."

Suddenly, I got it. "Yeah!" I said. "Me too!" Because once my parents had gotten some money, they'd changed, and I only realized it right that second. My parents now wanted more than good grades—they now had the resources to design my life the way people who thought they were great parents did. In other words, like 90 percent of the parents of the kids at my school. They took their kids on carefully selected foreign vacations; they helped them manage their extracurriculars; they tried to get them to do something athletic; and they wanted them to have friends who also had designed lives.

"What I mean is, I know what you mean," I told Lee. "Like, I told my family I want to major in history one day, so now they all send me history items."

"Exactly," he said. "They're building your history sidewalk."

Yeah! I felt like my brain was all sparks. "I get it! We don't want to live on the free-range farm, right?"

"Exactly what I'm saying, bro. They always tell you that you're the one doing everything that they set you up to do. They act like you're making the choices, but then you look at your life, and it's all the stuff they wanted that you're doing. It's them, not you. You can see that it's their design. The design don't lie." He paused. "They get you nice stuff, but they also make you work so you don't get spoiled, even though you totally are. But they don't let you act spoiled, because if you acted spoiled, that would mean they hadn't designed that part of you right. So you're spoiled, but everybody pretends you're not, because you don't act like it." He was getting really animated now. "Dude, you should read this article. I'll send you the link. Your parents design your life so you never hit bottom, but that means you don't hit the top, either, because your whole life now depends on this box they built for you."

"Yeahhhh," I said. "It's like . . ." I thought this over. "Yeahhh. The design don't lie."

Lee held up the paper again. "The box is mundane!" he cried out. "I don't wanna have a mundane life."

"Damn," I said.

"You can never be great, because they designed the life they thought you wanted. You're in the box, man."

I felt kind of sad, because I thought suddenly about some friends in Lombard I'd left behind. Their lives weren't getting designed. And some of those people were pretty dope.

But damn, living in the box. Was that what I wanted?

I looked at Lee, who was reading the article again. I'd never had a conversation quite like this before. You know, talking about our *lives*. I thought a moment. "But, I mean, you're gonna graduate straight into the greatness box. Because you're you."

He shook his head. "I dunno. I took a class at UCLA summer school when I was fourteen, and one of the guys there told me his parents just said, 'Luke, get online and figure out what college you want to apply to. We don't have time.' I would've enjoyed getting online and doing that."

He seemed a little sad for a moment. Then he said, "Welp. I just hope it's not too late for me to do something great." He hopped up and walked over to the PS4 and held up a controller for me to take. So I sat down in one of the mismatched chairs. "I don't remember it, but when I was first born, we lived in a one-room apartment," Lee said. "My parents built our whole life almost by willing it. Dad used to work until four a.m. They did it all for me and my sister. They built it all up like we were in the Sims, you know?"

I did know. But a minute later we were shooting the crap out of some enemies on the screen. I got killed and clutched at my heart and pretended to fall off my chair to the floor.

Lee laughed. "Good one, dude."

But lying there on the floor, I suddenly thought about the box again.

Damn.

SIX

Then Ben, me, Logan, Lee, and Anthony thought that the thing with getting into the schools these days was you needed to do something for society. Even though we'd rather be biking. That didn't mean we never wanted to do anything for society. It just meant we were kids. You know? What was the point of having those cool bikes if we didn't have time to ride them? Nevertheless, we needed to go to great colleges on account of we were Asian and our parents started thinking the words "Ivy League" the day our moms found out they were pregnant. All the extracurricular stuff schools offered was part of what they did to get you "experience," since the schools were part of the whole plan to design your life. I was worried that our high schools were designing us to hit doubles and triples. Lee's word "mundane" scared me.

Still, Ben, Anthony, Logan, and I started a business tutoring kids for free. The "free" part meant we were doing something for society. I tutored kids in math and essay writing. But did you ever try to explain to a thirteen-year-old how to write an essay? I thought I was pretty great with essays, but sometimes you just can't find the words to explain a concept to people. You feel you've used every set of words or phrases or sentences you can think of to explain to a kid why a paragraph that obviously doesn't make sense, doesn't make sense. But they still don't get it. In short, I sucked at tutoring.

Ben, Anthony, and Logan said they sucked at it too. Like, I've had two truly great teachers in my life, and teachers are trained. We weren't even trained, so what were the chances that we were going to be great tutors?

We started biking more and more. Mountain bikes are great for the city in terms of riding. The only bad thing is that you can't all go into a restaurant or store together, because you don't want anybody to steal your bikes. So when we wanted snacks, two or three of us would wait outside and the rest would go into the store.

We had one store we liked because the outer parking lot was sometimes empty, and we jumped from curb to curb—you know, those little curbs in front of each parking space? Ben took a while to get it, because you have to use not just your bike but your whole body as the suspension, and for some reason he couldn't time it just right at first. Once he got it, though, he really got it.

Biking is all about your body and the bike becoming one—your bike becomes kind of alive, and you become kind of a machine. It's pretty much a perfect feeling when you mesh with your bike.

Once, waiting on a bench outside a store, Lee and I were the ones guarding the bikes. People were walking across the lot pushing grocery carts, sipping drinks, carrying clothes to the dry cleaner nearby. "Where're you going for vacation this summer?" Lee asked.

"We don't really do that," I said. "I mean, we've been on vacations, but not on the regular. Where are you going?"

"Brazil. To see the Amazon jungle. . . . We went to Antarctica one year during Christmas vacation."

"Cool. Did you see anything weird there? You know, like there are all those conspiracy theories about Antarctica."

"Nah, it's kind of controlled. You can't just wander off."

"Do you feel different after you go there? Antarctica stuff was one of my favorite conspiracy theories when I was a little kid. Did you ever hear about the underground base?"

"Sure. It did feel like a different dimension almost. All that ice. It was pretty controlled, though, like I said."

"Were there penguins?"

"Yeah. The penguins were cute, but some of them were assholes, for animals. There was one who was just mental. He was strutting up to people like he wanted to fight them."

I laughed at the thought of penguins being assholes. Lee laughed too.

There was a homeless woman holding a baby near the curb. I watched people dropping bills into her can. There were hella homeless in California. They were everywhere. I used to have a friend in Lombard whose mom and dad met in a homeless shelter. When we moved, my mom gave them everything we owned that was still good but that we weren't taking with us. My friend gave me a funny look the last time we saw each other. At the time I didn't know what that look meant. I almost thought it might've been jealousy, and that made me like him less. But right this moment I wondered: Did he know that now my parents were in a position to design my life, and his weren't?

"Did you hear about those whales that are attacking boats?" Lee was asking. "I don't think they're being assholes. I mean, in that case I side with the whales. They must be ticked off about something."

"Yeah, humans might be the assholes in that scenario," I agreed. "It might be the wind farms bothering them. Also, I read once about captured whales in enclosures by themselves. They circle around day after day until they die of old age or loneliness. I'm surprised the wild whales never rebelled before this. Like, what if there was a war with the whales?"

Lee didn't say anything, but that didn't mean he didn't hear me. In fact, he was staring right at me. Not sure he saw me necessarily, but his eyes were on me. He did that sometimes when he was thinking. I figured it was because even though he was right there, he wasn't *there* there. He kind of had a foot in two worlds—the world we were both sitting in and the world in his head or wherever. Maybe the other half of his brain was in a completely different world than I even knew existed. Finally, he said, "The whales don't lie." He paused. "The whales don't lie. The design don't lie. Math don't lie. What else?"

I couldn't help laughing—you never knew what Lee was going to say.

"Math is the universal truth underlying all other truths," I said, but I was just shooting the breeze now. Some basketball players from school had driven up in a convertible, so we were looking at them. A minute later they walked past us, and we nodded. One of them was wearing a shirt that read: I'M 6'10". DON'T ASK.

When they passed, Lee said, "Did you know my sister is dating that guy? Evan, the one who's six ten."

"Su-Bee is dating a basketball player? What is she, like, five foot one?" Her real name was Susan, but she'd been called Su-Bee as long as I'd known her.

"Two."

"Wow . . . Do you have a picture?"

He showed me one on his phone. "That's amazing," I said. "She looks like she's four feet." But I was kind of surprised by how cute she looked in the picture, in a blue dress and straw hat. She always wore her glasses and sweats at home, and she was going to a different school for some reason. So I didn't see her that much. She seemed . . . odd, like Lee was maybe a little odd. They were both in their own world. You could ask them what time it was, and they would look at you like you'd just asked if there was a man on the moon. Then they would snap out of it and answer.

But, wow, she looked different when she stepped out.

I was pondering that when Ben, Anthony, and Logan came out with a bag of snacks, and we rode to my house, which was closest.

Then we sat around my bedroom with pretzels and Gatorade. Logan suddenly glugged down his entire bottle of Gatorade without stopping.

"Dude!" We all laughed.

He laughed too, then suddenly laid down flat on the floor with his arms spread out. "The college app thing sucks, and I haven't even gone through it yet," he said. "Why do we have to pretend to be helping society? Like, how can you help society if you're not even an engineer or whatever yet? I don't get it."

"You're trying to use logic," Anthony said. "Faulty thinking, dude."

"How can logic be faulty thinking?"

"Using logic at this moment is faulty thinking, dude," Anthony said.

Logan sat up, flipped his head back, spit a pretzel into the air, and caught it in his mouth. "If we got really good at engineering, we could do a lot more for society than pretending we're helping society when we're fifteen."

Ben said, "Maybe instead of Harvard, we should just go to Arizona State. My older brother goes there, and he says the Arizona heat isn't so bad."

Logan tugged on his long hair and said, "If everybody was helping society, there'd be nobody left to run stuff."

"My grandpa's a plumber," I added. "If he was helping society when he was fifteen, I dunno, maybe he wouldn't have been able to fix people's pipes." I paused. "On the other hand, my mom would jump off a cliff if I don't go to a top school."

"Same," Lee said.

"Same," Logan said.

"Same," Ben said.

"Same," Anthony said.

Then Logan threw a pretzel into the air a few feet away and lunged to the ground to catch it in his mouth again. And we all spent the rest of the afternoon lunging after pretzels.

Anyway, the very next week Anthony started hanging around with different people. Just like that. He got into expensive clothes. He did go feed the homeless to help society, though, with some new friends he'd made. But he got like some of the bougie kids at school. They fed the homeless, but they also looked down on them. Laughed at them, even. He may even have looked down on us now for some reason. That was the first time I ever wondered: *Do I actually know the people I know? You know?*

Still, we decided we hoped he was happy. Once a homie, always a homie. Like, I couldn't judge him, because he was just trying to make it in his own world. Right?

SEVEN

When Joshie turned four, my parents thought about putting him in nursery school, getting him a tutor, and seeing if there were any elementary schools that were "top-rated." But none of those things happened—I guess they decided that he was too young for them to start designing his life. Instead my dad asked me to teach Joshie to bike, so I picked out a balance bike for my parents to get him. I guess in my dad's time some kids learned with training wheels, so they learned to balance *after* learning to pedal—probably the opposite of the way you should learn. I learned on a regular bike with no training wheels. A balance bike has no pedals, and it's small so a kid's feet can lie flat on the ground.

The day the bike arrived, Joshie was like, "Now now now pleeeeaaase now now can we practice?"

"Ehhhh, okay," I said, even though I'd been planning to hang with my posse.

His bike was a fourteen-incher in the color he'd picked out: Totally Tangerine. In other words, orange, but for four-year-olds.

On a balance bike you push yourself along with your feet, and when you get more confident, you glide a little. Fortunately, we lived on a slight incline. So I walked alongside him saying, "Push, push!"

And he pushed his legs faster and faster before I cried out, "Pick up your feet, Joshie!"

Which he did, but then he didn't put his feet on the ground when he lost his balance. He fell over, jumped up beside his bike, stuck his finger in the air, and shouted, "I'm okay!" Even though his elbow was bleeding. For some families, it's a national emergency if their kid skins an elbow. My family was more like, whatever, skin grows back.

"Dude, good job," I said. "But my bad. I forgot to tell you that when you lose your balance, you need to put your feet flat on the ground asap."

"What's asap?"

"It means *now*. The second you lose your balance, put your feet flat on the ground. But don't do it if you think you're almost losing your balance. Wait until you're sure you're losing your balance."

He looked up at me skeptically. "Why?"

"Because the whole point is to learn to balance. So you have to, uh, learn to balance." This is what made me a bad tutor—I could *do* the thing, but I sucked at explaining how to do it. Because all the thoughts in my brain only fit in *my* brain, or something.

He was looking at me like he wasn't sure if I was making sense and he just didn't understand or if I really wasn't making sense.

Anyway, for the next hour, the second he almost sort of maybe possibly could've been losing his balance, he plunked his feet flat on the ground. Asap. So we made no progress. I mean, he looked cool with that madman hair bouncing and flying, his face screwed up in intense concentration. However, progress was not a thing that day.

Every so often, I glanced at Kiiro waiting patiently in our living room window. I swear, he knew I was kind of frustrated inside. But only inside. Outside, I was "chipper as a sunny day," as Grandma sometimes liked to say.

When I announced the lesson was over, Joshie's eyes got all shiny. "I'm getting really good, huh?"

"Sure thing, Joshie." We high-fived. Because, I mean, he was four, and who's gonna tell a four-year-old, *We may have just wasted an hour of life force.*

Which, actually, maybe we didn't, because he had a look on his face like that was just about the best hour ever, for anybody. In history. He petted his bike like it was a dog and said, "Thanks, dude," and I wasn't sure if he was talking to me or to the Totally Tangerine bike.

EIGHT

I was getting a little obsessed with the biking. I started wondering if maybe hitting a triple in mountain biking might be a cooler life than hitting a triple by going to school for another ten years or whatever. One day it was just me and Logan. I was on a bench watching the bikes while Logan went inside a drugstore to get Gatorade. I glanced at a homeless guy when he walked by, and he started shouting, "Why are you looking at me?" He took a couple of quick steps forward.

I looked around. "Me? I asked. I remembered my dad advising me, "Be cool if someone confronts you. You're a pretty big kid. They don't actually want a fight unless they're crazy." But was this guy crazy?

"You're looking at me now!" he shouted. I was pretty sure he was crazy.

But I heard my dad telling me to be cool. "Dude, you're talking to me, that's why I'm looking at you," I said. Crap. My heart was starting to race. He was a big guy. *Stay calm.*

"Give me a dollar for looking at me!"

That seemed like a good trade to me, so I reached into my wallet and pulled out two dollars to make doubly sure he'd back off. I gave him the money and watched him walk away, shouting at someone new, "Why are you looking at me?"

Then Logan came out, and as we drank our Gatorade, we watched the guy ask people over and over, "Why are you looking at me?"

Logan swigged from his Gatorade, then said, "My grandpa said they used to call homeless people 'hobos,' but they didn't bother people so much like now. There were a lot of them after the Civil War. Then a hundred years later hobos formed a gang called the Freight Train Riders of America. It was supposedly started by Vietnam War veterans." He paused. "I've been meaning to tell you that in case you wanted to write about it."

"Cool, thanks, bud." We high-fived.

The guy was heading back our way and stopped at our bench. "Are you still looking at me?" he demanded.

"Shit. Let's go," Logan said.

As we stood up, the guy gave me a little shove, and I shoved him back hard, because my dad taught me to stick up for myself. He stumbled backward, and Logan and I hopped on our bikes and sped off. I felt kind of pleased with myself for that shove. Not way too hard, but not soft, either.

At home later I checked out the Freight Train Riders of America. I check out any historical stuff that anybody tells me, just to respect them, even if I'm not that interested. Because it's cool of them to think of me. But it turned out some people thought the FTRA was more of a legend than real.

Might be interesting to write about the history of homelessness, though. . . . Like I said, our school did an assembly thing every month, where kids could perform or read or whatever. So I was always on the lookout for a good angle to write about—you know, make the assembly, pad my resume with that.

I guess if you look deep into anything, it becomes interesting. Sometimes I did that, spent an hour or two looking up something random. For instance, I might look up Dayton, Ohio, for no reason, just to test my theory that any random thing can be interesting. So far my theory was holding up. It turned out Dayton was once one of the richest cities in America. Who would've guessed? The city took a dive in 1960, though.

I mean, do you ever ask yourself who *were* those people in the past? Did the big names of the past have parents who designed their lives? For instance, a fifth-century historian named Priscus once wrote of Attila the Hun, "He was a man born into the world to shake the nations." He conquered a bunch of cities and nations and rewrote the history of those lands. Then, after he died, his three sons tried to take over for him, and they ended up destroying his empire. Is it possible that he designed their lives too much, on account of getting rich and powerful enough to do it? So they ended up in the box, but they weren't able to shake nations?

Like I mentioned, my relatives gave me any old items they had, like pictures and letters and stuff, and now my grandpa was saying I could write our family history one day. I liked looking at our past. I felt like I was trying to figure something out, but I didn't know what. On my mom's side we were a normal peasant family going way back in Japan. Emperors and wars came and went, and now here we were in Rocosa Beach. What if we were like Dayton, though, and went downhill again later? Dang, I hoped I wouldn't end up being the one to bring our family down!

NINE

So then one day my dad said out of the blue, "You gotta come see this."

"Sure, what is it?" I asked.

"It's a building."

We got in the car and hopped on the freeway and got off on the Westside. He parked and swept his hand toward a building that looked like . . . kind of like some luggage I saw once at the airport that was held together with duct tape. I kid you not, that's what it looked like.

"You read a lot. What's that all about?" Dad asked.

"What do you mean?"

"You're kinda a historian, right? I don't understand *why* they built that."

I tried to remember all the pictures of old buildings I ever saw. "I never saw anything like that from the past."

"We're in unprecedented times," my dad said firmly. "That's what I thought."

I had a bright idea! "It's like *Ubik*. It's a Philip Dick novel. The main character is trying to figure out what's going on during a confusing time, and little signs pop up. Like hints.

That building is a hint about something," I said. "Maybe from another dimension. They're trying to tell us something with that crazy building."

My dad looked at me in amazement. Then he laughed. "Sometimes your mom and I try to figure out where you get your thoughts from." Then this look flooded his face. Like, you know, *love*.

He started the motor and took off.

I know, it might seem like none of this is connected to anything. But I connected it all in my own mind—I took stuff out of different files in my brain and mixed it together. I asked myself stuff like, *Would Attila the Hun let a building that looked like beat-up luggage get constructed in his hometown, if he'd had one?* But he was a nomad warrior, so maybe he didn't care about something permanent like a building. I also wondered, *Why did nobody in the history of the world build ugly stuff like some of the buildings we build today?*

Because, *damn*, that building. WTF? There were some buildings from the past that you couldn't even believe were made by humans. They were fucking *exquisite*.

Not saying all these things are *necessarily* related to this story, just pointing out that they were on my mind all at the same time.

TEN

On my sixteenth birthday in July, we had a family barbecue on the strip of grass behind our house. Besides the grass, there was a concrete area about as big as Joshie's bedroom, which wasn't that big. We set up a few cheap Bluetooth speakers and some lanterns. Uncle Rob grilled steaks, since he considered himself the world's expert on perfectly grilled steaks. He was one of those people who has a secret sauce that he won't tell anyone the ingredients of. (It tasted an awful lot like A.1. to me.) The speakers were my grandparents' idea because they said Joshie and me needed to learn about "oldies." "Oldies" are music from your grandparents' time. Music from your great-grandparents' time would've been too old to be true "oldies," which makes no sense since they're even older. I don't make the rules, though.

But first Joshie made us listen to "What a Wonderful World" by Louis Armstrong about five times. Then we listened to the same song by the Hawaiian singer IZ. He was my mom's personal favorite, since she was born in Hawaii. My brother first heard the Armstrong version in a movie called *Madagascar*, which he watched nearly every day. Sometimes I watched it with him, because he liked to be around me. We practically knew that movie by heart and would both shout out at the same time, "The penguins are psychotic!" And, "All hail the New York Giants!"

I had a sudden thought. "Yo, Josh!" He looked up at me from where he was sitting cross-legged by a speaker. "Do you think it's a wonderful world?"

He smiled almost dreamy-like and nodded yes.

"Cool," I said, and it was.

At some point me and my twin cousins had a fistfight, which wasn't really fair since there are two of them. It started out as arm wrestling with Mike, and then, when I won, I pounded my chest. So they attacked me. I bopped Matt on the forehead, and Mike bopped me in the chest, and Matt pushed me, and I pushed him. Then I'm not sure what happened, but it was a bunch of pushing and a few punches and finally wrestling on the ground. Mom said, "Elijah!" Also, "Young man!"

Auntie Pam said, "You boys are too old for that!"

They were the same age as me, but Matt had skipped a grade. It seemed to me that we were exactly the right age for it. Anyway, we bumped fists and said, "All good."

Later Dad said quietly to me, "Good third punch. Pretty solid for not being trained."

Then the "oldies" started. Grandpa picked up a garden rock and sang into it like it was a microphone while Grandma looked shy. Even for old people, that was extremely cringe. He sang: "And you, my brown-eyed girl. You, my brown-eyed girl."

Then, I dunno, the sun was still shining, and we were all kind of sweaty, and not gonna lie, it was a good song. Maybe I would even say it was an awesome song, for old people.

Anyhow, standing there in the sun, I had a great moment. I squinted into the still-blue sky feeling the *perfection*, the absolute *excellence* of the heat, and the *outstandingness* of turning sixteen.

I sat down. My face felt a little bruised from a punch, but nothing too bad. "Dude," I said to Matt, "are you gonna get a mountain bike or what?"

"Nah, I'm into the guitar for now."

Mike said, "You don't have to do either a bike *or* a guitar. It's not a multiple-choice test."

"You know I can only do one thing at a time," Matt replied.

"Yeah, but why?" Mike asked.

Matt shrugged. It was true. His whole life, Matt would get into something really hard for a year or two, then get good at it, then move on to a new thing. But he couldn't do two things at once.

I looked around for snacks. I figured I would test the "birthday concept," so I ate three bags of Cheetos. Surprisingly, nobody got on my case about it. Grandma just told me to also eat an orange "for the vitamin C," so I did that. Grandma practically thought that if you hacked your arm off, you could fix it with vitamin C.

After that I ate steak, with some ribs on the side. And then some more steak. So meat and Cheetos was my birthday dinner. There were vegetables, but it was my birthday, so . . .

My mom had made her specialty, which was carrot cake. There was a single candle in the shape of the number 16. Everybody sang. I paused and closed my eyes. What popped into my mind was this: *I wish I could become a pro mountain biker before I go to college.*

I didn't expect that to pop into my mind, but it was too late now. I blew out the candle.

It was a windy night, and the sky was unusually clear. My mom was cutting the cake. But that was the moment when I *knew*. I had a chill, even. I just *knew* that being sixteen was gonna suck.

Later, when I'd been sixteen for a while, I thought back on that night and had a yearning that burned hot in my stomach. What I yearned for was to go back in time. Start the school year again. Follow me through this story, boys, and I'll explain it all. Think of me as the Priscus of our lives today. This book is for you. Hopefully I can save you some time.

ELEVEN

After dinner, Dad told war stories from his time in Iraq, and Grandpa told war stories from his time in Vietnam, and Uncle Rob told war stories from his time in Afghanistan, and all of them agreed that none of us boys should ever join the army. Uncle Rob said almost viciously, "All our wars turn to *shit*." Which was kind of surprising because he was mild-mannered and never used swear words on account of being a devout Christian. That is, never except for right then.

Grandpa nodded sadly and said, "The karma's coming. I can feel it. All those bad wars, the karma's coming back to us."

Dad looked up at the sky as if he could see something there besides, you know, the sky. "Yeah, it's coming."

I looked up at the sky to see if I could see what my dad saw. But I couldn't. "Do you really see it up there?" I asked him, gesturing upward.

"I see it everywhere," he said quietly. "I feel it everywhere, too." But he got up and put his arms around me from behind and pulled me close. He'd had a couple of beers, so he seemed a little extra emotional. "Happy birthday. I'm so proud of you."

Then he ruffled my hair and sat down again. His face was full of emotion—maybe he'd actually had three beers.

Uncle Rob added, "I had to shoot a kid once. He wasn't much younger than these boys. But he was pointing his rifle at my buddy."

I thought, *What?! A kid?!* Because I'd figured my relatives were all heroes just for going to war and that they'd killed some . . . not sure, but some really bad people. Some really bad adult people.

Dad said, "If there's ever a draft again, we gotta send these boys to Costa Rica or somewhere." That was a thing now among all the guys I'd known whose dads had served. A lot of dads were saying don't join up, it's not the same as it used to be, and don't let yourself get drafted.

"It makes a man out of you, or it breaks you," Grandpa was saying. "But there are other ways to become a man."

It's hard to explain to kids whose mom or dad never served. They never even think about it. But for us, even though we were into getting good grades, we'd also wondered if we should serve. Also, we didn't have much money at one time, so it was a thing a lot of guys who don't have much money think about. My cousins and I used to talk about it—when we were little kids, we always said for sure we would join up.

Mike, Matt, and I looked at one another. I think we all felt it: the men were talking to us like we were one of them now.

My mom was standing there with three empty cans and a couple of used paper plates. "Oh, of course, like we talked about!" she chimed in. She added passionately, like *really* passionately, "Costa Rica!" That kind of surprised me, because she wasn't a doomer type. She was pretty upbeat. Then she added, "We have to be ready for karma!"

I did feel a glimmer of understanding . . . sort of . . . of what they meant. Because karma's a real thing. Anyone who's read even a couple of history books knows that. Karma is a fact. All that karma swirling around the hills and mountains and rivers through the centuries: it's real. It can hurt people bad. My cousins and I looked at each other again. I think at that moment we all had the same two words in our brain: "Costa Rica."

Kiiro pawed me. I wondered if he could just *feel* that we were talking about me going to Costa Rica, if I ever needed to. I felt tears forming over the thought of how lonely Kiiro would be if I went away.

"Well, none of this depressing talk for me!" Auntie Pam was calling out from the food table we'd set up.

Then Matt played his guitar until we all got sleepy. Joshie was already out, curled up in a lawn chair like a caterpillar that's been poked.

I walked over to him, thought about needing to send *him* to Costa Rica someday, if that was still the right place when he got older.

That night I felt like it was my family against the world. I knew my dad and uncle would protect us from whatever we needed to be protected from. They would send me and my cousins to Costa Rica if they had to!

And so. So . . . the point is, like I said, your family is there. They're *right there*. And they love you, they would die for you, and they would kill for you if they had to, just like they did for their buddies during battles overseas. They would send you out of your own country to save your ass. And you love them.

And you can sit in the backyard and see the stars coming out and talk about karma and war and Costa Rica. But later you'll learn for reals and seriously how your family can't live your life for you. You gotta do that yourself. When you screw up, it's all yours.

TWELVE

The next day I took Joshie out biking again. I tried to be upbeat even though I was still thinking about Costa Rica and karma.

Biking practice was pretty much the same as last time, meaning Joshie just revved up his legs faster and faster but never balanced. So I finally said, "Dude. Maybe you should slow down your legs—it'll be easier for you to lift them up to glide a little."

But he got a stricken look on his face and said, "Elijah, I'm doing great!"

I hesitated. "Sure, yes, you are! I was just making a little suggestion."

His shoulders slumped, but then he said, "Okay."

So he tried slowing down, while I jogged beside him. After maybe ten seconds I called out, "Now lift your feet and glide!"

He lifted his feet, wavered very slightly, then immediately plunked his feet back down. After a few more times he seemed even sadder. So I said, "Do you like it better going fast?"

He nodded hopefully.

"Okay, go for it," I said.

After that, every time we went out, it was the same thing. On the positive side, his little legs were getting strong. I mean, his little legs got like one of those cartoons of someone running—just *bam bam bam*, super fast. He got so fast that I had an idea: I thought we should enter him in a balance bike competition for kids. I ran the idea by him one afternoon. "Josh, my man, did you know there are balance bike races for kids?"

He looked at me with pure rapture. "For real?!"

"Yeah, do you want to enter one?"

"DUDE!"

So his bicycle make was called Memphis for Balance. And they sponsored a race for two- to six-year-olds at a park in Los Angeles every summer. My parents entered him in it, and we all drove over—and by "all," I mean grandparents, aunt and uncle, cousins, and us.

The park was crowded—there must have been a couple hundred people there for what looked like about thirty kids. There was a racetrack set up with all sorts of orange cones and flags and balloons. There were booths under canopies and vendors for hot dogs and drinks. There were a couple of skill games, like trying to throw a quarter into a bottle.

Joshie held on to his bike just looking out at the park, gaping. "Wowwwww," he said. "Wowwwww." Then he paused and said, "WOW." He looked at Mom and Dad. "Can we do another race after this?"

"Of course we can," Mom said, then added quickly, "I mean, not today."

"There's a winter race in Ventura County," I said. "I looked it up." Once again, pure rapture on Joshie's face.

There were ropes around the track, and the families stood behind the ropes. The format was two semifinals with fifteen kids each, with the top seven in each group advancing. The race was about a minute long. The kids pushed their bikes down a straight track, turned, rode down another straight track, and turned again, straight, turn, and then running straight and finishing.

I felt my heart racing. "Wowww," I said.

All the kids lined up. A man called out on a loudspeaker, "On your marks! Get set! Aaaaand—GO!"

The next thing I knew, I was shouting at the top of my lungs, "GO, JOSHIE! RUN, JOSH, RUN!"

People were screaming all around me. "Bobby, push push PUSH!" "ALLLLLLEX!" Some people weren't even saying names, just screeching. I reached deep inside myself and bellowed: "GO, JOSHIEEEEEEE!"

He was in front, then fell behind a few places after the turn because everybody tried to glide except him. Three kids fell at the turn but picked themselves up. Joshie took the lead again around the middle of the stretch, but he lost the lead at the next curve. Gained it again on the straightaway. He was third at the next curve! I felt like I was levitating. "JOSHHIEEEEE, PUSH HARDER!"

He came in third! I saw him throw his arms into the air and shout with joy. Honestly, that might have been the new best moment of my life. I just watched those happy kids, listened to all the shouting around me—and suddenly felt I could cry with joy. Which I never felt before that, ever. I'd heard the phrase "cry with joy" but never thought it made sense.

The kids who advanced were all jumping up and down.

I saw Joshie, who was beaming, rushing his bike over. When he got to us, he started to go over the race. "And then on the first curve I pushed really, really hard. The kid on the blue bike fell down, and I almost hit him. And then I pushed hard like Elijah told me to do this morning. I couldn't catch up all the way, but then on the last part I went really hard. I pushed my feet down the hardest I ever did ever, and then I came in third!"

But the second semifinal was starting. We watched a few feet back, so the families of the kids racing could stand by the ropes and scream.

I watched all the parents and families screaming at their kids. And I studied who looked fast. There was one boy who must've been at the age limit who got ahead quickly. I wished they woulda made age four the cutoff. I made a mental note to try to find a race for just four-year-olds.

At the end of the race everybody got a ten-minute rest to wander, drink water, or just sit down. After a few minutes Joshie said, "I'm going to stand at the starting line." He took his bike over and stood there, waiting for the next race to start. They didn't seem to be assigning lanes, so he took lane five, for whatever reason. Some parents noticed him standing there, so they sent their kids to stand at the line as well. Pretty soon all the kids were standing in the line, even though it was still a few minutes from start time.

We decided to watch on the second straightaway, so we could remind Joshie to go hard.

I looked up at the cloudless sky, closed my eyes, and soaked in some late-afternoon sun. No exaggerating, I was in tune with the universe. Then the announcer cried out, "One minute!"

I opened my eyes and yelled out, "Remember to push hard, Joshie!"

He looked at me and bounced his body up and down a few times in excitement.

Then all these other people started yelling out things as if the race had begun. "TEN SECONDS!" the announcer cried.

Everybody fell completely quiet.

"On your marks! Get set! Aaaaannd—GO!"

A woman shrieked like she was losing her mind. "Jackyyyy!"

I realized I was squeezing my fists together. Joshie was flying! I jumped into the air. "Go, Joshie, go!"

Dad was waving his hand in the air in a churning motion. My mom was jumping up and down screaming—she wasn't even screaming words. I thought I was going to have a heart attack. Grandpa was holding both hands over his heart, and my cousins were shouting joyously.

Joshie was in fifth place at the final turn! I pointed my whole hand at him like I was zapping him with energy and shouted, "HARDER!"

He was in fourth place, his legs pounding the ground, and . . . he finished fifth. But that was pretty great, so my family and I yelled out, "Yayyyy, Joshie!"

Unfortunately, he was already crying. We all ran over there. He fell into Mom's arms and sobbed. Then he pulled away and said, "I'm sorry, I can't glide!"

We all said stuff like, "You did great!"

Grandma said passionately, "You were better than anyone else out there. Anyone!"

He stared at the ground for a few moments, then looked at me and said, "We need to work on that gliding."

I fist-bumped him and said, "Sure thing, my man. You're the boss."

Then we ate hot dogs and went to see the dumbest kids' movie ever made about a giant pterodactyl that somehow landed in Topeka, Kansas. In the year 1974 for some reason. Why would a pterodactyl land in Topeka? But the little kids made a lot of noise like they thought it was great and that it made perfect sense.

We drove home silently, as if we were all exhausted.

Joshie slept the whole way in his toddler seat. His face was dirty. He had a couple pieces of popcorn around his mouth. Pretty much, life doesn't get any better.

THIRTEEN

So, yeah. I was sixteen, and for a while it was so far so good. Me and the guys discovered a great, wide concrete banister-like slope on a city building, as well as some great stairways. We'd head over there after six, when the buildings were all closed. We'd ride our bikes down the stairs or down the concrete slope. Lee was the best rider among us. Dude was masterful. He would ride down that slope, spin, land. The rest of us could land backward but not do a full spin.

Then this one time I decided to try to spin all the way around, because I was really feeling it. Some days you can just tell you've got the magic touch. I was focusing hard, but then as I was taking off, a woman screamed. Which totally broke my concentration. And, crap! I spun halfway and barely managed to land without crashing. I landed hard, kind of clumsy-like, and grunted before falling slowly over.

The woman was pointing her phone at me. "I'm filming. I'm filming all of you! That's dangerous!"

Logan, who was usually chill, said with patient anger, "Ma'am, what's dangerous is to scream when someone's in the air like that."

Then we took off and just rode the empty side streets, rode and rode, going nowhere. And when we returned to the slope a few days later, there was already a sign right in front of the slope, blocking it, rising above it. The sign had a red circle with a bicycle inside it and a red line through the middle of the circle.

"Dang, my grandparents are always saying government works slow!" I said.

"Not when they don't want us to have fun," Logan said.

So then we found a place in a section of San Luis that was officially closed because there'd been a landslide—it was called the Sunken City. It was supposed to be fenced in, but the fence had been cut open, so we decided to go inside to do tricks. We actually dug a big hole—it took three days—and jumped our bikes over that. We called it a pit and pretended there were spikes in it. Yeah, I know that sounds like kid stuff to "pretend," but it was fun. In fact, it's hard to explain what this all feels like. You leave the ground, you're hanging in the air, over the pit with spikes, and you have so much confidence you feel like you could take over the world. You *know* you're not going to get hurt.

Lee knew it even more than the rest of us did. He knew it so hard that he had an idea he was going to do a flip over the hole. As in, go upside down. We knew he could do it, because he was Lee fricking Fang, straight-A+++ student and best bike rider in Southern California, probably. For sure in Rocosa Beach. We built a hill for him to ride up fast for his flip. I had a moment of doubt. There wasn't really enough height and space to gather momentum to do a flip. In my opinion.

Lee started as far back as he could, against some rocks, and as he pedaled, he had a look on his face like he was another person in another place—maybe in the Olympics, and this was his last chance for gold. He flew over the hole and flipped into the air with just enough clearance for a perfect landing on the other side of the hole. "Did you see that?!" he cried out after he landed. He beat his hands on his chest and shouted to the universe, "For I am the great and powerful Fang!"

The great and powerful Fang! That's *exactly* what he was. In fact, Ben beat his own chest and cried out, "The great and powerful Fang!"

Then Lee rushed back up the slope and did it all over again, except this time he overspun and couldn't quite make the landing, hitting the side of the hole and falling down into it, his eyes and mouth wide open in disbelief.

"Shit!" the rest of us said at once. We scrambled down.

"Don't touch me!" Lee cried out. "Ambulance! My leg!" His glasses were askew, and he was grimacing.

We all pulled out our phones but couldn't get reception. I jumped on my bike and rode as hard as I could, bouncing over the bumps, through the chain-link fence, and to a nearby park. I saw people! I kept pushing toward the parking area—I was *flying*. Then I spotted someone I knew, Ellory Bank. He was leaning on a car, and he had his arms around a girl. He'd graduated last June, and I'd heard that he wanted to be an EMT but that he hadn't passed his background check.

"Ellory!" I waved both arms through the air as I jumped off my bike.

He looked at me blankly, like he had no idea who I was.

"I'm Elijah Jensen!" I cried out, running toward him. "I go to Rocosa Beach High School! My friend broke his leg and needs to go to the hospital!"

The girl grabbed Ellory's arm. "You have to help him, Banker! I'll call 911!"

I rode Banker on my seat and pedaled while standing up.

When we got there, Lee was no longer in the hole. He was lying beside it, humming in a monotone. There was a smear of blood on his right pants leg. He didn't seem to notice anyone was there. He had an amazing ability to focus. When he was focused, nothing got through.

"Help him, Ellory!" Logan shouted.

"Don't call me Ellory," he snapped. "I'm Banker." But he was kneeling down. "I took classes on this stuff. Which leg?"

"Right," Lee said, and suddenly stopped humming.

Banker took out a utility knife and cut Lee's pants leg from the bottom up. The shin looked kind of warped, but only in one place and only kind of. I was with another guy who broke his leg, and Lee's looked the same as that time. A break, but not a bad one.

"How's your neck and back?" Banker asked.

"All good," Lee answered.

"Can you sit up?"

"Uh, yeah."

Banker supported Lee's back as he sat up. Ben was strongest, so Lee put an arm around Ben and Banker and hopped off between them.

Logan grabbed his and Lee's bikes. I reached for mine and Ben's but noticed something on the ground. I knew what it was—a vape pen. Must've fallen out of Banker's pocket. So I picked it up and put it into my pocket to give back to him later.

We all moved as fast as we could. When we reached Banker's

car, the girl said, "The ambulance is coming . . . supposedly. I don't know what's taking them so long!"

Banker had Lee put his weight on his good leg, then got in the driver's seat and started the car. Ben was exhausted, so Logan and I made a chair with our arms and lowered Lee toward the back seat while Ben supported his leg.

The girl climbed into the back too, squeezing onto the floor. "I'll make sure you don't fall off," she told Lee.

Lee called out, "Take care of my bike!"

"I got ya, homie!" I called back, and shut the car door.

And then they were gone.

"How are we gonna get his bike home?" Logan asked.

It was definitely too far to walk. That is, we could've walked, but it would've taken a long time.

"Call my mom, I guess," I said.

"I'll wait with you," he offered.

"Me too," Ben said.

I called my mom and sort of told her (basically) what had happened, and we sat down on a bench. A bunch of guys sauntered by, one of them saying, "You got a extra bike, dude." But they walked on.

And then a homeless guy approached. "Gimme that extra bike!"

Sometimes you could hardly sit on a public bench in California! This guy was one of the angry ones. Lee owned a top-of-the-line mountain bike, and even used, it must've set him back a bundle. *Dang.* My cousins and me had punched each other out a few times, but I'd never had a real fight. I stood up, though, because if I had to fight a homeless guy over Lee's pricey bike, then I guess I had to fight a homeless guy over

Lee's pricey bike. Logan and Ben popped to their feet as well, and the homeless guy was like, "Oh, three to one! Three to one!" He strutted off, still repeating, "Three to one. Ohhhh! Big man!"

We sat back down. "Your mom mad?" Ben asked me.

"Nah, just worried about Lee. You think yours'll be mad?"

Ben thought for a moment. "Yeah."

"He overrotated," I said.

"Yeah."

I knew a bunch of guys who had broken bones. I myself broke my wrist skateboarding when I was ten and got a concussion when I was fourteen from falling out of a tree trying to save a cat. But I don't know, Lee's mom wasn't as big on the biking thing as his dad was. It worried her. Lately there seemed to be a new thing happening, where getting hurt was a bigger and bigger deal. Like, all us guys' parents were always saying "Be careful" or "No, you can't do that because it's dangerous." But stuff being a little dangerous was the whole point. Otherwise, why would it be fun?

"It didn't look like a bad break," Logan said. "I mean, it didn't look like a good break, either."

"Yeah, it looked normal for a break," I said. "I've only seen one broken leg before, though."

Ben had one eye closed. It was a quirk he had. Sometimes he looked out of just one eye, for no reason. "Didn't like his vibe," he said, opening both eyes.

"What?" I asked.

"Ellory. Banker."

Everybody knew who Banker was, because a couple of years earlier he'd saved a kid's life by pushing him out of the way of a bus that was about to hit him. Banker had been knocked unconscious and ended up in the hospital for a couple of weeks. The kid had been hospitalized overnight, but he was fine. You'd think since we were all into "helping society" that Banker would've gotten some status after that. But he didn't. It surprised some people that he'd saved anybody, because he was one of the "bad" kids at our school, and I guess nobody would've expected him to do that. But somehow nobody admired him for it, and I guess I never understood why. Was it because they thought he was a chump? Or maybe because it embarrassed them that they knew they would never do the same thing? Even though he was a "bad" kid, and they were "good" kids?

Then I suddenly remembered the vape pen.

I put my hand in my pocket and pulled it out. We all looked at it. "Banker dropped this." You couldn't go into the bathrooms at school without running into a dozen guys vaping. But we'd never tried it. We'd talked about trying it, though.

Anyway, the pen was bright blue. I know this sounds stupid, but it was nice-looking, classy-like. Ben leaned forward. "Let's take a hit!"

"It's not ours," Logan said.

We all sat there for a second. "I dare you." Ben was looking at me.

I thought of all the guys at school in the restrooms. "I dare *you*," I said.

Ben took the pen from me and inhaled deeply. When he blew out, a heavy cloud of steam emerged from his mouth.

He handed the pen back to me. Logan and I met eyes, and then I took a hit. I immediately felt it, and inhaled again. It felt . . . good. It's hard to explain. It felt cool. Almost like riding a bike felt cool. Suddenly, the sky seemed cool. The ground seemed cool. Our bikes seemed super cool.

It must've been THC and not nicotine, because my dudes and I just sat there getting higher and higher. When it ran out, gotta be honest, I felt a twinge of disappointment. We weren't sure if the pen had run out of charge, or if the THC juice (or whatever it was called) had run out, or what exactly. Outside of a slight pressure at my temples, I felt good. Really good, in fact.

"I feel like things are moving in my peripheral vision," Logan said. He turned his head and moved his eyes as far to the right as possible, as if looking at the "things" moving.

Ben giggled.

"Ben, you're giggling," I said, and then I giggled too.

"Because Logan!" Ben exclaimed. "Logan, there's nothing there." And then we all cracked up. It was funny!

All of a sudden, we sat up straight—my mom was pulling up. I attached Lee's bike to the rack in back of the car as Mom got out asking, "Was it a bad break?"

"Dude, I dunno," I said. Which was surprising even to me, because I'd never called her "dude" before. She gave me a funny look. She pressed her lips together but didn't say anything more.

Then she left with the bike, and the three of us rode toward our neighborhood. I swear, we were so high that we almost got hit twice. It was hard to pay attention. I kind of didn't feel like riding. To tell the truth, I just felt like sitting around being high. I bumped into the curb once when I was looking at how red the setting sun was, and from behind me Logan called out, "Good one, Elijah!"

But we made it to our neighborhood and parted ways.

It turned out Lee needed surgery, but he had to wait a few

hours, because all the emergency operating rooms were filled. My parents went to the hospital for a while, on account of Lee's dad was out of town and his mom had a heavy accent, so Mom wanted to make sure the hospital understood her and she them. So I had to stay at my cousins' place with Joshie. I'd stayed alone in our home with him before, but I guess I was on some kind of time-out thing, judging by the way my dad had frowned at me before my parents headed for the hospital. And I had to leave Kiiro at home, because Auntie had cats. I felt like my emotions were ramped up extra high. So I hugged Kiiro like I was going away for a week.

I rode Joshie to our cousins' on my bike. Auntie Pam put him and me in the extra bedroom, which was full of shelves for Auntie's violet collection. She sold them on weekends at the farmers' market. One time she even won the Southern California African Violet Show. She seemed like she loved violets kind of like I loved Kiiro. I mean, she really, really loved them.

Joshie spread out on the bed, his arms sprawled like he was making an airplane shape. I figured he must be trolling me, so I said, "Joshie, can you take up less space, please?" But he was asleep. I had about eight inches to lie on my side. Then he cried out, "Put the boat in the fridge, Joshie!" Which didn't make sense even for something you were dreaming.

Last year Auntie had cancer, and it spread all over inside her. I prayed one night, the way we used to pray when we were little, back when I went to church every week with my cousins. And it worked, because after surgery she got better. The night before she had her surgery, my cousins and me had a big convo, and I mean it was deep. We talked about how we used to be babies in our moms' stomachs, and how someday we would do a lot of cool but as-yet-unknown stuff, and finally when we reached maybe eighty, we would just watch TV twenty-four/seven until we keeled over. "We might also golf sometimes after we retire," suggested one of my cousins.

We couldn't figure out what the purpose was, though. Like, why? Was there a purpose to it all? Like I said, we got really deep. And I said, "Well, the important part will be in that unknown stuff that we do. That'll be the why."

But my cousin answered, "I mean, going bike riding, or whatever, is a good 'why' too. It feels great just to ride in the sun. Or going swimming. But for sure we need to move to somewhere else someday to do some kind of big thing."

Auntie Pam had gone to New York for college, and she had fun and joined a sorority, and those girls stayed her friends forever and sent her flowers and candy when she was sick. But I'd wondered, *Is that it? You go away, and then come back after college?*

In the morning there were a few clicking noises, and a bunch of bright lights over the violets flicked on. I checked my phone: five a.m. I thought about unplugging all the lights, but then I remembered how when Auntie had cancer, she got kind of obsessed with these violets. And I thought about how much Matt had cried when she was sick.

So I went to the kitchen and ate Cheerios in the quiet house, and it was weird. I felt a pain in my heart so bad. That was something that hit me sometimes, my whole life. Before, I thought maybe it was because we were kind of poor and I wanted to be rich, but now that we had more money, I still felt that pain. I never told anyone, because these days parents were flipping out and getting their kids on meds at the first sign of a little bit of sadz. I didn't know any Asian parents who'd done that, but I knew three white kids on meds, plus three who used to be. I decided Joshie and me should leave—maybe that would make the pain go away.

So I left a thank-you note for my uncle and aunt, and I woke up Joshie. After he ate cereal, I rode us home, pedaling half standing. Rocosa Beach got foggy sometimes from the ocean. Even though we didn't live that near the beach, the fog rolled into our area too. As I pedaled through the fog, I thought about what it would be like when I left California one day. Joshie would be six or seven, and Lee would've already gone off to school. My cousins Matt and Mike would be going off to do the Ivy League thing. Right then I decided to do a wheelie. I shouted, "Hold on tight!" to Joshie super urgently. Then I did a couple more wheelies. Why not? Joshie squealed. And screamed out, "Teach me how to do that! Teach me how!"

FOURTEEN

My parents' car wasn't in the driveway. We went in, and Kiiro jumped on me and whacked my nose so hard, I checked to see if it was bleeding. He got upset when I was gone for too long. This time, in protest, he'd peed in three places by the TV. When I went to school, my parents had to keep him outside. It was crazy how much he missed me—the pee don't lie.

Joshie said, "Good night" and trudged as if sleepwalking to his room. Even his hair looked wilted with fatigue. He was one of those twelve-hours-a-night sleepers. I checked my phone. There was a text from Dad saying that Mom had wanted to stay with Mrs. Fang until Lee woke up from surgery, so he felt he should stay too.

Mom and Mrs. Fang had gotten to be friends after Lee and I became friends. I overheard them sometimes talking about that Asian-mom stuff, like this high school and that high school and this college and that college. I'd come home, and there'd be a bunch of Asian moms at the kitchen table, designing their kids' lives. They would talk about stuff like how there was some Asian kid from Las Colinas who got into Stanford *and* Harvard, and that was a surprise considering he didn't even get a perfect

SAT score like some other Asian kid who *did* get a perfect SAT and "only" got into the University of Chicago, which, honestly, was a hell of a good school too. But they wondered if it was because Las Colinas was a super, super, super exclusive gated community that none of us had ever even seen the gates of.

Anyway, I searched the whole house in case there was more pee that I'd missed. I wouldn't want Mom and Dad to get mad and punish Kiiro. I played my music on my *wired earbuds*, because of "electric waves" or whatever. My mom had to make sure my special brain ("*Nobody* understands history like Elijah!") didn't get hit with any cancerous waves or something.

I was the only person I knew who didn't have wireless earbuds. But what are you gonna do? She was a mom. And moms do their thing. Like sometimes when all the Asian moms got together at our place, they took turns bragging about how smart their kids were. My mom would take out my history prizes to show everyone, and I assume when she went to the other moms' homes, they took out their kids' prizes. You know how Olympic athletes have individual coaches? It was like that, except with our moms. And my mom happened to also have a thing about "electric waves."

I wondered suddenly what a smart dude like Elon Musk thought about wireless earbuds. Me and the guys, we kind of looked up to him. Sometimes we asked ourselves, *What would Elon think?* Right then, with a wet rag and soap spray in my hands, I thought about the Great Filter. Musk had tweeted about it one time. The Great Filter is the point of failure that stops a theoretical intelligent civilization from advancing into space colonization. Suddenly, I had this wild idea that someday I could figure out *why* there was a Great Filter. Like, *why* does history happen the way it does, over and over? Meaning, if you read Toynbee's *A Study of History* (which admittedly, I hadn't totally read, since it was twelve volumes), you gotta ask why civilization *has* to rise and fall. *Why* can't people save their world?

That's the kind of thing I thought about when I was cleaning up dog pee. Why not?

I used my mom's blow-dryer on the soapy spots I'd made, and I had just put it away when my parents got home. Mom went straight to the bathroom, and when she came out, she asked, "Did you use my hair dryer?" Even though I'd put it exactly as I'd found it.

I decided to tell the truth, because she's one of those moms who can see right through you sometimes. I could tell this was one of those times. "Kiiro peed because he was mad we left him alone." I said it a little accusingly, like it was someone else's fault, not Kiiro's. "So I cleaned it up and blow-dried it."

And she got that look on her face like, *Aw, that's cute.* So I was glad I'd told the truth.

"How's Lee?" I asked.

"The surgery went very well," Mom said. "It went perfectly."

She yawned a big yawn. Dad had already staggered to bed, and Mom followed him.

I looked in on Joshie. He was whining in his sleep, a new thing he'd been doing lately. I sat beside him and put my earbuds in his ears and played "Tegami," which was a hokey Japanese song that I used to really like when I was a little kid. The last line is "I wish you happiness." I mean, it was hokey for me now, but somehow knowing that I was playing it for Joshie, it didn't seem hokey anymore.

Later that day I just had a feeling that I was in trouble for helping to dig the pit, so I lurked at my parents' bedroom door, because I could hear them talking. And, no cap, they were saying exactly what I'd suspected. They were arguing, debating, and discussing. "I admit they do so many dangerous things." "Shouldn't they be growing up by now? They just don't *think*." And so on. Mom wanted me to get back into "something active that's also safe." Like baseball, which I'd played just one season. Dad was sticking up for me: "Sachi, he's a boy." When I was little, Dad actually let me jump off a friend's roof into a swimming pool. I just about missed, and he yelled and howled like he thought that was just about the coolest thing he ever saw.

Sure enough, the next day all four of us got grounded for digging the hole, for doing dangerous stunts, and for Lee breaking his leg. And when school started back up a few days later, in mid-August, my parents made me walk for a week instead of riding with Logan's mom, who usually picked me up. My mom wouldn't even let me ride my bicycle, which in general I didn't like to do for school because someone might steal it. It wasn't much of a punishment, since school was only twenty-three minutes away walking. But it was the best they could do, because my friends and I were basically good kids, at least compared to some of the other kids at our school, and for that matter probably at every school in America.

So we got ungrounded pretty fast, after which Ben, Logan, and I took our bikes back to the hole. Which was filled!

"Yo," Logan said. "Why don't we dig another hole?"

But nobody moved. Because we knew someone would just fill it up. "Lee would love it if we dug it again!" Ben insisted. "He would totally jump over it again when he gets better."

He would, that was probably true. But I said, "We'll get in trouble."

"So?" Logan asked.

Ben squirmed, then said, "Yeah, I don't wanna get grounded again." He drummed his fingers a moment. "Did you know I took Kaya to a movie last week?"

"Dude!" Logan and I both said. Kaya was a Singaporean girl I didn't even know Ben liked.

"Yeah, so I don't want to get grounded again."

So we each rode home and played PS4 with each other. Which I mean, I liked a lot, but kind of as a secondary thing to do.

A few nights later we decided to all go say "hey" to Lee. We'd visited him a couple of times already to sign his cast and just hang out, but both times he'd been on a painkiller and was kind of out of it. The doctor gave me a prescription for a painkiller when I broke my wrist and had surgery, but I didn't have much pain after a couple of days, so we ended up throwing it away. Same with Matt when he broke his arm. But maybe Lee's break had been worse than I thought.

Anyway, his mother let us in. Then, when we knocked on Lee's door, Banker opened it! Which was strange. I mean, I know he'd helped Lee out the day of the accident, but that seemed like it would've been a one-time thing—when a police officer or EMT helps you out, you don't start *hanging out* with them.

Banker was one of those guys who was constantly feening for chicks. So what was Banker doing at the house of Lee Fang, who was constantly feening for mountain bikes and homework? It wasn't like I was jealous. It was more a feeling that things didn't make sense.

The room was surprisingly clean. Lee's room was usually a disaster, messier by far than mine had ever been. His parents no longer cared about the mess because, he'd told me, a couple of years ago when they'd started making him clean up his room, he got OCD about it and focused on every little piece of dirt. They walked into his room once, and he was standing at the window with some Windex, consulting his phone. When his parents asked him what he was doing, he said he'd been trying to remove a certain spot on the window, but he couldn't get it off, so he was looking up how to remove difficult spots on glass. They walked over, and the spot was very small. Very, very small. So after that they stopped making him clean up his room.

"What happened to your room?" I asked. "I mean, it's clean."

"I cleaned it!" Banker said proudly. Then he frowned at me and said, "Dude, you broke my homie's leg." He kind of gently threw a pillow at my head. But also, it was kind of not gentle.

I didn't know why he focused on me, but he did. His eyes were friendly—but also, kind of not.

"Dude, I didn't do anything to him," I answered, but jokingly.

"Well, you did," he said, shrugging, and suddenly, his eyes turned to wood.

"It's all good," Lee said. "I overrotated."

"Nah," Banker said. Then he did this thing where he just stood there tapping his thumbnails into the pads of his fingers one by one, repeatedly. Later I learned he did that a lot.

"Give me that pillow, would ya?" he asked.

I reached down and picked up the pillow he'd thrown. When I tossed it over, Banker's eyes came back to life.

"Here ya go," he said to Lee eagerly. "Do you want it under your leg or behind your back? What do you need, bro?"

"Yeah, under my leg is good," Lee said. "Thanks." He seemed pleased at the attention.

Ben had a couple of cats at his house, and sometimes they lay around, regal-like. Lee was kind of like that now. I could almost hear him purring. So here's the difference between cats and people who are having their lives designed: When your parents design your life, they build the sidewalk in front of you, and all they ask is that you walk on the sidewalk they built for you to get from point A to point B in your life. Like, they build the sidewalk to college, and then when you go to college, they get super proud like you did it all yourself. But cats, man, they just sit around looking like art, and you feed them for it. It seemed like Lee was feeling exactly like that. He was just sitting around being Lee. No design, no sidewalk. Just lying there purring. Which now that I thought about it seemed like it might be fun.

Banker gingerly lifted Lee's leg with one hand. "Do you want me to help?" I asked.

"Nah," Banker said quickly. "I got it." He slipped the pillow under Lee's cast, then gently lowered the leg. "Is that good?"

"Thanks, yeah," Lee said. "That's really comfortable."

Banker looked at him almost the way Joshie sometimes looked at me, kind of admiring-like. Like *Lee* was the big brother. Even though Banker was a year older than Lee. Then he sat on the foot of the bed and just stared expectantly at Lee, like he was waiting for an order. And I could see he was sincere: he was genuinely waiting for an order.

Which didn't make sense, because what my homies and I did was ride bicycles and study. And Banker got high and chased girls. Ben, Logan, and I looked up to Lee because he did the things we liked to do, except better. But the cool kids—kids like Banker—had always ignored him, except when they wanted help with schoolwork.

"So how's it hanging, Lee?" Logan asked.

"Good," Lee said.

"He's doing good," Banker said to nobody.

There was an awkward moment. It felt like—like Banker filled the room. He had a presence like smoke, kind of every-where at once. You could almost smell him. I don't know how he did that. But his presence, it was big. I couldn't help turning to him. Wasn't sure what to say, though.

But I wanted to speak for some reason. "So what did it feel like saving that kid?" I finally blurted out. "Did your family feel all proud about it?"

Banker looked at me like I was an idiot. "I was unconscious, so how would I know?"

Nobody spoke after that. Someone in the house—probably Lee's sister—was playing music really loud. It sounded like club music, the kind some of the kids played at dance parties. Ben, Logan, and I started nodding to the music. Banker was giving us the coldest look. Maybe that was why, both at the same time, Ben and Logan popped to their feet. "I guess I'll get going," Logan said.

"Yeah, me too," Ben said. He looked at me. "Coming, Elijah?"

Banker looked at Ben, Logan, and me. "I gotta get going too. You kids need a ride?" Kids? He said it like we *did* need a ride. Which we didn't.

"We brought our bikes," I said.

He smiled like I'd just said our mommies had driven us.

"No problem. By the way, I know where you all live," he added breezily. "I know where everyone lives."

Uh . . . I couldn't think of a single thing to say to that.

"Let's let Lee get some homework done," he said next, as if he were Lee's homework manager or something.

We all walked silently through the hallway. I glanced into Su-Bee's partly open door, and she was dancing like crazy by herself to the loud music. I lingered a moment. Like I said, she was in her own world.

She must've felt my eyes, because she turned around suddenly. Her mouth dropped open, and she half waved. She was dripping sweat. She looked like she'd gotten into the shower in her T-shirt. *Damn!*

"Uh, good dancing," I said.

"What? I can't hear you!" she shouted.

"Good dancing!" I yelled.

She seemed embarrassed, so I half waved back and hurried after the others.

When we got outside, Banker got into his car without saying anything and burned rubber down the quiet street.

We stood watching him speed off. "Do you think they're . . . friends now?" Ben asked.

"Why would they be friends?" I asked. "I mean, maybe they are, but why would they be?"

Logan shook his head. "Dude, we're in the Twilight Zone. Nothing's making sense."

We all agreed on that, then rode off our separate ways.

FIFTEEN

I showed up at Lee's again the very next day, because yesterday had felt so weird and I wanted to check on him, and I recognized Banker's car outside. So ... they *were* friends now? I unconsciously stopped walking. I'd brought Kiiro with me, and after I stopped, he looked up happily at me to see what we were doing next. I hesitated—not sure why—then decided to go inside anyway.

Su-Bee opened the door. Lately I was a little embarrassed when I ended up face-to-face with her. We used to hang out when I first moved to the neighborhood, and a bunch of kids played casual softball in a big empty field nearby. On any given night maybe eight or nine of us might be out there. Sometimes she and Lee were both there.

But, I mean, she'd grown up, and . . . I mean, she was Lee's sister, and it wouldn't feel right to date a friend's sister, because it would seem like dating a cousin or something, you know? But if I could, well, she was really cute. And she had that long Asian-girl hair that fell to her waist. Also, she'd gotten contacts just the previous year, so you could really see her face now. She was kind of slender for my taste, plus there was the cousin thing. But very cute.

She seemed surprised to see me, even though I was here just yesterday. Maybe because she had blue clay stuff on her face. Not sure why that was cute, but somehow it was.

"Hi!" she said. She touched her blue cheek.

"Hi!" I paused. "Uh, don't worry, my mom does the same thing, except with white clay."

She took her hand away and said, "I can't smile. My face is frozen."

"Yeah . . . cool . . ." I was feeling sweaty. "Blue is my favorite color!"

She seemed confused, then said, "I haven't seen your dog in a while!"

"I bring him by sometimes, but I guess you weren't around . . . or maybe you were."

She glanced at her fingertips, which were also blue. "He's handsome! How old is he now?"

"Yeah, he's—" but then I forgot how old he was. "He's a few years old. Or maybe older."

She gave a single nod. "Yes. That's a great age!" We just looked at each other. "My brother's in his room. Anyway, I have homework. I mean, I'm not doing it now because . . . my face."

She walked off, tripping over the edge of a rug.

I walked to Lee's room, also tripping over the same rug, and then gave a quick knock on Lee's door before going in.

Lee and Banker were in there vaping. So I didn't mention this, because it was no big deal, but I had vaped twice since that first night with Banker's pen. I'd vaped nicotine in the school cafeteria with some kids at my table when the strictest teacher had lunch duty, and we were all laughing and trying to vape when he wasn't looking. Logan and Ben were there, but they weren't into it. To me, it just seemed like fun. I mean, we were in high school. There was still plenty of time to be serious. I never knew what people meant when they said life was short. Life was hella long.

Another time, a bunch of kids were vaping THC in the school restroom, and they let me join them. Even though I'd only gotten high once before that afternoon, I'd already found myself lying in bed at night sometimes, yearning for that feeling again.

So there I was, and Lee and Banker were vaping THC.

I just stood there, waiting and hoping for one of them to offer me the pen. And then Banker did, and it felt really great getting high. It made me feel like the "real" me. It was different from the previous times, though. I felt calmer than before. I felt peaceful happiness. I felt like a peaceful, happy wise man looking out at the world!

Lee had a crazy happy look in his eyes, meaning so happy, he looked almost crazy. He said, "Dude! I just did a physics problem high, and I felt like fucking Einstein. Right before you got here." Lee saying "fucking" was like—well, it would be like if my mom or Auntie Pam said it. You didn't expect it, is all.

Then it was my turn to take a hit again. "Isn't this stuff great?" Lee asked.

It was. Smooth-like. I felt joy flood my brain. I thought about an essay I was working on about emperor mythology over the centuries in Japan. I suddenly decided I would title it "Mythology and Meaning in Ancient Japan." I'd been looking for a title, and I felt like the vape had given it to me—*handed* it to me.

So I stayed.

SIXTEEN

There I was getting higher and higher and thinking about Japan for some reason. I could hear Lee and Banker talking in the background, but I felt like I could almost see Japan around me—that was trippy. I lay down on the carpet, Kiiro resting his chin on my chest.

"Does it make sense to say dogs have a 'chin'?" I asked out loud.

"They totally have a chin," Lee said. "What else would you call it?"

"It's the bottom of their nose," Banker said. "Dogs are all about their nose. Their entire body is just an extension of their nose."

Lee was inhaling on the vape.

I decided to jump in and said, "So there's this thing called 'fitness payoffs.' And we've evolved to try to obtain fitness payoffs instead of the truth. Our senses have evolved to perceive reality according to what helps us thrive in our community."

Banker looked skeptical, but Lee looked interested.

So I continued. "So a simple version is, if you lived in a society thousands of years ago where the king took a gold piece from you every time you smelled a rose, over time the people who had the most money and thus could afford to have kids would be people who couldn't smell roses. So over time nobody human could smell roses anymore. But the smell of roses would still exist, and dogs would still smell them, because nobody ever took anything from them thousands of years ago just because they could smell roses. If that makes sense. So your dog evolved to smell things you can't. In the scenario I just described, the reality of the way a rose smelled would still be there, but it wouldn't be in your perception. That's why humans don't really perceive reality."

"Dude, are you sure you have that right?" asked Lee. "Our senses aren't going to significantly evolve over historical timescales due to social norms."

"Hold up," I said. "Let me think about that."

Banker was looking at Lee like he was the actual Buddha or something. He said, "Wow . . ."

Myself, I was getting too high to be able to think about anything complicated.

"So can your dog smell good?" Banker was asking. "What's its name?"

I snapped back to reality. "Kiiro. Yeah, he smells great."

He seemed to be thinking about that, then went and said, "That's a dumb name."

He said it like a challenge, so I said, "Square up, buddy." Because that's what my cousins and I always said to each other when we were getting heated.

Lee pushed himself up. "Kiiro is cool," he said a little tensely. "So is Elijah."

Banker said eagerly, "You're right, Kiiro is cool, homie. He's way cool, and so is his name." But he did the thing with his fingers, and I felt like he was irate inside, but for no reason.

Then nobody was talking, we were just passing the pen around. And I was back to thinking about Japan. As in, what would my life have been like if I'd grown up in Japan? Because I knew my grandparents had always really wanted me to spend a summer there.

Japan is super busy and crowded, but it works for them, you know? If America were that crowded, we'd all have murdered each other by now. Tokyo is busy like the mall a few days before Christmas, except every day. But it's relaxing even though it's crowded. I think it's because everything is clean and *pretty*. Even their manhole covers have flowers and mountains and designs painted on them.

Also, in Japan nobody wants to screw with you, steal your wallet, or hit you on the head. "Nobody wants to screw with you in Japan," I suddenly told Lee and Banker. "Well, maybe they screw with you in some ways we don't, and they don't screw with you in ways we do . . . or something . . . uh, different fitness payoffs there, maybe?"

Then I got higher still, and I was feeling as good as when I was flying over our imaginary spiked pit on my bike. It was pure adrenaline. It was joy. I felt like I owned the universe. If you've ever ridden your bike at full speed over a pit, you'll know what I mean. I mean, it was all right there in that pen, and I didn't even have to do the work of digging a pit and riding over it. Because all that kind of stuff suddenly seemed like a lot of work to me. Literally that evening, everything I used to do that was so exciting was now work. Was it the THC, or was I maybe growing up?

Whatever—it felt good, it was that simple. And that was the way it really started. It felt good.

And work—homework—was a waste of time. I knew it that night as clearly as I had ever known anything. Now I wasn't even sure if I wanted to enter my essay on emperor mythology into the contest I'd been thinking about entering it in. I looked at Lee and saw that he knew everything was a waste of time too. I stared a moment at where I had signed his cast when he first got back from the hospital. It said, *Yo, bud, when you get better, we'll dig a new pit, and this time we'll put real spikes in it!* No, we weren't really going to put spikes in it. But for sure we would have dug a new pit to ride over if Lee wanted. This night, though, reading what I'd written on his cast, it seemed like a different person had said that. It seemed . . . quaint.

The higher I got, the more I thought all this. By the end of the night I felt like some kind of philosopher king. Elijah Ichiro Jensen, the Philosopher King.

Then my mom texted me: *It's a school night.* I thought about my homework. A Waste of Time. "It's all a waste of time," I said out loud. "Studying."

"Yeah," Lee said. Then he looked serious. "Well, no."

I saw his eyes drift to Banker, and I looked at him too. Banker seemed proud—of what, I didn't know. Of us? Of himself?

Then Banker said eagerly to Lee, "Dude, homework is never a waste of time for *you*. You're gonna be like Feynman or something. He's a physics dude."

I cringed, because nobody had to tell Lee Fang who Richard Feynman was—that was like telling a high school basketball star who Kobe Bryant was. Plus, Feynman was his hero. One of the most brilliant physicists in history. Still, after Banker said that, Lee looked shy and modest and pleased and proud all at once.

As would occasionally happen over the next couple of months, I could feel clarity trying to make its way into my brain. Something . . . about . . . Banker. But he handed me the pen and, his voice all amused, said, "You look fried."

Did I? Was I? I inhaled deeply and exhaled. I was suddenly sleepy. I looked at Kiiro, who looked back curiously at me. And then I just wanted to be in my room with my dog. Damn, I missed my room so much!

But I could still feel that clarity trying to reach me, almost like there was physical knocking on my skull saying, *Hello?* So I concentrated. But I couldn't find clarity. Finally, I blurted out to Banker, "I—I think it's cool that you saved that kid. I always meant to go up to you and tell you that back when I first heard about it."

A touch of life washed over his face. "Yeah? The kid's parents gave me a car!"

"Really? That's so cool."

But Banker looked dejected. "But it's a shitty car. It breaks down all the time." His eyes turned to wood again. "So I got a shitty car, knocked unconscious, and the kid didn't even say hi to me when I saw him at the 7-Eleven. He doesn't even realize I'm the guy who saved him. It's like . . . I dunno . . . at the time I did it without thinking about it. But it wasn't like in the movies where you're the hero."

Lee sat up straight. "But you *are* a hero. I don't know anybody else who's a hero who hasn't gone to war or something."

He stared at the floor, frowning. Then he shot me a look.

"Why did you bring that up? I don't like to think about it."

"Really, you don't?" I asked. Which was actually a dumb thing to question, because it was his thing, so if he didn't like to think about it, that was the final word. Everything felt awkward, so I rubbed Kiiro's head, because I'd read once that petting your dog increased your oxytocin levels, which in turn stabilized you. And I felt like I needed to be stabilized. Because the room felt out of whack.

Something pounded, and I raised my head. Banker was glaring at me. He pounded his fist over and over on the floor. At first I thought he was angry at me, but then I saw that he was just angry. "I still get backaches, man. The impact when I got hit screwed up my back. It's not cool to talk to me about it."

"Sorry, dude." I thought about getting up. At the same time, getting up seemed like it would probably be a big, big effort. However, I for sure had to get home. I felt a powerful desire to be at home.

So I pushed myself up. "G'night, Lee," I said.

Surprisingly, Banker fist-bumped me, his whole demeanor totally different than it had been a minute earlier. "No hard feelings, Elijah." I didn't quite understand why, but I felt strangely important now. It was like "no hard feelings" made me feel I was a part of this new group, the way I'd been a part of my old group.

Then Banker said loudly, "I wouldn't do it if I could live that day over again. The kid's fine, and I'm not, and nobody gives a shit about that except for me. Some people think I was a dumbass for doing what I did."

Tears started falling down his face. It was startling. Then he wiped them away, said "Fuck you" to me, and his face filled with hatred.

Of me, maybe. Or the kid he saved. Or himself. Then I thought I might be imagining the hate.

"Sorry I brought it up," I told him. "Seriously."

"His parents too . . . they didn't say hi to me at the 7-Eleven either."

Lee's head was swaying. "Yeah, I know who they are. Someone saving their kid isn't part of the perfect life his parents are designing for him. It's *awkward*." I wondered if I looked as fried as he did. "They've moved on. The design don't lie."

I was standing up. "I guess I gotta go, guys," I said.

"See you, Elijah. Crap, I got homework," Lee said with a groan, reaching for his laptop. "So much homework." Then he kind of froze and just stared at the wall, his mouth still open from the last word he'd said. "I just saw it. Sometimes I can see it."

I waited, but he didn't say more. "See what?" I asked.

"That thing Einstein theorized, that the universe is finite, but unbounded. Sometimes I can't see it, and sometimes I can. I can see finite or I can see unbounded. But to apply finite and unbounded to 4D space-time like in Einstein's physics? That I find hard to imagine. Sometimes I can almost see it, though."

I looked at the wall he was staring at. "I can't see it being finite either way, bounded or unbounded," I said. "That's why I'm gonna major in history. See ya."

As I left, Banker caught up with me. We walked through the house silently. Kiiro ran a little lap around the living room, jumped on the couch and off, ran to the front door, and sat down.

"So are you kind of Lee's best friend?"

"Maybe. We're good friends."

Banker's face took on a knowing expression. "You know . . . homework is bullshit for you."

I hesitated. "Yeah," I finally said.

"Unless you're going to Harvard, I mean. Are you going to Harvard?"

"Probably not," I said.

"That's what I thought. So for you, homework is bullshit."

I thought that over. It might have made sense. I wasn't sure—my head was too cloudy. He actually laid his hand on my shoulder, like my dad might.

"You're in the sweet spot we're all in—too smart for homework but not smart enough for Harvard. Guys like us, we gotta make our own path." He licked his lips and did the thing where he pressed his thumbnails into the pads of his fingers. "Did you like that brand of THC? It was wax, not oil."

"Sure," I said, though I didn't know the difference between wax and oil.

"I thought so."

We stepped into the cool night air. Kiiro trotted ahead to explore a bush.

I suddenly thought of something. "What about Lee? He might go to Harvard."

"Might," Banker said with a shrug. "But what if he doesn't? Then all that homework would be a waste of time."

And I actually had the thought, *Wow, that's true.* Even though Lee had never mentioned Harvard, because he wanted to go somewhere "different," he'd said. He was talking about Duke if he got in, which, how could he not? I guess he visited Duke once, and there were lots of trees or something. Why would you go to college for the trees? Just go up north and visit the redwood forest if it meant that much to you. But that was Lee for you. Dude could've graduated college by now, and he was worried about trees.

Anyway, I asked, "How about Duke?"

Banker shook his head firmly as he got into his car. "Only Harvard."

"Huh."

"Yeah, see you later." He lifted a hand in the air in a half-hearted wave, then squealed off like last time. I got the feeling for some reason that he made the car squeal to impress me. I wouldn't say I felt impressed, but I felt like there was a whole world out there that I didn't know anything about, and it might be worth exploring.

I decided to go down to Gardner Park with Kiiro, to think. Walking by the Johnstones', the couple who got divorced and then remarried and then divorced again, I remembered seeing the wife once running through the street in a robe. She was crying. Then the moving van came a week later. A little way down lived the Pattersons, who had a loud party nearly every Saturday. There was also a family whose dad was a university professor and whose son somehow became part of a gang from South Central. I heard the kid was involved in a shooting but didn't pull the trigger, and he got off.

When we moved here, it seemed like a perfect place. But I dunno, it was no different from Lombard in ways, you know? People got divorced there too, and I saw a woman crying downstairs once in her nightgown. And people threw parties all the time. And became part of a gang. There are hella gangs in California. But, you know, you had to design your own life in Lombard. Your parents didn't have the cash for extracurriculars.

That was rich-people stuff. I kept thinking about things Lee had said, how maybe if you designed your own life, you had a bigger chance of failing, but also a bigger chance of not landing in the box and kind of going all the way, in whatever it was you wanted to do.

When we reached the park, I walked across the grass, with Kiiro running in a huge circle around me. We crossed the path and sat on the cliff looking down at the water. It was a great night, cool the way I liked it.

Kiiro lay beside me, and I could feel his vibe—how much he enjoyed just lying there next to me. I felt a pang: I missed Lombard. I missed having to yell "I'm home" to get into the apartment. I missed looking out at the people walking by with their plastic shopping bags from the 99-cent store. I missed having nothing and wanting more.

I lay my head on my dog, thought about going to sleep right there. I felt a rush of love for him. And for the wind, the waves, the stars—the night seemed *intense*. Was that real, or was I just wasted?

SEVENTEEN

I spent too long at the cliff, waiting to come down from my high. But when I got back home, I was still feeling out of it. Then at home it suddenly felt a little *off* to be with Kiiro. I guessed it was because I was high, and with him, and at home. Maybe I felt ashamed of myself. But he didn't care—dogs don't judge. He sniffed curiously at me, then licked my hand.

And wouldn't you know it, as we headed down the hall to my bedroom, my mom was standing in the doorway of her and Dad's room, waiting for me. She studied me hard in a new way. One of those looking-into-your-soul things. I should have checked what I looked like on my phone.

"Are you okay?" she asked. "You weren't crying, were you?"

"Crying? Nah. Why do you think that?"

"Your eyes are red."

I made a mental note to get some Visine. Some of the kids used it when they got high, but I hadn't because someone told me your eyes could get addicted to it and then stay red unless you use it. And I had to admit that when I heard that, I'd thought it was bizarre that kids would risk their eyes in any way just to hide vaping from their parents. But now I was thinking I should get some.

I kneeled down and held Kiiro's head in my hands, avoiding looking at my mom. And it was messed up, because even though I could tell through being high that I still really, really, really loved my dog, I also felt detached from him at that moment. Like I was just going through the motions of loving him. I felt for a second like I *missed* him, even though he was right there.

"You seem different," Mom was insisting. Then more firmly, "You seem off."

An unexpected and intense annoyance rose up inside me. I got mad sometimes, and I got annoyed sometimes, but this was something new. I felt so annoyed by her that it was like I was going to levitate with the energy of it. I went from "I feel chill" when I'd walked through the door to wanting to break a hole in the wall. But I wanted to stay chill, *needed* to stay chill, so I said, "Nah, just tired."

"Yes, it's late." She was eyeing me like she was trying to put her finger on something but couldn't.

"Come on, Kiiro!" I said, and jogged toward my room, feeling her eyes on my back.

"Honey!" she called out. "I need to tell you something."

I turned around, holding in my anger. I did not want to talk, about anything. I felt if I stood there too long, my brain might explode.

"Joshie got a little pushed around today in his playdate group, so if you could be extra nice to him for a while, that would be great."

I felt fury rise in me over him getting pushed around. He'd

recently gotten his long hair cut, because some kids had made fun of him over it. And now this. Instead of saying anything, though, I just grunted and looked down at the floor trying to calm myself. Then I said, "Okay."

I forced myself to calm down before slipping into his room. He was asleep, his face lit by his half-moon nightlight. Except for his wide-set eyes, he looked like your typical cute hapa kid. When they're little, some hapa kids look almost fragile. And I dunno, that made me need to sit on the floor with my head in my hands. I didn't know why. Was it because I was high? Was it because I suddenly could see the ways that life was gonna get harder for him as he got older? Because it would. He was way too sensitive, for one thing. Like, dude, you don't have to cut your hair because of some stupid kids in your playdate group. And I just *knew* it would be hard for him someday.

Back in my room I pounded my fist on the bed, over and over, just to let off some excess energy. Kiiro was staring at me. "It's okay, boy," I assured him. He came over and licked my hand again. And suddenly, everything was all right. It felt good to be alone. The ceiling seemed cool . . . for some reason. Kiiro seemed cool. My bed seemed cool. There was a spider on the ceiling—that seemed cool as well.

I decided not to do my homework—it was way late for that. In general, school was okay. I liked it because I liked having people around during the day. But I wasn't like some kids who thought school was fulfilling or something. Maybe if we could do history all day, it would've been fun. Math was okay too.

Then I got to wondering: If you write about history, are you doing something as important as the people you write about? Do you need to do some interesting stuff as well, in order to really understand what you're writing about? Otherwise, you'd be writing about history from a blank slate. Which, is that even possible?

Lee was different; I was sure he could create something from nothing. Like invent some kind of new rocket ship, and then after he got tired of that, he could teach at one of those big-time schools. He was on *the* national physics team the previous year, and he got a gold medal at the International Physics Olympiad. You know how smart you have to be to do that? He didn't do the team this year because he was a moody guy and just didn't feel like it. He said he was born happy and got sad at some point. My parents said it was hormones, whatever that means. Like I said, he coulda finished college by now, but he just took advanced classes instead. He could have skipped three grades, honestly, and gone to college when he was fifteen, but his parents wanted to keep him normal. I guess they were worried about how the Unabomber went to Harvard when he was sixteen, because he was some kind of walking brain. And look how his story turned out—he got experimented on by some psycho Harvard psych prof, and it broke his brain.

I walked over to the pictures on my wall. My dad with his buddies in Iraq; my grandpa with his buddies in Vietnam; my uncle with his buddies in Afghanistan; my great-grandpa with his buddies in World War II, before he got killed in Italy. Dang, the guys in those wars looked young! I thought about Costa Rica, about hanging with my cousins on the warm beaches while some kind of useless war was going on that other young American guys were fighting in. Getting killed in.

I turned off the lights and got in bed. Kiiro was already asleep under the comforter. I hadn't done my homework and didn't feel guilt about it. I thought about that, and about the time I was getting the flu a couple of years ago, felt like crap, and finished an hour of homework anyway. Now I searched my mind, but nope: no guilt.

As I tucked the blanket around my neck, I had the sense that I was in a different world now. Like I had walked through a door. Guilt on the other side, but not on this one.

I wasn't sure how it had happened, but I wasn't in *The Truman Show* anymore.

EIGHTEEN

The semester had barely gotten started when we went on a trip to Japan. It was because my great-grandmother—my *hii-obaachan*—was sick. Probably dying, and the only thing my parents would've ever let me take two weeks off school for was if somebody in the family was dying. Because family first.

My grandparents in Japan—Obaachan and Ojiichan—hadn't visited America for a couple of years, and Joshie had never seen Japan and never met Hii-Obaachan. As we took off from LAX, I saw him gasp and clutch the armrests. We shook a lot during takeoff, and for the first time ever, and for no reason, I wondered whether it would really be so bad to die. It popped into my head, just like it had popped into my head that I wanted to be a pro mountain biker.

But I was worried that if I died in a plane crash, my other grandparents might give Kiiro away. I didn't think they would, but they might. They had promised me they would take good care of him, but even if they kept him, he might be depressed if something happened to me. I didn't like to think about him depressed. I knew people from school who got super depressed, and it sucked.

Also, I have to admit I didn't want to go to Japan because I knew I would miss getting high. Even on the plane, I already missed it. Japan has hella strict drug laws, so I didn't want to risk bringing any THC. But I didn't think vaping was necessarily a bad thing. It was more like it was a new thing that I was getting into, is all. And, like, if it felt so cool, what could be wrong with that?

We arrived at night. I trudged behind my parents, holding Joshie's hand. After a few minutes of that Dad suddenly turned around and lifted Joshie up, and afterward we moved much more quickly.

So the thing about Japan was, nobody was fat there. Everyone was thin and everyone dressed nice and practically nobody in the entire city of Tokyo wanted to steal your wallet. One thing about Japanese people that was funny, though, was that every single one of them seemed to think they could speak English, but hardly any of them actually could. Like, they looked at you so sincerely while they thought they were speaking English to you, and you had no idea what they were saying. They were Japan Japanese, so they wanted to speak English if that was your language, and you didn't want to hurt their feelings. Therefore, you ended up pretending to understand, and you both got more and more confused. At some point I would kind of bow and say *arigato*, and that would be that. I told Joshie that *arigato* meant "all good, bro," and then Mom told him it meant "thank you." I raised my eyebrows at him like we had a secret between us, and he raised his eyebrows back.

A lot of the signs on streets, doors, in parks, and so on were in both Japanese and Engrish. Engrish is English that makes no sense, as in NO PEDESTRIAN ONLY or DO NOT ATTACH HAND TO DOOR. Which, who would ever attach their hand to a door? Or a pair of plain socks in a store might have a tag on them saying, *These socks will make you most popular dazzle at party*. Which, who notices people's socks at a party? I was pretty sure that anyone who went to Japan for the first time laughed and laughed at all the Engrish. I honestly didn't think the Japanese cared if you laughed at the Engrish, because they were secure in themselves in that way. They weren't gonna spend all day trippin' like Americans who were constantly trying to figure out if laughing at something was racist. I tried to explain all this to a teacher once, but she just couldn't comprehend. Her argument was, "How could the Japanese *not* think that laughing at Engrish is racist? The word 'Engrish' itself is racist." I swear, way too many teachers believed that everybody else in the world was trippin' over the same things they were.

We moved silently among others going to get their luggage. I was tired, so it was kind of cool to still be a kid, and my parents had to take care of everything as I just followed behind. In customs someone said something in incomprehensible English to my dad, and my mom answered both "yes" and "*hai.*"

The airport was forty miles from my grandparents' small apartment in Tokyo. Joshie and I fell asleep in the taxi, and when I woke up, I could see the skyscrapers ahead of us. There was a really tall building-thing in Tokyo called the Skytree. Tonight its lights were blue and white. The Skytree was one of the tallest structures in the world, and some scientists found out that time moved a little faster at the top of it than on the ground, because time is different at tall heights, because, uh, gravity . . . or something—Lee would probably have understood it. Gravity was something that seemed really simple, and then the more you learned about it, the less you really got it.

The streets were not crowded at that moment, even though there were almost as many people in the Tokyo metro area as in the entire state of California. Like I said, if there was anyplace that crowded in the United States, everybody would kill each other. They would. But in Japan people mostly got along. Because for them, what was there to be mad about?

At the apartment building we let the taxi driver take out our luggage, and then Mom and the driver bowed to each other and said "thank you" a few times apiece as he unloaded the trunk. You weren't supposed to tip in Japan, so I just gave a little bow with my head and said "thank you." Including Joshie and my dad thanking him, I think I counted seven "thank yous." What were you gonna do, it was Japan.

When we got up to my grandparents' apartment, right after saying hello, first thing Baachan did was hand me a perfectly wrapped present, shiny silver paper with a silver bow. When I opened it, inside was . . . a sweater. I honestly couldn't remember a single time I, or any of my friends, had ever worn a sweater. But I said, "WOW, A SWEATER," like they'd just given me a Supreme T-shirt. A collector's Supreme T-shirt was something I'd asked for on my Christmas list for three years in a row, but I hadn't gotten it yet. I wrote it down for every single relative who requested a list. But nada so far.

Baachan was instantly really upset, because when I held the sweater up, we could all see it was too small. She apologized:

"I'm so sorry! Ohhh, so sorry! I take back for best size. This not best size!" The sweater was not even sort of something I would ever wear, *ever*, but I told her it was the best sweater I ever saw, *ever*, and thank you so much. I guess I overdid it, because she got so excited that she said she was going to buy three more sweaters and send them to me in America. And I didn't even wear sweaters. Did anyone wear sweaters anymore? I honestly didn't know. All the guys I knew wore hoodies to stay warm. Then when you had a girlfriend, she wore your hoodies, kind of like my grandpa said he used to give his girlfriends his ID bracelet, and then when they broke up, she gave it back to you. Or maybe even threw it at you if you broke up during a fight.

Anyway, this was the thing about Japanese people who were actually from Japan. Even if you secretly didn't like their present, you had to be polite to them at every moment, and sometimes they didn't realize it when you were saying something only to be polite. They thought you meant it. Possibly there was more to it that I didn't understand, and I just didn't do the white lie correctly, and that was why I was now going to end up with three sweaters I would never wear. I was pretty sure the three sweaters were going to set back Baachan a few hundred bucks, on account of when your Japanese relatives bought you presents, they always bought you expensive ones. So I needed to straighten this all out before I left.

I would've been fine with some kind of cool *tishatsu*—the Japanese have all these words that are just Japanese versions of English words. So *tishatsu* is T-shirt. But if I asked for that, she would probably get me some kind of hundred-and-fifty-dollar Facetasm *tishatsu* that was bright orange and said FACETASM across the front, like she did last Christmas. And which I'd brought, so I could wear it for the first time.

Then Baachan took Joshie in her arms and talked really fast in Japanese. She and Jiichan talked excitedly to each other, and then Mom joined in while Dad looked on enthusiastically, and I had no idea what anybody was saying. I was pretty sure Dad understood about as much as I did. Joshie seemed a little confused but excited by all the commotion. Then they all calmed down and started talking in English again.

We were on the fortieth floor, and outside the living room window I saw hundreds—probably thousands—of tall buildings out there, all lit up. The lights didn't seem real. I imagined Mount Fuji in the distance to my left, but it wasn't visible in the night.

I tried to concentrate, to figure out if even at only forty stories I might feel a little different than if I was in my one-story house—in other words, to see if the Skytree effect worked at just forty stories. And I swear, I did feel different, my life passing slightly faster than usual. It was like being in the middle of a sci-fi movie.

There were only two bedrooms, plus a tiny room for Hii-Obaachan, my great-grandmother who also lived there. My family slept in the second bedroom, on two different beds. There are all kinds of lights in Tokyo, so my grandparents had given us silk eye masks to block the light, and my parents also pulled the shades down. I lay there wide awake. I mean, I was glad to be in Japan, but I gotta admit I felt a pull inside me. I thought about how cool it would be to stand at the window looking at the city while I was high. I wouldn't have to be completely fried. But a few hits of THC, just to have that kinda different perspective on the world. Getting high was not a negative thing, it just gave you a different way of seeing things.

It was hard to sleep because of that pull, though. A brief worry flickered through me that I was starting to like vaping too much. I thought back on not doing my homework after getting high at Lee's. If I could've, I would've vaped myself to sleep that night. But I'd woken up the next morning with the guilt back, so I got out of bed early and finished my homework.

Then I was hit with a massive craving for THC. I started to think about the last time Jiichan and Baachan had come to visit us in California. They had heard about Skid Row in downtown Los Angeles, and they wanted to see if it was for real. So we took them there, driving slowly through the homeless people and the people shooting up whatever people shoot up—heroin, I guess, or meth—and I remembered they'd gasped at one guy who was walking with his whole body bent forward, just because he was so out of it. He had drool coming out of his mouth. He looked like he was twenty-five, tops. It seemed like he saw us, because he waved a hand like he wanted us to stop looking. That made me feel bad, so I looked away.

There was a girl, and she was maybe twenty and kind of pretty, and she was just sitting on the curb staring into space. With my grandparents that day, I never for a moment thought, *That could be me someday*. But, you know, lying there in Japan, I realized that that could be anyone someday. It could be you. It could definitely be me. The only one it wouldn't be is Joshie, because I would for sure rescue him.

My grandparents were surprised by what they saw. I could see it in their faces. Japan had a small number of very tidy homeless people, but they were surprised at the *scope* in California.

I'm not criticizing America, exactly. I'm just saying. It seems like we took a wrong turn at some point.

Every day Baachan cooked for us. She made the best sukiyaki since sukiyaki was invented. She knew I loved it, so she made it five times while we were there. I also sat every day with my *hii-obaachan* in her very tiny room that wasn't really a bedroom but had a bed in there.

Mostly she didn't wake up. Regardless, I sat with her for an hour every afternoon the way my mom told me to. Mom said not to be on my phone in there, because that wasn't respectful. Hii-Obaachan was ninety-nine, and she had lived in Japan when Tokyo was getting the crap bombed out of it in World War II. She wrote a diary, but it was in a museum basement somewhere with a bunch of other diaries from that time. I asked her once if she could get it back so I could have it, and Baachan called the museum to see. But no go.

Hii-Obaachan used to be out of bed more when I was younger. She was my height when I was ten or eleven—we could look eye to eye. This trip she was in bed almost the whole time. When she was sleeping, it got boring, so I did look on my phone, but I tried to look at pictures from World War II, since maybe that was more respectful—after all, that was her time. Plus, I loved those old photos! Hii-Obaachan told me once that was the time she remembered most vividly in her life. She'd almost died during bombing raids. She was running to a shelter when a bomb fell, and a piece of a house flew at her, knocking her down with a big *whack* sound. Her back hurt like hell, but she got up and kept running, because that was just what you did—you didn't give up. It seemed amazing actually to be sitting in that room with someone that old; someone who'd run through bombing raids.

Whenever Hii-Obaachan was awake, she talked to me, and sometimes I would sort of understand what she was saying, and I would answer her in English, and she would go "ahh" like she understood, which I don't know if she did.

At one point she got agitated and kept saying, "Tegami, Tegami." Then I realized she was saying that because she had taught me the "Tegami" song last time I was here. I don't know where she heard that song. It was a hit, but not a big hit. The lyrics are in the form of a letter to a fifteen-year-old. The first line is: "Dear you, who's reading this letter." Like I said before, it's hokey, especially the part sung in English about believing in yourself. But Hii-Obaachan seemed satisfied once I found it on my phone and played it for her. She sang along. After she sang the last line, she sang it one more time without any music: "*Shiawase na koto wo negaimasu*"—that's the "I wish you happiness" part. She was really calm after that. I guess she just wanted to get it out of her system, on account of she knew how old she was. Who knew if we would see each other again?

In middle school I wrote up a history of Hii-Obaachan for a project, and at the end I quoted the ancient Chinese philosopher Chuang Tzu: "And the greatest man is nobody." I thought that applied to my great-grandmother, because everybody who knew her when she was younger was gone, and she never got famous or anything, so you could say she was nobody. And she raised five kids through extreme poverty and stayed a good person through a lot of super-hard stuff. So she was basically nobody, and also the greatest.

That trip did turn out to be the last time I ever saw her, because she died a week after we got home. I just kept thinking about how much she had wanted to sing that line to me. Not gonna lie, it was nice having people who cared about you. It kind of made you feel worse about yourself sometimes, but it was still nice.

NINETEEN

I hadn't gotten high for a couple of weeks, and when we got back from Japan, I was surprised how motivated I felt. I started thinking about buying these pricey Shimano biking shoes I'd seen in the mall that maybe I wouldn't even bike in but just put on my desk to look cool. They were a crazy green-and-black design. So I knocked on doors up and down the neighborhood offering to mow lawns. I'd done our lawn a couple of times, and I had the energy, so why not?

I did five big lawns in one Saturday for sixty bucks apiece. These were not small lawns like ours. They were *big*. On the last lawn I could tell my arms and legs were gonna be aching tomorrow. But it felt good.

It was getting to be evening when I called my dad and asked him to pick me up. He drove over in his pickup, and I heaved the lawn mower in.

"How much you got?" he asked.

I handed him three hundred dollars. "Can you get me the shoes?"

"Sure thing. Good job, Elijah!"

At home I trudged into the bathroom and looked in the

mirror. I'd never seen my face so dirty before. I thought of how Ben Matsumoto's grandpa had been a gardener for decades. My body hurt. I wondered if his body had hurt like this all time. Even today, the times I'd seen him, it seemed like his body still hurt.

Well, not "today" today. I hadn't been to Ben's for a while. I thought about giving him a call right then, which used to be so easy. But for some reason it didn't feel easy right now. Grandpa had told me that he was in Vietnam for only a year, and when he got back, everything looked exactly the same, but somehow everything was totally different. I guess the change for me wasn't that dramatic. But when I looked at my phone and opened it up, I *couldn't* call Ben. And that was just nuts.

TWENTY

Lee had gotten his cast off the day I flew to Japan. When he realized I'd returned to America, he texted, *You're back right wanna go to the mall my parents got me a car for getting my cast off.*

What? Whose parents got them a whole car to celebrate getting a cast off? But I replied, *Sure what kind of car*

Used beemer it's nice

Cool

Half an hour homie

Sure

I was doing homework even though it was only four o'clock—I did homework early on Tuesdays because I usually played PS4 with some other guys I knew from online on Tuesday nights. I didn't even *want* to go to Harvard, so maybe, like Banker said, the homework was a waste of time. But it made my parents crazy happy. So I did it. I wouldn't have enough time to finish my trig right then, but I figured I could do it before I went to bed.

"Going to the mall," I called out to my mom as I left the house.

Lee pulled up in a silver BMW. It looked practically

brand-new. I guess it was cool, for a modern car. I was sorta into classic cars, but most cars today were kind of meh unless they were for rich people. That was another thing I saw from old pictures. There was this *something* about older vehicles that wasn't around anymore. Let's see if I can explain . . . a lot of old cars had this look like, *I know I'm a cool car.* And today's cars mostly had a look like, *I can get you from point A to point B.* And going back farther, a stadium from Rome had this certain look: *I will be here forever.* And if you walked into a stadium today, it felt like, *This'll last for a while, and when it breaks down, whatever.* I learned a lot of stuff from old pictures. I learned about the people in a certain time period, even if there were no people in the picture. For instance, I learned that we weren't people with so many cool cars anymore, and we weren't people who built stadiums that'd last two thousand years. Which kind of sucked. Probably sucked for future archaeologists too. They would wonder what the frick we could've been thinking.

I walked up to the passenger side, not noticing until the last second that Lee was sitting there and someone else was driving: Banker.

Seemed a little "off," but I rolled with it, because it wasn't *my* car. So I opened up the back door, and another guy was just sliding over. I didn't know him.

"Yo," the guy said.

"Yo."

We fist-bumped.

"Davis," he said, pausing before he added, "Whang."

"Elijah," I replied. "Jensen."

I noticed he didn't have his seat belt on. I put on mine anyway.

"Nice car," I said to Lee. "It smells new."

"Yeah, I know," Lee said. "It only has thirteen thousand miles on it."

Banker pulled away from the curb, and then Lee reached back, handing me a vape pen. Banker glanced at Lee and said, "Hit it, Elijah."

I found myself reaching out eagerly—I hadn't been high for more than two weeks! I inhaled the THC and passed it to Davis. A few rounds, and I had that great feeling again: like I could jump off a mountain and live. But also something new. I could see the entire world; I could understand it, too. I was like some kind of wise man from history.

"How late can you stay out?" Banker asked.

I came back to Earth, a high school student again. "I still have homework, so not that late." I felt dumb after I said that. Not dumb, but young.

"Homework?" Davis said, kind of sarcastic.

He handed the pen back to me. It wasn't my turn, so I tried to hand it forward, but Banker said, "That's okay, you guys share one."

I felt flattered; that stuff was expensive. So I inhaled, watched the cloud of steam come out of my mouth. And just like I had before, I got it: Homework was a waste of time. A lot of things were a waste of time. Maybe just about everything.

TWENTY-ONE

We never did go to the mall. We rode down Pacific Coast Highway, all the windows open, and when we got to Malibu, Banker parked in a lot at a restaurant. Then he said, "I'm gonna take you guys to an expensive restaurant. It costs hella money."

Lee glanced at him. "For real? You have enough money for that?"

Banker took out his wallet, opened it up, and showed us how fat with bills it was. I was impressed. I wasn't *that* into money, but on the other hand, I mean, his wallet was *bulging*. It wasn't easy to get that much money. Banker looked like he had a thousand.

We were at a place called Blue. I saw a Rolls Royce in the parking lot, as well as a bunch of Mercedes. As we approached the entrance, the other guys got into a discussion about whether you were supposed to say "Mercedes" or "Mercedeses." I felt kind of excited, because I had never been to a high-end restaurant without any grown-ups, and even then only twice.

The lady with the menus looked like a girl from a few decades ago. I think all guys today should have been sixteen in about 1980. That would've been great! Punk and later heavy metal and muscle cars and girls with big hair. The menu lady had long hair that was kind of poofy on top, and she wore maybe a little more makeup than I liked, but other than that she was almost perfect. Total 1980s look.

Banker confidently followed her through the restaurant, with Lee, Davis, and me following less confidently. Lee was limping slightly, I guess because his muscles were still weak from having a cast on for so long. Davis was trying to look like he came to restaurants like this all the time, but I could tell he didn't. We sat at a table on the patio, the beach below us. The water was bright blue and calm, and it looked like it had diamonds on the surface.

"Order whatever you want," Banker said, looking up momentarily from the menu. He waved his hand like he owned the place. Lee and Davis each ordered a lobster dish that cost more than seventy-five dollars.

So I thought, *Why not?* and ordered the same. No cap, it was about the best meal I'd ever had. I'd had crab a few times at Japanese restaurants, but I'd never eaten lobster. It was cooked in butter, but it didn't taste buttery so much as it tasted *clean*, and it was soft. It tasted less fishy than fish, but still kind of fishy. Like, I'm a teenage guy, and there I was thinking about how to explain the exact taste of lobster. And the waiter treated us like we were rap stars.

When we'd finished, Banker asked for a dessert menu. The waiter brought it, telling us, "The crème brûlée is to die for."

"Thanks," Banker said, and the waiter left us alone. "Dessert?" Banker asked magnanimously.

"Nah," I said. I was stuffed. Also, I was starting to get worried about the bill.

It turned out that Lee and Davis were also stuffed. So Banker made a show of pulling out his wallet. He set it down, pulled out more bills than he needed to. And they were all hundreds. It was more than I'd thought, for sure. That made me really think. Like, really, really think. Where would Banker get all that money? And why would he show it to us? But then I saw him smiling proudly to Lee, and I saw that he wasn't showing off for all of us. He was showing off for Lee.

He laid down four hundred dollars, and we got up to leave.

When we got to the parking lot, Banker said, "Hey, why don't you sit in the passenger seat, Davis?" He glanced at Lee, and I had the sense that he was trying to make Lee jealous or something. Which was strange. In the car, nobody said anything for a good ten minutes. Then Banker smiled into the rearview mirror. "Hey, Lee, what did you think about that?"

"Uh, what?" Lee asked.

"What we just did. I did it for you."

Lee licked his lips a couple of times, finally answered, "Me? Well. The food was good." He paused. "What do you mean, for me?"

"I dunno, I do everything for you, homie." Banker was beaming into the rearview mirror.

Nobody spoke, maybe because that was a weird thing to say. Like, why would Banker do everything for Lee?

Then Lee tapped my arm. "I've been wanting to tell you. Remember that guy Chien Lu, who graduated last year? He wanted to major in molecular biology?"

"The one with the pierced ear?" Banker was giving me a dirty look, but I ignored him.

"Yeah. I ran into him the other day. He goes to Johns Hopkins now and says his classes are lit."

Johns Hopkins had one of the best molecular biology and genetics programs in the country. "What's he doing back?"

"Someone in his family died. But anyway, you know how I never got the molecular biology guys?"

"Yeah."

"When I was talking to him, I got it."

That made me interested. I could see that intense look he had in his eyes whenever he was really thinking.

"You know how a lot of normies think the universe is gigantic, and you look into a telescope, and it might as well be infinite even if it isn't, although maybe it is? I'm talking about how everybody just assumes."

Banker had actually pulled over to turn around to listen. On the shoulder of the freeway the Beemer shook every time a car sped by. There was nothing but a dark warehouse on the side of the road.

"Sure," I said. I thought it was dope when Lee felt like geeking out and discussing the stuff he thought about all the time.

"Yeah, so talking to Chien, I realized that every step smaller, reality is just as complicated," Lee went on. "In other words, just like outer space may go on forever, no matter how high the resolution of your microscope, there will always be something smaller than you can see. Reality effectively goes on forever into smallness. In that respect, it's just as unlimited as space." He paused. "Some people think it's fractal."

"Maybe it's finite but unbounded," I said. I was just talking, repeating back what he'd told me that one time—I wasn't even sure what that meant.

But Lee leaned back and stared at me like he was impressed. "Maybe," he said. "I'm gonna think about that."

I chuckled inside, because I wouldn't even know how to think about that. And then I did, sort of. "It's like history, where you have an unlimited number of factors shaping reality. I have a theory, though!" That came out more excited than I meant it to. So I continued coolly, "I have a theory that history is fractal. It occurs in complex patterns on both a large scale and smaller ones. So, like, you might have the same pattern in a group of twenty people as in a city of a million people as in a country as in a civilization. But the pattern's hidden, because we can't see the recurrent motifs through the complexity."

"That's bullshit," Banker said.

But Lee exclaimed, "Oh, yeah! Dude, you should try modeling that on a computer. I know a guy at Caltech who might be able to help you."

Banker had turned completely around, studying Lee. "It's cool the way you're so smart. I never knew anyone like you. I just want to show you the other side of the world before you go off and, you know, become a working genius."

Davis handed me the vape pen. "Chill, bro." Even though, how did he know I wasn't chilling? I inhaled hard and passed it back. We got higher and higher, and I felt more and more faded. I thought back on the evening. The more faded I got, the more I started to think it had been a great night.

Banker decided to drop off Davis first. He lived in a Santa Monica town house. There was a police helicopter overhead, with a searchlight pointed down, and what looked like every police car in Santa Monica blinking on the road. Santa Monica used to be nice, but now there were parts where the U.S. Postal Service said they couldn't deliver to anymore, because the mail carriers were getting attacked.

For a paranoid moment I thought the police were looking for us! I actually got pretty nervous.

"All the cops are *right here*," Banker observed. "This would be a good time to rob somewhere!" But he laughed, because he was kidding. I hoped. I wondered again where he'd gotten so much money.

But then Davis said, "Let's do it!" I felt sick. I just wanted to get home.

Thankfully, Lee leaned forward and said, "I gotta get back. I haven't done my physics problem for class tomorrow."

I did a quick prayer in my head: *Please, God, can we just go home?*

"Sure thing!" Banker said. "See ya, Davis."

"Yeah," he replied, getting out.

Banker screeched off, Lee and I still sitting in back. Banker brought up the food again, looking at me in the rearview mirror. "That lobster was kick-ass. Come on, what did you guys really think? Lee?" He paused, then added, "Come on, Elijah, chill. Geez."

"Yeah," I said, just to get him to stop talking. I tipped my head back, exhausted. Lee and I lived about a mile away from each other. Banker lived in Bell City, but he and his brother had used their aunt's friend's address to go to our school, because Mr. and Mrs. Bank had high hopes for Banker's younger brother, Alex. I think they thought that Alex was smarter than he really was. I guess he'd been pulling all A's at his old high school, and then he came here and got five B's. There were actually students who thought it was the end of the world if they got a single B. In fact, I'd heard that Mr. and Mrs. Bank had hired Alex a tutor after he got the B's. The way

I look at it, it would have been better if Banker and his brother had stayed at their former school. His brother would've gotten better grades, and Lee and I would've never met Banker. Then after a year with a few B's, the Banks sent Alex to prep school back East.

Sometimes I thought about fate and stuff like that. The way how, if I had done this or that, and Lee had done this or that, everything would have happened different. But you couldn't think that way for long. Because there were a million interconnecting lines out there, and maybe by walking along one line, things happened that were messed up, but it could've been even worse along ten other lines. And maybe some stuff just had to happen. Like you could move to the middle of nowhere or to the biggest city in America, and maybe there were just certain things you had to go through.

When I got home, Grandpa and Grandma were babysitting Joshie. I looked at them, surprised.

"Hi! Where's Mom and Dad?"

"Your aunt and uncle had their car stolen in Valencia, so your parents went to pick them up."

"Wow," I said. "That sucks." It made me kind of depressed, actually, because my aunt and uncle were pretty cool.

Joshie was staring at the TV. *Madagascar*. I stood there for about ten minutes, waiting, and then at the same time as the TV and Joshie, I shouted, "The penguins are psychotic!"

Joshie looked at me excitedly. "Do you want me to replay the part where I know every line by heart?"

"Sure thing."

So Grandpa said, "I'll find it." He played around with the remote, then started the section. And Joshie recited by heart for about five minutes. He looked at me like he was about to bust open with pride.

And I was able to say, and completely mean it, "Dude, you are just about the coolest kid I ever met in my life. In fact, you *are* the coolest."

He seemed amazed by the compliment, then cried out, "Thanks, Elijah! I'm going to learn even more lines for you, okay?"

"Sure thing," I said, and we high-fived.

I went to my room with Kiiro, sat at my desk. I thought about all of Banker's money and still wondered where it had come from and why it worried me so much. Then someone knocked on the door.

"Yeah?" I said.

Grandpa walked in. "Homework? Am I bothering you?"

"Nah," I said. I tapped my fingers on my laptop. I had one of those raw-edge desks, so the wood in front wasn't cut straight across like most desks. It wavered. The top was empty except for my laptop and cord, my lamp, a container of vitamin C from Grandma, and my new Shimano shoes. I did my math, English, and science on the laptop, and I did my writing all in my head before ever sitting at my desk. I tried to hold a whole essay in my head before I typed it out. Usually for writing stuff, I skipped over the pen and paper part.

Grandpa was nodding at the floor, then looked up. "You okay, Elijah?"

"Yeah. Why?"

"Just a feeling I had."

I wanted to say something, wasn't sure what. So I asked, "Do you think there are good people and bad people?"

He nodded again, this time confident, like he *knew* he knew the answer. "You have to live like there are." He paused. "But sometimes you have to treat bad people like they're good and good people like they're bad."

"What do you mean?"

"The first time I shot someone dead in Vietnam, I lay in the grass later trying to sleep, and I thought about the guy I killed. For all I knew, he was a good person. And I had a couple of assholes in my platoon. I realized that someday I might have to kill a good guy to save an asshole. You see?"

"Yeah . . . that really sucks. And what about here? Like, now?"

"I don't know. It's complicated. . . . You sure you're okay?"

"Yeah. Just tired, I guess."

He studied me. Sometimes with your relatives, you feel like they're looking right through you. I felt like I had a tattoo on my forehead that said I'M HIGH. I tried to hide my face by acting like I was studying the desk, something in the wood.

Grandpa said, "People look like they're good, and they're good today, and then three weeks later something happens, and they do something crappy, maybe to you. You don't know who they are until you know." His eyes went hazy. "And a guy might be a great guy in an office but an asshole in a war. Or vice versa." He seemed to really be concentrating now. "You learn more in a war than you learn in fifty years of living. But it's not what your dad and I want for you." He choked up a little as he said that.

"So how do you learn all that without going to war?"

He shrugged. "Some people never learn it." He held a hand

to his mouth, fingers partly curled. Thinking. "Are we talking about you?"

"I'm not sure," I said honestly.

"The only way out is through," he said. "No matter if we're talking about you or someone else."

He'd told me that before many times. He said when he was in-country, he would look ahead at the terrain his unit was trying to cross, and he didn't know if he would make it to the other side alive, even if it wasn't that long of a walk. Maybe it was only a hundred yards, but he thought about how he might die before he got to the other side. He told me he'd thought constantly during the war, *The only way out is through*. Once he was in Vietnam, the only way out for him was to go through it, to cross *through* his life a hundred yards at a time, hoping he didn't die, doing everything he could not to die and not to let his buddies die. And, apparently, sometimes having to kill a good guy in order to save a bad guy. But, I wondered, did that make Grandpa a bad guy, in that moment? Even though he was a good guy now?

I studied my desk for a full minute, this time for real, not speaking. An old man who was into wood had made it for my grandpa for his high school graduation, before he got drafted. And then Grandpa gave it to me when I was born, only I didn't know it at the time. It had been in storage. When I first started school, he gave it to me officially. I hadn't really liked it in my small room in Lombard, because it took up too much space. But now I got how cool it was, handmade and everything.

"I feel like I gotta go through," I said suddenly.

"All men gotta go through," he answered quickly. "They don't teach you that in school." He strode over with those funny long strides of his and squeezed my shoulder. Then he laid his hand on the desk, seemed to be admiring it—his hand, not the desk. He had gnarled hands. I knew he'd been strong once. Now he had arthritis, and his fingers didn't straighten out all the way anymore. "You'll do fine, Elijah. I got your back."

TWENTY-TWO

One fine day I needed money to get high, and I didn't feel like working for it. Because stuff like that was now a waste of time. So I sold a cool surfboard my dad gave me one Christmas when he wanted me to try surfing, but then I almost drowned and never tried again. I'd kept it in my room as decoration. The graphic was a big fish eating a smaller fish, which was eating a smaller fish, which was eating an even smaller fish—it was a pretty brutal design, if you really thought about it. But it was a gift from my dad, which was why I'd kept it so long. My dad hated shopping, but every birthday and Christmas I knew he thought a lot about what to get me and Joshie. Dad was kind of complicated on the inside, but on the outside he was a simple guy. He didn't talk about deep stuff. I knew he felt deep stuff; he just didn't have the words like my mom did.

Anyway. Seems Lee started thinking about money too. He was over at my place one afternoon, and he said, "Where's your surfboard?"

I looked around, then lowered my voice like my room might be bugged. "I sold it," I said softly.

"Who'd you sell it to?" He spoke quietly as well.

"Some guy from Craigslist. I turned off our security cameras, and he came over while everybody else was out."

He looked thoughtful. "I wonder what I could sell. I've got my car . . ."

"Dude! What would you tell your parents if your car went missing?"

He smiled, but just a little.

I didn't think about it at the time. I thought at the time that we were having a perfectly logical discussion. But later I realized that when you're doing drugs, the moment you start thinking about how you're gonna get the money for the drugs, that's the moment everything changes. Because after that anything can happen. You want what you want, and you need money to get it. So how do you get the money?

TWENTY-THREE

All of a sudden, Lee started hanging out at Banker's house a lot. As in, all the time. Maybe because Banker was giving him free stuff. I was there too a lot of the time. Lee and I were getting high daily. At first I was only getting high with them, but after a while I kept a vape pen someone at school sold me under my pillow in case I got the urge in the middle of the night.

Banker had started out acting like Lee was a really special super-genius guy who he just wanted to be friends with because of his super-genius-ness. Which totally flattered Lee. I could tell it pumped him up the way Banker thought he was so amazing. And then something changed. I'm not sure when. It's kind of like you don't know exactly when day starts to turn into night. But all of a sudden, you realize it's getting dark. More and more, Banker was kind of bossing Lee around but subtly. Like he was teaching Lee how to be a different person. Like he was *tutoring* Lee. Banker had a certain skill set, just like Lee did, and he was trying to teach his skill set to Lee.

Lee kept asking me to come with him to Banker's, though, and whenever he asked, I did. Because Lee, he *was* special. I knew a lot of smart kids—I was one of them—but he was something else. Maybe he wasn't born to shake the nations, but I felt like maybe he was born to shake science. And like I said, Banker had seemed like maybe he thought the same. Early on, Banker said to Lee over and over, like he was bragging, "I'm teaching you so much good shit."

Anyway, I went over to Banker's with Lee one Friday night. Davis was already there, and Banker's mom made about five jokes about how we were an Asian posse. She was Asian, and Mr. Bank was white.

He was one of those dads who lived on the couch. That was kind of an American thing. My trig teacher said Americans watched more TV than any country in the world. Had nothing to do with trig, but he liked blurting out details about whatever. I thought it was kinda cool, but some of the kids thought he was mental.

Mr. Bank watched sports and the news and Hallmark-type stuff, and then when he got tired, he fell asleep during a talk show. The Banks had a white leather reclining sofa with thick cushions. It must've been super comfortable, because I could tell Mr. Bank felt like a king on it.

Banker's house looked beat-up outside, but inside, everything was really nice. I guess some people thought that might fool burglars.

Anyway, Banker had a long room jutting out on the side of the house, so there was a window at the back and a long window on the side that was covered in aluminum foil. Don't ask why, I don't know. Otherwise, normal room except for a splotch on a wall, like somebody had thrown a mud ball and it dried. Banker was always asking us to sleep over, but we never did. It just didn't feel right.

So this one night, we were chilling, getting high, watching a movie, playing a little PS4. There was a hot girl there named Sophie. You could feel the heat coming off her, no kidding—I swear, the air was wavering. I didn't know her, but when we were watching the movie, she was leaning against Banker, and he had his arm around her. And he goes, "Lee, go grab me some water from the kitchen. I'm kinda busy here, thanks."

Maybe he meant he was busy with Sophie. But there was something disrespectful about the way he said it. It caught my attention, because (1) it was Lee who was gonna, you know, build satellites and stuff someday while Banker was still getting high; and (2) he'd previously been super respectful toward Lee.

But Lee said, "Sure," and hopped up to get water. He came back with a cup that he handed to Banker.

Banker was like, "Dude, where did you get this water?"

"Uh, from the tap. Your mom said you have a built-in water filter."

"I keep a special bottle of water in the fridge," Banker said, an edge of impatience in his voice. "I only drink cold water."

Lee stood there a moment. I jumped up and said, "I'll get it!" And I did.

Then Banker started making out with Sophie, and Lee and I got up to leave. Davis was busy trying two different vapes, ignoring everybody.

Outside, I asked Lee, "Why can't he get his own water?"

"It's cool," Lee said, waving a hand like he was brushing the question away. "He was just showing off for Sophie."

He dropped me off at home. We hadn't talked much in the car, and when I got out, he just said, "See ya," and I said, "Sure."

I was thinking about something. Banker got his hair cut

into a fade last week. Then Banker told Lee to also get a fade. And Lee said, "Okay." And he did. Like, does that make sense? Is that normal to tell someone how to cut their hair, and then the person does it? It seemed like shit was getting real.

At the same time, getting high kinda took my mind off most things. Even riding my bike through a homeless camp one day under a freeway, I didn't feel the impact like I used to. I used to be like, *Wow, there's* hella *homeless in California.* Now it was just like, *Well, they're everywhere, so what?* Nothing mattered that much anymore.

Also, homeless people came in handy. One day I tried to get some THC on my own. I stood outside a dispensary in San Luis, waiting for a homeless person to wander by. I finally spotted one and said, "Excuse me. If I pay you three dollars, can you get me a couple of vape pods?"

"Make it five bucks—what do I look like, anyway?"

"Uh, you look fine. I want one Stiizy Sour Tangie pod and one Strawberry Cough. They're both sativa, cost is about twenty-two each plus tax. I'm going to give you fifty, and when you come out, you should have almost two dollars left, and then I'll give you three more so you get paid five."

He reared back a bit. "Do you know how much tax there is? This is California, man. For marijuana, we got taxes on your taxes."

I didn't think "taxes on your taxes" made sense, but on the other hand, what did I know about taxes? I handed him another five, but he rubbed his fingers in the air. So I traded the five I just gave him for my last ten.

"Got it, boss."

He hunched down suddenly like he was going to run off

with the money, and for a second there I thought I was going to have to chase him down. Which I totally would've done. But he went into the store, and in a few minutes he came out with a plain white bag. I checked inside: perfect. I looked at the receipt he handed me, and he was right—taxes on taxes, California, etc. I gave him his five.

"Thanks, boss. I'm here every afternoon around the same time, because the bagel shop gives me leftovers when they close."

"All right, catch you later. Thanks."

It felt cool—I felt like I'd accomplished something. I was making my way in the world!

I looked around, opened my package, and clicked the pod into my pen. I'd charged it up earlier and took a hit now. It felt good. Strawberry Cough was my favorite. The THC flooded my brain. It was like jumping into a swimming pool and going deep under without drowning. I loved that feeling. You entered an alternate reality that was way cooler than regular reality. So why would you even want to *be* in regular reality?

TWENTY-FOUR

One day in the middle of September, I was vaping in the backyard and really getting off on the outdoors. I squinted up at the sun and said, "Hey, sun."

"What is that?" I heard Joshie call out. "It's pretty."

I jerked my head around. My brother was running toward me. I guessed he meant the cloud of vapor. I slipped the pen into my hoodie pocket just as he arrived in front of me. He seemed unsure if we were playing a game. Or what. Then he realized it was "or what." He hesitated, then lit up and said, "What are you doing?"

"Uh, just relaxing," I said. "Hey, wanna throw the ball for Kiiro?"

He nodded vigorously before grabbing a ball from the ground and heaving it pretty well for his age. "WHAT a throw!" I exclaimed.

He looked genuinely and completely and extremely pleased that I'd said that. I looked up at the blue and the clouds and the white cloudlike moon in the afternoon sky. I felt an ache like . . . like I could feel every person's ache on the planet. It was like my whole insides were in pain. For some reason.

Joshie suddenly gripped my wrist hard, his nails digging into my skin. "Are you okay, Elijah?"

I flashed back to when Ben and I were kids, and he took a brutal fall off his skateboard. His eyes had rolled back, and I'd grabbed his arm the same way. I remembered the burst of worry I'd felt. Now I looked at Joshie's face, and I could see how much he, you know, *loved* me.

Kiiro was standing behind him, the ball in his mouth, his tail wagging. "Hey, lemme see if I can throw as far as you!" I said with pretend excitement to Joshie. I threw the ball just a little less far than my brother had. Joshie squealed so loudly that Kiiro stopped to look back at us. Then he saw everything was fine and trotted to the ball.

Joshie fell against me, and I caught him. It was a game of his, trusting me to catch him. I wrapped my arms around him. "Good throw," I said.

"I know," he agreed. "I'm such a throw-bro."

But Mom was calling him, so he ran in.

Kiiro stuck with me, of course. By the way, he'd suddenly started to get white around his muzzle, even though he wasn't even eight yet. And it was like I could see he was getting white, but it didn't seem real. Everything that used to seem real no longer seemed vivid anymore. So that was really, really sad, that my dog was getting old and I wasn't totally there for him. But I couldn't find the place to really be there with him anymore. I didn't know where that place was.

I could tell Kiiro somehow knew all this, but he couldn't say so. Kiiro was happy when I was happy. Which was not lately. That's dogs for you; they know your insides.

I was about to throw the ball again when I saw that my

mom was walking toward me holding something in her hand. She was wearing some flowery thing. I swear, half her clothes had flowers on them. She was such a *mom*. When she was in Japan, she acted really Japanese and was always giggling and bowing and saying no when she meant yes. But in America she was very direct. When she reached me, the first thing she did was turn around, as if to check that Joshie had gone inside.

Then she held up a vape pen.

"Shit," I said. I mean, what else could I say, right?

I had three pens by then, including the one in my pocket and the one she was holding—which I knew she'd found in the fake water bottle Banker had bought me for twenty bucks on Amazon. Which was nice of him, I guess. It looked like a Dasani bottle, but if you twisted it, there was a secret compartment inside.

"I know what this is," she informed me. "I looked it up on the internet."

I didn't say anything, because the only thing I could think of was to say "shit" again.

"I *knew* something was off about you lately, so I searched your room. It was in your jacket pocket." Oh . . . I'd forgotten about the one in my jacket pocket. At least I still had the one in the fake water bottle!

"Welp. Uh. I mean, Mom, it's just like weed. Didn't you smoke weed when you were young? Be honest."

"No, I did not."

Wow, just my luck to have the only mom in California who never smoked weed when she was young.

She seemed to be waiting for more. I suddenly realized that this conversation didn't matter. Because I wasn't going to stop. She didn't know that, but I did.

"Elijah . . . what is going on with you?"

I pondered that but realized I didn't know the answer. So I said, "Mom, all the kids vape, and most of the parents don't even care." A bunch of kids had told me that their parents were like, "Well, we'd rather you didn't, but on the other hand, we smoked pot when we were your age."

"Honey, you don't belong to those parents, you belong to your father and me."

I stared at my bare feet. Kiiro pressed his chin into my thigh, and I rubbed his head. I looked up, saw Joshie peeking around the back doorway. "But it's not that big a deal."

"But you don't seem like *you* lately. I don't like that. I don't like it at all."

Hmm. I decided to try apologizing. "I'm sorry, Mom. I won't do it anymore. I swear it!"

Her face immediately looked relieved. Like I'd flicked a switch. She believed me! "Thank you, Elijah, that's all I wanted to hear." She was really proud—I saw tears in her eyes—and then she leaned over and hugged me. "I'm so proud of you."

"Thanks, Mom. I'm really sorry."

Then Joshie ran out, and we threw the ball awhile, and that was that.

TWENTY-FIVE

I mean, it wasn't *that* that. Dad came by my room later as I lay in bed. He sat on the edge of the mattress, the way he used to when I was little. "So how're things at school?"

"Okay," I said.

He nodded. "All right." He nodded again. "Hey, did you know I had a drinking problem after I got back from Iraq? A lot of us did."

Wow, I could not imagine my dad with a drinking problem. "No . . . really?" I said. Although now that I thought about it, I *could* imagine it.

"Yeah, it was hard times."

"What made you not have a drinking problem anymore?"

"You." He paused.

I thought a moment. "I ain't having a baby. I don't even have a girlfriend yet."

He laughed. "Yeah, you don't need a baby yet."

"Wait, so was that after you got married even?"

"Yeah."

I thought about that a second. "Wow, live and learn." I heard myself saying that kind of flippantly, even though I could see my dad was trying to talk serious.

"So what's this vaping thing all about?"

"I dunno." But he was my *dad*, so I added, "I like it."

"Yeah . . ." He took a big breath, flexed his back. "I know that feeling. But you're gonna try to quit, right?"

"Sure." But I hung my head and decided to say an honest thing. Sometimes you kind of just need to say an honest thing, just to feel something, you know? So I added, "I don't know if it's too hard to stop, though."

"Yeah." He hung his head too. Then he looked around my bedroom, his eyes landing back on my bed. "Is this better?" he asked.

"This?"

"I mean, you have a full bed now instead of a twin."

I looked down. I still had my same blanket, which was a white Japanese comforter with a gold oval shape in the middle. It was a twin comforter for my old bed in the Lombard apartment, but I'd kept it because Hii-Obaachan made it a long time ago for her first son, who died in a fishing accident. "Yeah, it's much better," I said. "What do you mean, Dad? Don't you think it's better?"

"Yeah, sure," he said.

"But really, don't you?"

"Yeah, I really do. I guess I do. But sometimes I can't tell: Is it home?"

I wanted to help him out here, but I wasn't sure what he meant. So I said, "I think it's great. It's definitely home." Even though, was it?

"I hope so," he said. Then he got up. "So you're gonna try to quit, right? You're gonna try hard? Because I can tell you from experience that at some point you're gonna have to ease up— you won't have a choice. And sooner is better."

"Yeah, I—" I was going to say, *I promise*, but instead I said, "I will definitely try."

He left the room, and I held Kiiro for a minute, wishing I'd gotten him as a puppy. I buried my nose into his neck and smelled his dog smell. Then I took his head in my hands. "You've got white around your muzzle already," I said. It just seemed wrong the way dogs get old so fast.

TWENTY-SIX

I did try for a couple of days, but then I stopped trying. I missed it too much, due to the world seeming boring without it.

And then one day I got a whole new level of mad. It was a level of mad I didn't even know people could get. I had biked home from school as fast as I could, so I could get super high. The door to my bedroom was open. I scanned the room: my Shimano shoes were not on my desk! I had tried them on only once! I rushed into Joshie's room feeling almost like I was ready to smash a hole in a wall. And there he was sitting at his computer playing Minecraft IN MY SHOES.

He turned quickly, looking shocked and scared—scared of *me*.

"WHAT THE FUCK ARE YOU DOING IN MY SHOES?" They were like five sizes too big for him!

"I'm sorry, Elijah!" he cried out, yanking them off and holding them out to me. I knocked them out of his hands, so hard they flew across the room. Not exaggerating, the anger explosion was unreal—it was like being transported to another dimension.

"WHO THE FUCK TOLD YOU YOU COULD TAKE MY SHOES?" I stared at my Shimanos, at the cool green design, and I thought for a moment I was going to black out.

He'd turned to stone, gaping at me slack-jawed.

Those shoes were one of my prized possessions. Anger was exploding inside me. My fist clenched; I wanted to sock my little brother across the room.

Then a part of me started being self-aware and watching myself being furious. I saw Joshie's eyes move to behind me. My mom was standing there, also gaping.

She didn't yell. She just said my name softly: "Elijah?" Like she wasn't sure it was me.

That was it for my parents—no more Mr. Nice Guy, as Grandpa would say.

Eight days, and my mom had found a rehab, the insurance had okayed it, and I'd cleared a three-day waiting list that we were told was "unusually short." And Mom, Dad, and I were all sitting in what's called an IOP, which is Intensive Outpatient Program, which is rehab with a different name.

Basically, for an hour an ex-addict would lecture a bunch of us kids about how addiction was terrible and caused all our anxiety and depression and anger, and was destroying our IQ, and we'd better stop asap. Then for another hour we had a talking group, where we spoke about our issues as they related to drugs. Then for another hour we had either another lecture or another discussion group. Occasionally, there was a meditation or stretching class.

The main room was kind of homey, like your living room

if you lived in an IKEA set with extra chairs. Nature scenes decorated the walls.

Anyway, I kid you not, you have to do this IOP thing every day for three hours from four to seven. It's like a job! All us kids slumped in our chairs and acted bored. Even if we'd been interested, I'm pretty sure we would've pretended to be bored. Because, what were we even doing there? There were people out on the street smoking meth and shooting up. There were people addicted to fentanyl. There were people *dealing* fentanyl and meth. And quite a few of us were just vaping. Okay, there were also kids drinking and taking pills. On the other hand, for some reason we all accepted being there. I asked around one day, and none of us even put up a fight about coming. Maybe deep inside we wanted to stop? Or was it that we liked seeing that we weren't the worst kid in the world—there were plenty of others like us?

Once a week the parents came and we all met together, on top of which there were twice-weekly parents-only meetings, as well as a meeting with parents, their kid, and a counselor. Not to mention, the place my mom had found was forty-five minutes from home. So it was kind of a job for them as well. During the second parent-kid meeting one guy stood up, and he was different from the rest of us. Because, honestly, we were just there because our parents were making us, or at least we thought that. But he was there for reals, taking it seriously. He was seventeen and had been in and out of rehabs since he was thirteen, and he actually *wanted* to quit doing drugs. And he couldn't.

Not gonna lie, I sat up straighter when he first said it. Because a lot of us still felt we could quit, if only we *really* wanted. And here was this guy who *really* wanted to but couldn't. He vaped both nicotine and THC, depending on his mood. He did some pills. And I was thinking, *Dude, it's just vaping, and it's just a couple of pills here and there.* Like, every parent in that room besides my mom probably smoked weed when they were young. They took pills, they snorted coke. And here they were, living their normal lives. So what was the big deal? I didn't get it. But the ex-addicts all said vaping was different, and even smoking weed today was different, on account of how potent the THC was now. It wasn't like the stuff that kids used to smoke in the old days. Like, at least three times a session, different ex-addicts told us that there were studies about how today's weed and vaping made adolescents psychotic, whatever that means—I mean, aren't all adolescents a little psychotic?

But anyway, this guy—his name was Martin—started talking passionately about how his parents were sorry they ever had him. "They think I'm a bad influence on my brothers! My teachers think I'm a bad influence on the other kids. My therapist thinks I'm a bad person!" He was standing up, pacing back and forth. "But I know I'm a good person!" he shouted. "I know I'm still a good person inside!"

His parents both touched his arm, and his dad said, "We know who you are inside, Marty. It was like a religious revival. There were tears falling down my dude's face—it made me really feel like I gave a shit for the first time in months.

Day after day, I could see how hard Martin was trying. He always sat up really straight in one of the harder chairs, like having good posture would keep him sober. Then during group therapy he did a lot of the talking. "Even though everybody at school knows I'm trying to quit, they keep offering me stuff. Why does everybody want me to fail? I thought they were my friends." He slumped down suddenly. "I don't even know if I have friends."

I knew that was a thing—those people who wanted you to be high for some reason. You'd think, what do they care? But they did care, and they wanted you high like they were. My mind flashed to Banker, the look of eagerness he sometimes got when he watched Lee and me get high.

On Wednesday nights we always had the session with the parents, and everybody went around the room and said how their week was going. When it was my turn, I said, "My week is going all right. I mean, I've been grounded, to tell the truth, so I mostly just went to school and came here. It was okay."

Britney did what she did every week, which was hold a stuffed rabbit with big ears from home and talk about how she wanted to go out and her parents wouldn't let her, and how was she ever going to grow up if they didn't let her go out, and then it turned out she'd wanted to go hang out in Hollywood with a bunch of older kids. I happened to know that Britney had a private Snapchat account with grown men in it. I mean, I think it was only her and these grown men. Which, how did that fit with this girl holding a stuffed rabbit right that second?

Also, rehab was where I found out that it was a thing for some kids into drugs to go to parties with grown-ups there. Britney did that, but her parents didn't know. Martin had done that as well. He said so in a group chat some of us had formed.

Anyway, when it was Martin's turn, he was kind of rambling about wanting to quit. I was zoning out, to be honest, because he said this stuff every time he talked. Then OUT OF NOWHERE Martin broke down in sobs and started talking about an older guy who used to fondle him and pay for this fondling by giving him pills and vape pods. In fact, this guy was the one who got him started on pain pills. Martin was telling this story, and then he suddenly strode over to a wall and started pounding on it over and over. I swear, I could feel the room shake every time he pounded. Then he looked at his hand and said, "I think I broke my hand." I saw his fingers hanging at an odd angle. His parents didn't say a word, just each took a side and put an arm around him. The father called out over his shoulder, "Pardon us, we need to go to the hospital."

After they left, I just . . . I looked at my mom, then at my dad, and I . . . I couldn't comprehend that this was real life and that Martin may have broken his hand because he was so upset about what he was upset about. I just . . . like . . . the world truly sucked. I wondered if he could be lying. But I knew he was not, because I'd seen the truth in his eyes.

At the same time, there was also a part of me that didn't understand why I was there. I was nothing like Martin! I wasn't even like some of the other kids at the rehab who were pretty bad with the pills and one who was doing meth. Like, yeah, I had lost some motivation, but I was sixteen. What was the hurry? Why couldn't I take a little life detour to be a normal kid and party a little? Why did all the Asian kids at school have to be so well-behaved? I mean, I was only half Asian!

Still, I gotta say, Martin's story shook me up. The way you know something shook you is that afterward you feel like you're not exactly the same person you were beforehand. The lead counselor told us that there was a lot of sex abuse in the drug world. I honestly hadn't known that. I mean, it surprised me. Yeah, so like I said, I knew that some of the kids went to parties where adults were present. But, I mean, this other stuff was all new to me. In other words, I'd known grown-ups were at some of these parties, but I didn't know grown-ups were there AND there was sex.

I touched eyes with some of the other kids, but nobody was reacting much—we all sat stone-faced. The counselor said sometimes you got abused, and that made you stay an addict, and sometimes you became an addict, and then in the process you got abused. He said an advantage the abusers had was that some of the parents got really uncomfortable about the possibilities—they had never even considered that it could happen to their kid. They got so uncomfortable, they shut their minds down and acted like zombies.

When we got in the car after the meeting, Dad didn't start the engine at first. He lit a cigarette, which—didn't he stop smoking when my mom was pregnant with Josh? He smoked the cigarette all the way to the filter. Then he said, "Geez."

"Geez," Mom echoed.

I just leaned over with my head in my hands. I couldn't stop seeing Martin hitting that wall. I had this weird feeling like hyperawareness of my crotch—like spiders were crawling between my legs. I knew that what happened to Martin went on in the world, but damn, seeing him that upset . . . *Damn.* Just *damn.*

I felt myself transported to a darker place. I looked out the window, and it wasn't the same parking lot anymore, and then wasn't the same street, and then wasn't the same freeway. Wasn't there some book where there are layers of hell or something? I had just seen a lower level. Maybe I had even skipped a level or two somewhere and sunk deeper than I ever intended.

As we drove, I sat quietly, watched as we passed a Home Depot and then a Staples and then a row of apartments close to the freeway. And I felt like, even though the stuff had happened to Martin and not to me, I was still in that lower level.

"I feel so bad for Martin," Mom was saying.

"Yeah," Dad replied. "If I were his dad, I would kill that fucking bastard. I would."

"Well, but then you would end up in jail," Mom said. "Nobody wants to go to *jail*. It's horrific."

The parents, they're funny. Like the way jail was this mythical place where someone else went, but never anyone *you* knew. But, like, some of the counselors had told us *they'd* been in jail. These days you could just join a crew and rob some fancy store in a smash-and-grab, but some of these counselors had *robbed banks*.

We were quiet the rest of the way, quiet as we walked into the house. Grandma and Grandpa were watching TV on the couch, babysitting Joshie. They did that every day now, so Mom and Dad could drive me to the program. A lot of the parents hung around the parking lot while the kids were in sessions. I guess it was because they were so worried about us. Plus, all the meetings, and how far some of us lived from this place. But maybe also just to be there by their kids. Like, I'm pretty sure my mom would've sat in that parking lot for three hours, even if we'd lived ten minutes away, the same as if I was in the hospital having an operation and she was in the waiting room.

My grandparents both stood up like they did every time I came home from rehab. Like they were worried. I looked at them and continued on to my room. I was shocked when I turned on my bedroom light and saw Joshie in my bed, hugging Kiiro. He opened his eyes. "Hi, Elijah. Are you okay?"

"Yeah, what do you mean?"

"I dunno. I felt worried."

"I'm good. Hey, dude, sorry about the other day. With the shoes, I mean."

"It's okay—Mommy said you didn't feel well. I shouldn't have tried on your shoes."

I relaxed and pulled my desk chair to the bed. "I'll take you out on your bike soon to make up for it." Kiiro had walked up to me and was nuzzling my hand. Dogs are such bros, always there for you.

Joshie looked like he was going to cry, but he nodded. "Yeah, I miss my bike lessons." But then tears were falling from his eyes. "I asked Mommy why I had to stay with Grandma and Grandpa so much now, and she wouldn't say. But then I asked Grandma, and she said it was because you were sick but you were going to be fine. Are you okay?"

"Yeah, I'm not sick. I'm . . . I'm okay." Then I reached out and rubbed the top of his head. "Why don't you go to bed, I'm fine," I said softly.

He looked up at me so sincerely. "Are you going to die?"

"No! Nah, I'm not going to die. I'm not really even sick."

"Grandma was lying?"

"No, I mean . . . I'm gonna be fine," I said.

"Can I go with you?"

"Where?"

"Wherever you go? Maybe I can help the doctor make you better. Are you going to a doctor?"

"Nah, I just, uh, I just talk to some people about bike riding and stuff." I could see that didn't make sense to him, but lying is like once you tell the lie, you kind of have to stick with it no matter how dumb it is.

So when he asked, "Bike riding?" I firmly replied, "Yes, that's right. We talk about which bikes have better suspensions and brakes and stuff like that, and how you have to adjust to each bike. And that makes me feel cheerful." Like I said, you stick with the original lie into absurdity.

"But can I go with you?"

There were a couple of younger kids who came to family group sometimes, one who looked as young as Joshie. But I would've felt embarrassed for Joshie to be there. Ashamed, actually. Me slouching, occasionally smart-assing like we all tried to do sometimes to show we didn't care.

He stood up. "I want to help you get better." He stomped his foot for emphasis.

I twirled the chair toward him, and he leaned into me. I held him like that, resting my cheek on his hair. "I'm gonna take you out biking soon," I said. "I promise." But at that moment I just didn't know if I *would* take him biking soon. I could no longer even make a simple statement like that and know if it was true. Because suddenly, I knew: there was no sidewalk anymore. Your parents could build your sidewalk to where you took your SAT, to your extracurriculars, to college, to a job. But not for this.

TWENTY-SEVEN

Then the very next week I got hit on myself by a drug dealer creep Banker knew in Hollywood. It was after I snuck out when my parents were asleep. I walked right out the front door and met Lee at the curb. Lee had been getting into this begging mode with me—he said I just *had* to come with him sometimes. And he was still my homie, even if I'd barely seen him since I'd been in rehab. Just because rehab takes so much of your time.

Anyway, back to the creep—my first creep encounter, I guess you could say. I'm not even great-looking or anything. I'm okay. I have this kind of typical Asian thick straight black hair that sticks out and that I have to use product on to make look acceptable. And the typical hapa skin that isn't quite gold and isn't quite white. Kind of gold-white. I wear a lot of T-shirts and plain jeans or workout shorts. I guess I'm strong from all the biking, but I don't lift. And I've always thought I look, I dunno, like a basic half-Asian guy. There's probably thousands of them in California.

But this dealer looked at me like I was *delicious*. I felt this weird almost paralyzed sense that the air was thickening, turning into quicksand or something and I wouldn't be able to move through it. I couldn't even believe it at first, but then I saw it clearly: he wanted to touch me, or for me to touch him. Some of these guys don't care if you're a boy or a girl—I learned that later at rehab. Some do care, but some just want you to be young. Like these guys act like they're aquiring some special life force by getting a blow job from a young person. I thought of how upset Martin had been and wondered what kind of voodoo these guys worked on you.

Banker and Lee were both there, inside an apartment, but they just watched as this fresh hell came at me. The guy said "Hey" to me and touched his crotch. He actually licked his lips like a cartoon bad guy. I had to ask myself if this was truly happening. So I asked myself, and it was in fact happening.

I just about puked, but I tried to look cool. I was like, "Nah, I got money." I still had money left over from selling my surfboard.

The guy told me he knew a really gorgeous girl who could get any drug on the planet, anytime she wanted. Her dad thought she was a good kid. "Your parents think you're a good kid," he said, like he knew my parents. "You want five Percs? Ten?"

Banker was nodding yes at me.

My lips felt dry. I just said, "Nah, I'm good," then went out to the front walkway to wait for Banker and Lee to finish the transaction they were making with the guy. This apartment complex was a little like the place where we used to live. I used to look at people like that guy walk by, except from the other side of the metal door. Now the palm trees were rustling like giant birds, and the world felt like black magic.

Nobody came out. Five minutes passed. Ten. Fifteen. Then Banker and Lee finally came out. The creep guy came out right behind them and put both his hands on Lee's shoulders and gave a squeeze, kind of leaning in. "See you, sweetie," he said close to Lee's ear. Right then, right as he spoke those words so close to Lee's ear, so intimate-like, I entered the lower level that I'd only *thought* I'd entered previously.

TWENTY-EIGHT

I know, girls might have a big discussion about what had happened. Or not. But we just sat in the car silently. Because that's the way guys roll. And because there's no sidewalk. You're just not really sure what the fuck. You know?

A few days later, in rehab, Martin showed me pictures of his house—you could see the ocean from the living room, his bedroom, *and* the dining room. You could see the city lights from another window. We were on a couch looking at his phone while one of the counselors set up a short movie about addiction we were going to watch.

Martin lived in Las Colinas, which I never even met anyone from there. It's one of those ridiculously super-superduper wealthy gated communities in California. I mentioned it before. The one where I had never even seen any of the gates.

I guess some of the homes there had stables. Martin showed me a picture of his horse, Red. The program I was at used to have equine therapy, where the addicts would take care of horses. So I was really interested in Martin's horse, because I didn't get what becoming unaddicted could possibly have to do with horses. The horse was red-brown except for all four ankles, which were white. Did horses even have "ankles"? The red shone in the sunlight. I didn't know anything about horses, but this one looked amazing. Gentle and not gentle at the same time. Domesticated and not domesticated. Martin was leaning his head against Red in the picture he showed me.

And, so. The night he showed me those pictures was the last time I ever saw him, because he OD'd the next night. He didn't show up at rehab for a few days. And then on Monday, Mr. Kevin, the director of the rehab, came in and told us the news.

He was wearing a backward baseball cap, even though he also had on a suit. "I have sad news. Martin is no longer with us."

"Did he change rehabs?" I asked.

"No. He overdosed at a friend's house. Only you can't really call a friend like that a true friend. Let's say a prayer." He took off his cap, held it to his chest, and looked down. "Dear Lord and Savior, I ask that you forgive Martin his sins and remember his good heart as you welcome him into heaven. I ask that you watch over his family and especially his mom and dad, who, as you know, are good people—the best. The best of the best. Thank you for giving me the chance to do your work, and forgive me for failing. Amen." I looked up, but the director's head was still bowed. He didn't lift it for a long time. In fact, the counselor started the session while the director's head was still bowed. Mr. Kevin stood there until we were about halfway through the hour, then put on his hat and left.

We had Pac-Man for this session. His real name was Patrick Gilmore. He'd told us he'd been in jail seven times, including for beating up people. But mostly for drugs. He was the baddest dude of the counselors. He took the confrontational approach, along the lines of "You think you're pretty tough, don't you?" Each of the counselors had their own strategies. Pac-Man was hard-core. A guy named Jack took the detail-oriented approach, telling you what to do if you felt a craving (go for a jog, do breathing exercises, etc.). A couple of the women took the "Honey, I'm on your side" approach. Jeannie tried to scare us with her tales of being in jail and how awful it was. She told us she'd stabbed someone once, for seven dollars. Like, she just suddenly announced in the middle of a lecture, "I stabbed someone once for seven dollars. I would've killed her if she had a hundred." Then she went back to her presentation.

Actually, they'd all been in jail, except the director.

A guy named Dr. Peterson did the "You're hurting your parents" thing. He wasn't a medical doctor, but he had a PhD in English. And so on. Mr. Kevin was my favorite. He was kind of all-knowing, like he'd met every addict who ever was and ever would be. But I guess he still didn't know how to help them, so he seemed kind of sad and tired.

Pac-Man was saying, "The egg or the peach with the pit inside, the egg or the peach. Are you hard on the inside or hard on the outside? I was both—I was a rock. I was hard down to my heart."

"So then why'd you get sober?" I asked.

"To help you kids," he answered.

"You didn't help Martin," one guy said.

Pac-Man said, "Tough guy, right?" He took a big breath. He had a grizzled look, even though he was only in his forties. "You know the ones that hurt me? It's not even the kids. It's the ones who get sober after years, they're trying to be happy. And they go out and get a job—managing a coffee shop, warehouse worker. They get a girl. Years go by, and then someone offers them some shit. They take it, and two weeks later they're dead. I always wonder: Why didn't they call someone?"

"Martin said because they don't call back," someone said.

We were all supposed to have a guide, someone you could call at any time of the day or night, and they would take your call. But Martin had told us his guide never called back, because he was also guide to about ten other kids. So, no time. But I would hate to be the guy who didn't take Martin's call.

I thought of his parents, and of how that night when he said he was still a good person, they had told him solemnly that they still knew who he was inside. But I'm not sure that they *did* know. Because the drugs kind of make you somebody who maybe your parents don't know so well anymore. His parents became Christians during all of Martin's troubles, I guess for good luck or something, and also because they kind of pushed a "higher power" at this rehab.

One of the things about the Bible is that they sell it to you like it's goody-two-shoes stuff, but when you actually read a little of it, it's like, *Goddamn*, people have been acting like assholes since the beginning of time. They killed Jesus for no good reason, just to be assholes. But I mean, there are also some guys in the Bible who were the GOAT. I wished people would talk about how these guys built arks and killed giants and created entire nations. You know, like when we used to go to church, everybody talked about doing the right thing and how to make decisions keeping God's words in mind. But me, I was interested in someone like Noah. He built a whole ark and kept humanity alive. I would still go to church if they talked about inspiring stuff like that. But they talked like hall monitors. You know, don't swear, don't covet whatever, make sure to respect your parents.

Pac-Man was saying, "You kids think you're tough. I've died three times, one time in jail after I got knifed. Twice from overdosing. I was so addicted to fentanyl, I could ingest enough to kill any of you three times over."

See, that was the kind of remark that was extremely unhelpful. First of all, you can't be killed three times. Second of all, none of us even did fentanyl. As far as I knew, anyway. But then I glanced around the room and realized I didn't know anything about anybody. Because that was the way the world worked when *The Truman Show* ended.

One of the guys said, "You can't die three times."

"I did," Pac-Man shot back. "The doctors said I did."

"Well . . . you didn't."

"I was you once," Pac-Man said. "The smart guy." He looked like he wanted to break some heads open, but I couldn't tell if he was just doing that to scare us or if he really wanted to break our heads open. "I have seven friends who died. Four overdoses, two suicides, and one car accident. The car accident was his fault, and he took out someone in the crosswalk too. You know what I did after he died?" Nobody said anything, so he continued, "I had his key and went to his house and stole his shit. . . . I knew him since third grade."

I thought of something. "Did you see a bright light when you were supposedly dying?"

"I *did* die," he said, even though it was pretty well established that he didn't. "No lights. I wasn't going to the place with lights." He was a buff guy. His left eye was glass, because he'd gotten stabbed in the eye. Not in jail—that was a different stabbing.

"I got stabbed once," a girl said. "I also got raped once when I passed out at a party." She spoke matter-of-factly. "But I just really like getting high." She shrugged.

"I do too," Pac-Man said. "We all do, that's why we're here."

"So how'd you get sober?" I asked.

"My dad didn't know how to get through to me, so he took some fentanyl himself to see what it felt like. It took him almost a year to get off it."

"How did *he* get sober?" I asked.

"He got on a plane and flew to Wisconsin in the middle of winter to go to residential. He came back sober a year later." He gestured his index finger at the girl who got stabbed and raped. "The next step for you is residential. Hardcore residential, too, not one of the places that are like hotels."

The counselors were always warning us about kids who got sent somewhere hardcore. Some of the places didn't even let you make phone calls. How was that even legal? But I guess the parents got so they would try anything.

"If it gets to be either you're gonna be Martin or you're going somewhere hardcore, I know what I would do if I were your parents."

I studied the girl. She was dressed in baggy pants, because she'd shown up in short shorts, and that was against the rules for rehab. They kept extra clothes there just for that reason. It had happened several times. I didn't know why the girls kept dressing that way—they knew they were going to end up having to put on something else. But at least two of them had traded sex for drugs. So maybe dressing that way had got to be a habit.

We had a whole conversation about that one day in group. It was strange how apathetic we all were that day. The girls had seemed bored, like, *What should we feel? We wanna get high.*

Anyway. At the end of the night I heard Martin had died, I went to the blackboard after the room was empty, and I drew a gravestone and a horse. I wrote *Red* over the horse and *Martin RIP my Dude* on the gravestone. Damn, that horse was gonna be bummed. I'd heard horses were emotional like that.

Every day when I showed up for rehab, I sat somewhere different than the chair Martin had last sat on. One day, just to see what it felt like, I sat where he'd sat that last night. I thought of the things he'd said then. Like how the horse was his best friend.

The American dream—his family may have thought they had it in their hands. That's what Martin's mom said once in group. But now I bet they hated life and they hated their amazing house that reminded them of Martin.

Then I felt like I could almost see the guy who'd done that stuff to Martin. He was almost taking shape in front of me. What did he look like? He looked like anyone. Just a guy. Then I couldn't take sitting there anymore, so I got up to sit in the only free chair, which was this slanty one that you almost felt you were going to slide off of.

So I know this is old-people stuff, but I started looking at homes on Trulia. Some of the houses looked alike, but some of them were just plain special. And then there was a level beyond that, where the homes really were more like castles from the times in Europe when they had kings and queens and dukes and all that. But bad shit happens—that's just facts. People get wrecked. If the demons decide they want your kid, they want your kid. The gates blocking off your neighborhood can't stop them.

In fact, I wouldn't choose to live in a place like that if I could be anywhere, anytime. Maybe . . . maybe if I could be somewhere else, anytime, anyplace, it would be back before my great-grandpa died when I was six, or back when Joshie was born, or back when I got Kiiro. That was cool stuff. That was real. That *mattered*. As Grandpa would say, that had *value*.

Anyway, I looked at those houses on Trulia. I looked at them and looked at them, and I always remembered something Martin had said in group. He said this: "My parents thought I was missing once, but I was sleeping in the stable, like I did another time when Red was a colt and he got sick. I miss those times."

"I got ya, homie," I'd told him. "The Before Times, right?"

He nodded. "Right. The Before Times."

You would think getting touched by a creepy drug dealer wouldn't hurt you that much. But I couldn't unsee Martin when he told us about it, his face filled with rage—his whole body tensed into one big rage. I wondered if it was really worth it to the guy who did it: did destroying somebody's life get him off so much that it was worth it?

Unfortunately, the obvious answer is yes. It was worth it to him. Quite simply, that was why he did it.

You don't *have* to learn these lessons. You can skip them by sticking to the design. You can walk on the sidewalk your parents build for you if they have the money. But us guys in rehab, leaning back like we were bored . . . Like, I asked myself if we were all wondering the same thing: Is this all there is—the design or the demons? What else was out there?

TWENTY-NINE

When I got into the backseat of the car after rehab, I said, "Martin OD'd."

"Oh," Mom said. She was quiet a moment. "Did he . . . die?"

"Yeah."

"Oh my God!"

"Yeah," I said again. I paused. Both my parents turned around to look at me. "I wrote 'RIP Dude' on the board and drew a picture of his horse." I looked down at my hands, compared them in my head to Grandpa's. These hands, if I followed the design, would never look like his, or like Ben's grandpa's.

"Aren't you upset?" my mom was asking incredulously.

I didn't answer.

Dad turned even farther around than he already was. "When Basketcase died in Iraq, the guys gave the sarge a DC comic book to put into the coffin. It took us all day to come up with that comic book. I mean, it was Iraq. He was always talking about how DC was better than Marvel. But I wouldn't say anybody acted upset." He laughed, but sadly. "What's that movie where the coach says there's no crying in baseball? We were in a war zone, man."

"Tom Hanks, in *A League of Their Own*," Mom said, but quietly. She reached behind her seat and took my hand in one of hers, then reached over to pick up Dad's hand with the other. Closed her eyes. "We will get through this together. We *will* get through this."

But I knew she didn't know that, didn't know what would come next. Dad agreed with me. I could tell by the way he met my eyes and raised his eyebrows after she let go of our hands. All through history, nobody's ever known what comes next.

And something always comes next.

THIRTY

So after Martin "left" rehab, a new kid showed up, because there's always a waiting list at these places, apparently. I was surprised to see that the new kid was a guy from my school's basketball team—the best player, in fact. He was Evan's friend—Evan was the player Lee's sister, Su-Bee, dated. When he walked in, he nodded at me and I nodded back. Didn't really know each other but had seen each other around.

"What're you in for?" he asked.

"Different shit," I said. "Mostly I lost my temper."

"Oh, yeah, it's hard to stay cool when you're feening," he said. He was about six foot five, named Noah. "This is my seventh one," he added.

"Seventh what?"

"Seventh stint in rehab. When I turn eighteen, my parents told me they're kicking me out. The exact second. They're gonna be watching the clock on my birthday."

"Wow, really?" I tried to squint into the future—did I have more "stints in rehab" ahead of me? God, I was tired.

I thought of this doctor I read about who used to give addicts money for drugs in return for them letting him do unnecessary surgery on them. Then he would charge their insurance company for the money for the surgery. He eventually got arrested. It seemed like if your parents kicked you out, that could be your future—selling surgeries on your body for drug money. But I was far, far from that—I was only a junior in high school!

I asked Noah, "Yo, dude, how do you play basketball if you're high?"

"Some NBA players play high. NFL, too. Sometimes they admit it after they retire. But I dunno, maybe they don't get so mad like I do." He lowered his voice. "When I can't get the pain pills, that's when I feel crazy mad. My sister is scared of me, you know?"

He yawned.

They were trying a new thing today in rehab. They were using therapists to lead some of the groups instead of drug counselors. We had two therapists in our first group. They told us to look for the trauma we all must have suffered at the hands of our parents that made us into addicts. One of the therapists, who was pretty young, said she had learned in grad school that all addicts had been traumatized.

And then the parents came in, and the therapists talked further about our trauma. Noah's mom started crying out of nowhere and shouted, "I would let Noah cut off my hand with a steak knife if he would stop doing drugs!" Which, I mean . . . what an insane thing to say! Because (1) there was no way that would even help; and (2) like, WTF, what was the point of even saying that?

And, actually (3) no way was she kicking him out of the house when he turned eighteen. She'd cut her hand off before she did that! Because where would he go?

But at the same time, I got it. The pain in her face, that was the point. She was just expressing the pain she was in. And that maybe Noah was in? And yet Noah was yawning again as she said that. Then he leaned back in his chair and closed his eyes.

His mom looked very upset. That was the thing about being in those rooms with the parents and kids. It was like being in a room full of pure pain. Every shade and color of pain. The moms' pain out in the open and kinda ostentatious; the dads' pain expressed like they'd been thinking about it for a month; and, maybe, ours was deep inside.

"Sweetheart, can you open up your eyes, *please*?" Noah's mom was saying.

So then Noah opened his eyes and shouted, "Stop pressuring me!"

Even I could see that he was wrong, but the one therapist looked excited and leaned forward. "Noah, tell me more about how it made you feel when your mother said that just now." And then they spent the next five minutes talking about Noah's feelings. Even though his mom was the one who would let her hand be hacked off.

Noah acted like he could not give less of a shit.

"It's because of Pavlov's dogs," the other therapist was saying. "Because of his dogs, we know how people act under stress. His dogs were caged in a room that flooded. For hours the dogs survived by sticking their noses just above the water. *Just* above. After they were rescued, some of them wouldn't eat. In the weeks that followed they wouldn't play anymore.

And you know how Pavlov had conditioned them to salivate when they heard a bell? You've heard that story? Well, they no longer salivated when they heard the bell. A single high-stress incident had broken all their conditioning and turned them passive. Pavlov spent the rest of his life giving dogs nervous breakdowns to figure out how to fix them."

"Damn!" I said. "He's as bad as the guy who fucked up Martin!"

"Damn," Noah said. "What an asshole. I would fuck him up if he came near my dog."

The therapist looked frustrated. "I'm trying to explain what trauma and high stress can do to you. So, Noah, you're under stress and traumatized, and that's why you're yawning."

"Maybe I'm not stressed, though."

"Maybe you're more stressed than you realize."

"Maybe I'm bored with life," he said.

My mom leaned forward intently. "Do you mean to say that all these kids here were traumatized?"

"I believe so, yes," the therapist answered.

My mom was looking at me like, *Is my son traumatized?*

"Pavlov found that every dog was different. Some were easy to break, and some were hard. However, every dog could be broken—every single one."

"He sounds like a real dickhead," I said.

Noah lifted his hand, and we bumped fists.

Another guy said, "Fuck Pavlov."

"Okay . . . okay, this isn't about Pavlov, this is about trauma."

But by now you could see that all the kids were thinking about what a piece of work Pavlov must have been. And all the parents were thinking, *Wow, is my kid traumatized?*

In short, the therapists had lost control of the session. Only the parents were interested, which was kind of annoying, because now they were all thinking we were traumatized instead of thinking we simply liked getting high. Because Noah was onto something: Sometimes we were just bored.

But the thing was, even though we sat in rehab kind of hating our parents, one of the reasons we hated them was that we really loved them, and that made us hate them. Because you just can't stand sometimes how much they love you, and how much underneath it all you're maybe hoping that they can do something to help you out. Meanwhile you can't stop yourself from being an asshole. Something just takes over you. You become an entity instead of the kid you were.

I could see it in some of the tweakers in rehab, but especially in that one weirdo dealer—he'd become an "entity" instead of a "human." Banker later told me and Lee that the guy was "nothing and nobody." He'd said, "You just gotta close your mind off. Don't let them touch your mind." Much later I thought about what an evil dude Banker was, but there were guys who were way worse. Going into drugworld and going into demonworld are pretty much the same thing. In fact, you may think this is crazy, but what I've learned throughout all this is that there are actual demons in the world. And it can be hard because they look just like you. Just like your best friend. Your teacher. Your neighbor. What I'm saying is, you wouldn't always recognize them until it was too late.

Like, one of the guys in my group who got to rehab before me said that a friend of his had met dudes who were really nice at first—super-nice, stand-up dudes. Guys in suits who worked in offices. And they turned out to be from demonworld. "Like, how?" I'd asked. He said I'd be amazed how many guys in suits wanted blow jobs for cocaine, or for whatever. "Most of them do." Even I knew it wasn't "most of them." Or was it? Because not gonna lie, you get paranoid. I did, anyway. One kid told me about a grown-ass woman he'd banged in exchange for drugs. He said she had on too much makeup and a hard face. I started looking at people—women with too much makeup and hard faces, friendly guys in suits—and I wondered who they were, *really*.

But the thing that was creepiest of all was that at some point you're lying in bed, and it kinda dawns on you that *you* could become a demon. I don't mean molest some kid, I mean find a way to destroy someone's life. I knew it was possible because I read an interview once of a guy who survived the Omarska concentration camp during the Bosnian War. The guy's interrogator in camp was a former middle school teacher who had been a very nice person and who he'd liked a lot. The guy said that when he was imprisoned he'd had no feelings about it as he watched people taken off to be tortured. "Extraordinary circumstances make you react in ways you can't explain." And he said people didn't want to believe it, but "There's a very thin line between becoming a perpetrator or a victim."

Yeah, he said that. I thought about it a lot. What I mean is, that guy's real talk haunted me as Lee and I descended into the next ring of hell.

THIRTY-ONE

The therapists instead of the drug counselors
ran most of the groups for a week. We didn't know if this was
going to last or was just a trial. They asked a lot of questions
about our feelings and didn't talk at all about drugs. In fact,
it seemed like you weren't even supposed to mention drugs,
you were just supposed to talk about your feelings. Then one
day Mr. Kevin came in and asked us to fill out a questionnaire
about the groups with therapists versus with drug counselors.
Turned out the guys mostly liked the counselors better, and the
girls mostly liked the therapists better. I never thought I would
say this, but I missed Pac-Man and his real talk.

After rehab was over, Mom and Dad were waiting in the car.
They turned to study me.

"Are you okay?" Mom asked.

"What do you mean?"

"I mean, have you had a trauma?"

"I don't think so," I said.

"Well, maybe think about it," Dad said, "and let us know
what you come up with."

Then he started the car.

"Are we getting anywhere?" he asked nobody in particular as he maneuvered through the lot. "Are any of them? They're all just like when we arrived, except now they can talk about their feelings more."

Some of the dads were *truly* bad at therapy—they didn't like talking, they liked results. Don't get me wrong, being "good at therapy" doesn't make you a good dad, and being bad at it doesn't make you a bad dad. But it was just noticeable that some of the dads were there to figure out what was even going on and what to do about it, while the moms threw themselves into it. I mean, the moms . . . wow, they just let loose. They cried, they gave passionate speeches, they shouted out "My child will NOT die before me!" They blurted out every emotion they had and every emotion they'd ever had and every emotion they thought they would have, ever. I mean, wow . . . the moms let loose.

Sometimes in the car my mom wanted to find out what happened in my sessions that day. But tonight she was quiet. I could hear her sniffling, though. I wondered if some of the other moms were also sniffling in their cars at that moment, because the moms were in some kind of mind meld together or something. Like I was pretty sure at that exact moment at least half the moms were thinking, "I would totally hack off my hand if it would save my kid from drugs." Because the moms were like that.

THIRTY-TWO

Even as I was going through all this rehab crap, I had promised Joshie I'd take him biking, so one Sunday morning I finally got off my ass to do it. First, to prepare Joshie for his next race, I picked out some videos on how to glide for us to watch together, and it turned out the videos were a better tutor than I was. He threw his hands into the air and shouted, "I get it!" Then we went out with his bike, which Dad had gotten him orange rims for, because, why not? Kinda crazy, because some days at rehab stuff felt *existential*, like an actual battle for life against the actual forces of darkness, and then right alongside that I went to school and Joshie rode his tangerine bike and my mom experimented with recipes and Dad ran his business.

I set up cones, because Dad wanted to alert anyone who might be driving faster than they should. We didn't get much traffic on our street, but these days, with half of California probably high, the cones seemed like a good idea.

So we stood at the top of the hill, and Joshie tilted his head a little and got a look in his eyes that was kinda alien. As in, interplanetary alien. This was a new expression I'd never seen.

Head tilted, neck stiff and awkward, teeth bared. He looked like he was about to metamorphose into Godzilla. Intense focus. Then he pushed off on his bike as I jogged beside him.

After maybe seven seconds of running, he lifted his legs, tottered, but kept his legs raised as he discovered the magic of balance. If you've never done anything that takes advanced balancing, I can tell you that it really is magic every time you discover a new level of balance. You're finding something in yourself that you didn't know was there.

He balanced for about ten feet! When he finally set his feet down, I was right there beside him. His mouth was stretched into an amazed smile. "I'm great," he said with pure astonishment.

"You *are* great," I assured him.

"Wow! I never knew I could be great."

He had a look in his eyes like he could see his whole future of greatness. Then he started running again and after a short time glided to the end of the block. We ended up out there until it was getting dark, and I didn't even get high that night. It felt good that Joshie had done really well. I mean, for a little kid, you really could say he did great.

When the next big race rolled around, we all drove to it with big expectations, especially Joshie. He was looking forward to his life of greatness. But Mom seemed concerned as she buckled Joshie into his seat. She got in the car and looked at him worriedly as Dad put the car into reverse. Dad seemed excited and even went a little over our lawn as he backed out of the driveway.

We drove quietly until the freeway. Then, as if she'd been holding something in, Mom turned to look at Joshie and said,

"I'm sure you're going to win, but don't be disappointed if you don't, okay? But I'm sure you'll win. I mean, just in case. Even if you come in second, or even if you come in last—which you won't—it's the effort that matters. Always try your best."

Joshie said with hurt in his voice, "You don't think I'll win?"

"No, I absolutely think you'll win. Elijah says you're great. I just mean in case you don't, don't worry about it. But you will win. Elijah said you're great."

"Wait, don't put it all on me," I said. "I mean, if he loses, it could be because there's somebody even greater. But don't worry, Joshie, you're gonna win. You're the greatest, it's just that sometimes someone is greater."

"Greater than me?" Joshie asked.

"Nobody's greater than you," I said. "You're the greatest. But you never know; there might be someone really great there."

Dad piped up. "You're the greatest in our eyes, just remember that."

There was a silence. Then Joshie said, "You're filling up my head."

"Sorry, dude, carry on!" Dad replied.

Josh pulled up "What a Wonderful World" on his iPad and played it all the way there.

When we arrived and parked, the scene was similar to the last race, with one big difference that I hadn't realized was going to be a big difference. Namely, the course had small hills. I stared, felt glad I had brought a vape pen, because I needed a hit or two right about then.

I held off going to the porta-potty so that I could say to Joshie, "So what I'm thinking is that you need to push hard to get up the hill and then glide down. Okay?"

He was staring at the course like he couldn't believe it. "Think about this," I told him. "You're Godzilla, conqueror of worlds. Look at those little hills and understand you're Godzilla, and those hills mean nothing to you."

He turned to me. "You didn't tell me there were gonna be hills."

"Yeah, dude. I didn't know. I'm sorry."

He turned back to look at the course and said quietly, "I'm Godzilla, conqueror of worlds."

So I went into a porta-potty, took two big hits, and went back outside into the bright sunlight. Put on my shades. Kids were strapping on their helmets, parents leaning over to give them advice.

Joshie had landed in the first heat like last time. We stood about halfway through the course. I felt a little far away from it all, like all the eager parents and their kids were in one world and I was standing just outside of it.

The announcer was telling the kids to geeeet ready. "Aaaaannd GO!"

Joshie's face turned into the interplanetary being's face again. He was pushing with such force, I thought he was going to lose his balance even though he hadn't even lifted his legs yet. Then he reached the first hill and crested it easily, but wobbled big-time gliding down. Some people with VOLUNTEER written on their T-shirts ran over to push a few struggling kids up the little hills.

Nobody could pound the straightaways like Joshie! He was in second place!

At the second hill he was still pushing too hard. And he did fall over while gliding down.

"GET UP, JOSHIE!" I bellowed at the exact same time my dad bellowed the same thing.

He did get up, made the same mistake at the next hill, and got up again to pound the straightaway like a bat outta hell.

He finished eight of sixteen, so he made the final!

When he came over, he looked like KMS, but it turned out he was fine. "I've never been so tired," he said. "Bed."

"Do you mean you want to go home to bed?" Mom asked.

He looked confused. "No, I mean lie down."

So I got sent to the car to get a blanket. When I opened the trunk, I looked around, then took a couple of big inhales from my pen. Then took one more for no reason. I was flying. For a second I wasn't sure what I was doing standing in the parking lot with a blanket in my hands. To make it worse, the blanket had Christmas trees on it. It was a . . . Christmas blanket. What?

Then I came back to Earth and closed the trunk, heading back to my family. I spotted them on a field filled with other families. Beyond that, there was a baseball game for kids going on. I could hear the parents yelling for their kids, could see them filming the game on their phones.

"Can you spread it out, Elijah?" my mom was asking.

"Okay, sure."

I shook the blanket a couple of times—it seemed strangely heavy—and laid it on the grass. Joshie dropped down and crumpled into a ball. "I'm imagining," he said, his eyes closed.

"What're ya imagining, bud?" Dad asked.

"What went wrong."

I wanted to tell him he'd gone too hard up the hill, but my eyes were also closed, and I felt like I could take a nap for five hours. I lay beside him, draping an arm over his shoulder like I used to when he was a baby and crying about something. As I drifted off, I heard Dad and Joshie discussing his ride. Like, strategies. Dad would take care of it. . . .

"Aren't you getting up, Elijah?" Joshie was saying.

My dad tapped me with a foot. "C'mon, come watch your little brother."

My mom was saying something about going to get waters.

Forgot where I was for a second, but I pushed myself up anyway. I started to walk unsteadily toward the track. Dad said, "Elijah, can you grab the blanket?"

I felt anger rise in me. Why was the stupid blanket my responsibility? But Dad and Joshie were already walking off. I gave them the finger behind their backs and grabbed the blanket. Then I tried to get ahold of my anger. Because this was Joshie's day. I needed to say it out loud to calm down: "This is Joshie's day."

I trudged to the track with the blanket. As Joshie started pulling his bike to the starting line, I said, "Josh!"

He stopped to look at me. "Don't push so hard at the top of the hills, okay?" I said. "You're getting too much momentum."

"What's that?"

"You're going too fast over the hills. Okay?"

He looked suspicious. "But it's a race to go fast."

"Buddy, you're losing your balance when you start gliding," I said a little impatiently.

Dad looked at me curiously. He reached over to ruffle Joshie's hair and said, "Actually, that's good advice. Okay? Go up and down the hills with intention. Do you know what that means?"

"Yes . . . No."

"Don't lose focus. You need to get up and down as fast as you can without losing your balance. Sometimes that means going a little slower at the right time."

"Wait, let me think," he said. And then he stood there and seemed to be thinking. Dad and I watched him thinking. Then he nodded. "Okay."

So he trotted beside his bike to the starting line.

"Aaaaannnd, GO!"

It went great at first. He slowed it down on the first three hills and was in third place at the last hill. "YEAHHHHH, JOSHIE!" I was yelling.

Finally, he pushed as hard as he could on the top of the last hill, losing his balance and skidding onto the track. He lay there not moving, so we ran over. The volunteers ran over too. He was lying there with his eyes open.

"You okay, bud?" Dad asked.

"Yeah," he said. He sat up. But his body was all slumped over, and he declared, "I failed."

"No, you didn't," Mom and Dad and I said.

"Then why did I fall down?"

That was a very good question. All I could think of to say was, "There was one hill too many, dude. That's not your fault."

"Whose fault is it?"

"You'll do better next time, I promise. We're gonna do some work."

We knocked fists.

We trudged back to the car, Dad pushing the bike because

Joshie was angry at it. He was in a bad mood. I was in a bad mood. Mom and Dad seemed like maybe they were in a bad mood. I wanted to say something to cheer them all up, but the only thing I could think about was how I shoulda found a place to take a hit before we headed to the car.

THIRTY-THREE

So. After the therapists took over the groups, the rehab program started getting different kinds of kids—namely, kids doing drugs but also kids having mental health issues without drugs.

Noah and I were talking one afternoon between our group sessions. "Why do you think they changed everything up?" I asked.

He looked around and lowered his voice. "My dad says it must have something to do with the insurance companies. Maybe they're more willing to pay out over mental health than drugs."

"Why does he think that?"

Noah leaned in. "Because our insurance company told them since I'd been through so many rehabs, they weren't going to keep paying out unless there was some kind of acute issue." He was practically whispering now. "The insurance company was making us pay for a while. It's like a thousand dollars a day for IOP. Then my dad convinced them I was suicidal, so they'd keep paying. And Kenny—he's the dude with blue hair—told me his mom told the insurance company he was traumatized by some shit, so they'd keep paying."

Everybody was coming back into the room from walking around the hallways, checking their phones, using the restroom, etc.

I got up to check my phone for notifications, but nada.

Anyway. I guess all this meant that the insurance companies were more into trauma and suicide now than drugs? So now the rehab started getting substance abusers, suicidal kids, kids who were cutting themselves (three girls), and kids who were changing genders. And the program changed its name from "rehab" to "recovery center." There were still a bunch of druggies. Also, I asked around, and it seemed like maybe 75 percent of the kids were on meds. I even had to get interviewed by a new psychiatrist who suggested to my parents I get on antidepressants. He also suggested they "might want to think about" going to a therapist for the trauma they were apparently going through that was caused by my supposed trauma.

My mom said absolutely not on the antidepressants. She didn't add this, but that was more of a white-kid thing. For some reason. Some of the white kids said their moms were on antidepressants too. Which my mom would never do, because she was kind of a radical health fooder. I only ever got chips when I bought them myself. At home, if I wanted a snack, it had to be a piece of fruit, unless we were having a party with snacks. But with my homies I ate whatever.

Listen up, I have a lot of theories about some of this stuff. It's a fucking industry. Because America has more than one hundred thousand overdose deaths a year, while some other countries have hardly any overdoses. Japan, for instance. So clearly, it can be done—it's possible to have almost no overdose deaths.

I kind of missed the lectures from former addicts, even though they'd seemed boring at the time. Because now the therapist was making us go around the room and introduce ourselves for all the new people. "Say something real," the therapist was saying. "I'm not pressuring you to say anything you don't want to. I want you all to feel safe. By 'real,' I just mean try to be truthful, even if it's only a small truth. But only if you feel safe."

When it was my turn, I said, "I'm Elijah. I'm here for drugs." I thought about what I could say that was "real." What I came up with was, "I have this theory that nobody really wants to stop the drug overdoses in America. Because one of my cousins who wants to be an engineer says the rule is, 'The purpose of a system is what it does.' So the acronym for that is, uh . . . POSIWID. If you have a system that you say is to create canals and pipes and a new water department full of new employees, and you say the purpose of your new system is making water cheaper for the people, and then three years later the price of water has tripled, then the purpose of your system is to raise water prices. Because POSIWID. It doesn't matter what you say your system is for. That's not the purpose; it's just what you say. If you create a system that you say is trying to help addicts, and you run your system, and more and more people become addicts, then the purpose of your system is to create addicts. And like with addiction, the drug dealers and drug makers and drug counselors and drug therapists are all parts of the same system, just like pro athletes and jersey makers and stadium builders and kids in sports and elite trainers are all parts of the same system. Just like the candy manufacturers and the acne medicine makers and the diabetes drug makers are all a part of the same system. I've been thinking on this a lot. I have an uncle with diabetes, and he's always sneaking candy. He can't stop! And the world doesn't want him to stop, on account of how much profit he's making someone in the system."

The therapist was holding up her hand like, *Stop*. So I did. Because I got it—nothing I'd said had anything to do with therapy.

"Try to use the 'I' word," she said.

The next person who was either a girl or a boy said, "I'm Max. My pronouns are he/they. I'm here because I think about killing myself when I wake up, when I go to sleep, and about twenty times during the day. That's all I feel safe saying."

And so on. The parents weren't in this group. Not gonna lie, if my dad were here, he would've pulled me outta this place in about two minutes. He would not be down with this. He's a practical guy. If he were here, he'd be having practical thoughts like, *Is this really gonna help my son?* Pretty sure the answer he'd come up with would be no. Because POSIWID.

When it was Noah's turn, he leaned back in his seat, putting his hands behind his head. "Yeah, so to elaborate on what Elijah was saying. *I* learned about POSIWID in my business class." He emphasized the word "I." "And here's what *I* figure. *I* think the parents are the target—the ones everybody's squeezing to make money. They're what make the system go round, because they're the source of the money. So the whole system revolves around them, not the kid." He paused. "I'm saying the 'I' word."

"Say your name, Noah," the therapist said.

He paused. "Yeah, I'm Noah. POSIWID rules the world, man. I guess that's all *I* have to say."

Noah and I smiled at each other and dramatically high-fived.

As people kept introducing themselves, I started thinking that whoever made the drugs and sold them *lived* to destroy people's lives while making money. Just like Kiiro lived for petting and Frisbees and walks and dog food. And me. He lived for me. I figured those big corporate drug executives were like the dealers in that they got excited from making money and messing up your life at the exact same time. They went through their daily activities, and no matter what they were doing, in the back of their minds they were feeling happy that they were making money while destroying someone's life. The cigarette assholes did that, and the OxyContin assholes did that, and the vape assholes did that. The fentanyl assholes. The heroin assholes. The Valium and Xanax assholes. All of them. All assholes.

The therapist was listening intently to a girl mumbling something about pulling her hair out strand by strand. She took off her hat and showed us a bald spot. She was wearing gloves, "so it's harder to pull out my hair."

"Why do you do that?" Noah asked.

The therapist looked like she was about to say something, then didn't.

The girl in the hat said, "It feels so satisfying."

She was the last person in the room to speak. The therapist pulled at her chin-length hair a couple of times, then said, "Thank you. Thank all of you. That was so real." She pounded her right fist into her left palm. "We're here to help you! You have to do the work, but we're here to help you get better!"

"Did you ever?" I asked.

"Ever what, Elijah?"

"Help anyone get better."

But she was looking at the door. Mr. Kevin was coming in with Martin's parents. "Martin's parents wanted to come talk to you kids and say goodbye and thank you for supporting their son."

Did I mention how small Martin's parents were? She was maybe five feet tall, and he was about five five. They looked like you could flick them over with a finger.

"I wanted to thank you all for listening to my son," the dad said. "It helped him to know you cared. It helped me, too." He nodded, then added, "Keep fighting. Your parents love you very much." He glanced to his wife.

She seemed very shy, and her shoulders were kind of pulled in close like she was scared. "We are selling our home and moving to Portugal. I have cousins there. America is not the right place for us anymore." She took her husband's hand. "I will miss all of you."

It seemed like someone was supposed to say something, but nobody did. So I said, "Uh, Mr. and Mrs. Martin's parents. Martin seemed like a great kid. He was very emotional, in a good way. Uh . . . I hope his horse is doing well."

His mom looked really happy at the mention of the horse. "We are taking Red with us to Portugal. We are flying him over. I would never leave him. Some nights I sleep in the stable with him. I bring Marty's blanket and pillow and lie in the stable at night, and sometimes I feel so peaceful out there."

Mr. Martin's dad closed his eyes against the tears that were now streaming. "Red, Red, Red. Thank you for asking about him. My son loved Red. Thank you. You're good kids. Thank you for supporting my son."

"Have a good life in Portugal," Noah said. "I went there once. It's a cool place."

"It's a beautiful place!" Martin's mom said. "We have two more sons, so America is not the right place anymore. It is not the right place!"

Martin had been a living kid, and now he wasn't. He said once that his grandparents who lived with them had come from Granada, Nicaragua. I looked up Nicaragua after he told me that. A lot of stuff had happened there, a lot of fighting, and not all that long ago. A revolution, even. There was still unrest. But his grandparents had been thinking of the future, and they thought that meant getting to America. Would you rather have unrest and an uncertain future in a place that had had a revolution, or would you rather end up living with your kids and grandkids in a beautiful house in one of the richest gated communities in the country, but where your grandson died of a drug overdose? Pretty much, if you could have a do-over, you'd pick the place that had had a revolution. Not to mention we had hella unrest here in America too.

THIRTY-FOUR

We never did talk about Martin, like officially in group. After Martin's parents came to say goodbye, I asked a therapist, "Can we talk about Martin at some point? To process?" "Process" was the therapists' word for "discuss and then deal with it." At least that was how I thought of it. She said yes, we could process what happened to Martin. But we never did.

So I still couldn't quite picture it. Like, why there was no coming back from what had happened to him. I would sit in rehab and try to process it on my own. Here's what I figured happened. When Joshie would listen to "What a Wonderful World" over and over, I kind of got into it sometimes—I could see from his point of view what he was feeling that made him love that song. And it was just like all great songs, where you're kind of living the song as you listen. In other words, you're listening, and it really is a wonderful world, because you're inside the song. And you grow up and you see the bad stuff, and sometimes you see the brutal stuff. But you can still think it's a wonderful world, just complicated. But what the demons do when they touch you is they take away the wonderful world inside you. It's just *poof*. One touch, and it's gone. Maybe you can live after that, and maybe you can't. Maybe you can process and move on as a stronger person or even as a weaker person. Or maybe you die.

My grandpa told me once about crossing fields in Vietnam, and all anyone wanted to do was get across in one piece. That was your only goal for the day. His whole day was walking . . . walking. One of those days he heard an explosion, and a few yards behind him was his now-dead buddy. Why him and not Grandpa? "No reason," Grandpa told me. "None at all."

THIRTY-FIVE

One day I was sitting at my desk trying to focus on homework. But I couldn't. So I got up and looked out my window into the backyard. I saw the two nectarine trees. My mom was sitting there cross-legged in front of them. Every so often she would wipe a couple of tears from her face with a cloth she was holding.

That's it. That's the chapter.

THIRTY-SIX

Whenever a new family showed up, they were almost eager, like it was the first rehab—even if it was the third or even the seventh. I was still on my first. But kids would come in who'd been to a bunch.

Columbus Day was a school holiday but not a rehab/recovery center holiday. So as my parents drove me to rehab the second Monday in October, my mom was saying excitedly, "They just added on their website that the success rate of this rehab is that four months after graduating the program, close to half of grads are still clean."

Nobody spoke for a moment. Then my dad asked, super unimpressed, "That's it?"

"They kicked out some dude the other day for having oxycodone in his urine for the third time," I said. "Three-strike rule. And that girl, I think her name was Trina, quit because she moved. They kicked out that guy who started a fight on his first day. And Martin died. So that's four right there who won't be counted, because they didn't graduate. And there's only fourteen of us. I mean, do the math."

"Yeah, sounds like a fail to me," Dad said.

"Me too."

"Four months is four months," my mom insisted stubbornly. "You can't get to a year without going through four months first."

And, I mean . . . that was a pretty low bar for three hours a day and however much the insurance companies were paying. And, also, POSIWID. Say two-thirds of the kids made it to graduation. The purpose of the program was to keep half those two-thirds clean for a few months. Not to mention, I'd already failed two drug tests, so I was about to be in the one third that wouldn't be a part of the stats. My parents were super calm when I failed my tests. One thing about the parents was that the more you failed, the more determined they became. Not angry at all, just more determined to help you. You could see the same thing in all their faces. They were gonna see this thing through. They were gonna save your life or die trying. It was like that story of the dad whose three daughters were drowning. He jumped into the current to save them one by one, and after they were all safe, his last words to them before he died were, "I got you." That was every parent with a kid in rehab.

Anyway, THC stays in your system for a long time, so the way they measure is, they send your test to a lab once in a while, and the lab figures out if your level has gone down since the last time. But they don't send to the lab every day, because it costs money. One thing I didn't understand, though, was how come I saw program kids vaping in the parking lot sometimes, and they hadn't gotten kicked out yet. Some of the kids thought they only kicked you out when your insurance was used up anyway. But I guess there was also some kind of stuff you could ingest to hide the drugs in your system. You could buy it online. Also, some of the kids gave each other clean pee. It had to be warm for the temperature gauge on the tests. Don't ask me how they worked it out. I was an amateur next to some of them.

So, yeah. When I got to rehab, I went in for my first group. There were three therapists in the room—usually there were just two—and all three were women, even though there were eight guys and six girls in the program right now.

First thing, we went around the room "affirming" the person to our right. When it got to me, I looked at a suicidal girl to my right. She'd only just arrived last Thursday and had hardly said anything so far. She had this kind of blocked vibe, like you didn't know what she was thinking or feeling. Like, I had no idea. So I said, "Your hair is dope." She had long, curly hair that stood up naturally about two inches on top of her head.

One of the therapists said to the whole group, "Can you please not comment on what the other person looks like?" She smiled at me. "Go on."

I looked at the blocked girl, took a big breath. "I could bring my dog one day. He might make you feel better."

"I'm allergic, but thank you."

She spoke in a monotone. Monotone was a thing for some of the kids. I guess it was the Pavlov dogs effect, where they'd been through bad stuff and were now passive.

"So that was very nice of Elijah to offer to bring his dog. And thank you for letting us know you're allergic," one of the therapists said.

Then Noah, who was to my left, was up. He said to me, "Hit me up if you ever wanna talk, homie."

"Thanks," I said.

"So Noah generously offered to let you contact him if you're ever needing affirmation, and you very nicely thanked him."

And so on.

After that was done, another therapist said randomly, "How did hearing all that affirmation make you feel? Let's see, who should I call on? Elijah!"

I was leaning back comfortably and didn't move.

"Uh . . . when we signed up, my mom said we were going to work with horses. I guess I'd rather be doing that."

"Thank you for your honesty, Elijah. I appreciate that. How did *you* feel about all that affirmation, Maria?"

I guess this was supposed to help us "grow." And—this is facts—that just wasn't what a lot of us guys were into. What I mean is, maybe we didn't "grow" by thinking all the time about what we were feeling. Why couldn't we work with horses? The therapists kept wanting us to talk about our feelings and to listen to everybody else say how they were feeling. But, I mean, people have been discussing their feelings more and more, and is the world getting any better as a result? Pretty sure the answer to that is no.

Then the director pulled me out of group to tell me that I'd failed my lab test from last week. I wasn't surprised—in fact, the main surprise was that it had taken this long. "Pack your bags, Elijah, pack your bags," Mr. Kevin said. He patted my shoulder. "But I wish you luck. Believe me, I've seen kids a lot worse off than you, and they got sober. So there's hope, okay? We just don't want you to hit rock bottom like so many people have to. That's why we all do this. Hopefully, many of you are not going to ever hit rock bottom. But some of you are. Try not to make that you, okay? Don't think because you're basically a good kid, you'll be all right. Lots of kids were good kids like you, until they weren't."

We shook hands, and I said, "Thank you. Um. Is that it?"

"That's it."

So I texted my parents to come pick me up from wherever they were—probably eating dinner nearby—and waited for them in the parking lot. They didn't even look surprised as I slid into the backseat. "Kicked out?" Dad asked.

"Yeah."

Mom immediately said, "I've already been looking over other places, just in case. I think I have a good one for you."

My parents didn't seem too disappointed, although my dad drove a little faster than usual.

"Are you guys mad?" I asked at a stoplight.

"When I was in-country, I didn't get mad much," Dad said. "But later I did. Maybe I'll be mad when we get through this. We'll see."

"I'm proud of you!" Mom said passionately. "And I'm optimistic about this new place!"

But I thought of her crying at the nectarine trees. And I could see how tired my dad was lately.

But, you know, getting high was more important than all that. If it wasn't, I wouldn't need to be in rehab. There wouldn't be people shooting up in the streets. There wouldn't be kids dying.

The high was the god of all things.

THIRTY-SEVEN

Although my grandparents knew I was in rehab for vaping, they didn't know that a few weeks before I got kicked out, I'd started stealing pain pills from Grandpa on the regular. The reason I'd started was that the other kids at the program thought pain pills provided a really good high. Again, POSIWID: part of the purpose of the program was for us to teach one another new bad stuff, like how grandparents were a premium source of prescription drugs. Anyhow, Grandpa didn't really think about stuff like how many pain pills he had left in the prescription bottle. I, on the other hand, always knew exactly how many he had. I visited them every weekend and started checking out their bathroom cabinet every time I was there.

But for some reason, when you abuse people's trust the way all us kids in rehab did, it made you mad—at *them*. Maybe you were mad at them for standing between you and your high. Because anything standing between you and your high was just really fucking annoying.

One day I was high on Grandpa's Vicodin and was standing at a window at the end of the hall at school. I just felt like looking out at how green it all was. It was just a quirk with me, but I kinda enjoyed looking at trees and grass and stuff when I was on pain pills. "Hey, Elijah."

I turned around—it was Logan.

I must've looked surprised, because he said, "Sorry, am I bothering you?" I felt kinda happy and kinda embarrassed and kinda wary and kinda like I wasn't really me anymore, so it was strange that he recognized me. "How you been, Elijah?" he asked.

"Pretty good. Or not. I'm okay. How about you?"

"I'm good. . . . Did you hear that Ben broke his arm?"

"Really, how?"

"Cliff jumping."

"Bruh . . . I hate cliff jumping!" For a moment there I felt like the old me again. But it was maybe the fastest moment in history.

"Me too, dude! I tried it once and landed in about four feet of water. I thought I'd broken both my ankles, it hurt so much."

"Bruh!"

But the bell rang for the next class. We stood there awkwardly.

"Uh, see ya," Logan said. He moved like he was about to walk away, but before he did, he said, "Are you okay? You know, you can still call me anytime you want."

"Sure," I said. "Thanks."

I popped another pill right there in the hallway. I was lucky my grandpa had a prescription. These days you didn't know what you were getting, although maybe for some kids, that was part of the thrill? And sometimes I wondered if some of the kids were addicted to fentanyl without even knowing it was in some of the pills they took. There was no way you could know what was in the pills if you got them somewhere like the beach.

By the way, you would not believe how many drugs there were at the beaches in California. It was like the mall.

THIRTY-EIGHT

There was Halloween stuff hung up at the new recovery center my parents had enrolled me in. The receptionist was wearing a witch's hat. She asked my name, then said, "Welcome, Elijah. Happy Halloween! You were assigned Aiden for your mentor. He's in that office." She indicated a door, then turned to my parents. "I'll take you to the director so he can introduce himself."

I knocked on the office door, and a guy said, "Come on in, Elijah."

I walked into the smallest office on the planet. Aiden said, "Go ahead, sit down." He looked down at his notes. "So just the THC with you, right? Tell me the truth, I'll find out anyway."

"Sure, yeah, just the THC."

He tilted his head at me. "I'll find out anyway."

"I know."

He set his pen down. "You're too smart for your own good, buddy. I used to be that way." Then, knowingly, "You'll fall off your high horse one day, and then you won't be so smart anymore."

So he was doing the tough-guy thing right off. Which, whatever. I looked at him skeptically. "What is your percent success rate?"

He looked up at me, then returned to a file. *My* file, I guess. He wrote something on a paper, then lifted his head and said, "I hear this is not your first stop. It may not be your last, either." But his expression abruptly softened, which I didn't expect. "But you'll be okay. I can't always predict, but I have a feeling you're gonna get out of this. Every so often you meet a kid who you just know ain't gettin' out. He's not even in deep yet, but you know in your gut that he ain't gettin' out." He shook his head, as if trying to get a memory out of his brain. "I have your phone number already. I'm gonna text you right now. You can call me any time of the day or night." He looked directly at me. "I mean it. Especially if you're in trouble; call me. Got that?"

"Sure."

He wrote a few more things down, asked me a few questions, and then sent me to a big room with a lot of chairs. These were hard folding chairs. My parents were sitting with a seat between them, so I took it.

More female therapists. Two of them. "I'm Wendy," one of them said. "This is an open group today. To the kids, we're just going to let you debrief about your day, your week, your month. Whatever you want, we're here to talk about it." She smiled like she just remembered she was supposed to. "To the parents, I know this is hard for you. Your kids have been traumatized. You've been traumatized too. We heal the whole family here. We have three new families here today, so I want to talk briefly to the new parents about listening. Because when you talk to your children, they can't always hear you. So in order to help them heal, you need to listen. Just knowing that they're really being listened to helps them to heal from their trauma."

A suddenly crying mom said desperately, "But tell me how

I should be listening to her. Should I just not ask her any specific questions at all? For instance, is it better just to ask more general questions like, 'Are you having a good day?' Or is even that too specific and might trigger her?" The mom wiped away tears. "Please tell me how to listen to her! Tell me how to talk to her too!"

This new place had both substance abusers and kids having mental health crises. Also, the longer I sat there, the more I realized that more than half the kids were there for gender confusion issues.

Apparently, once a week at this place they held three separate sessions at the same time: a girls' session, a boys' session, and a gender-neutral session. So when it was time for us to separate into the three groups, me and a few other boys went into the boys' room. We had eight kids in our group—four of them girls who identified as boys.

I said, "Yo, I'm not trying to be rude, but are you sure I'm in the right group? This is the group for boys?"

A therapist named Melanie exclaimed passionately, "It's the same thing. IT'S THE SAME THING!" I'm not kidding, she wigged out. Her eyes got super wide, and she started waving her arms through the air.

One of other guys went, "*What's* the same thing?"

We looked at each other.

"You are ALL boys. IT'S. ALL. THE. SAME. THING." Then Melanie calmed down and fake smiled and continued.

"Then why separate the groups into girls and boys and gender-neutral in the first place?" I asked.

Another guy held up his hand to me. "Believe me, you're not gonna win this one. I've been there, done that, you know?"

Melanie said patiently, "Elijah, we separate into these groups because each group has different issues. Boys often have different issues from girls. Any other questions, kids?"

Another guy raised a couple of fingers in the air and said, "Yo, I have another question."

Melanie seemed to be evaluating him but didn't invite him to ask a question. "I was thinking today we could discuss how boys deal with their depression."

Wendy was nodding fervently. She didn't talk as much as Melanie and seemed more like an apprentice. So the other guy lowered his fingers.

Melanie asked sweetly, "Are we all on the same page now?"

"Not really," the guy said.

The other guy said, "Me neither."

Wendy finally spoke. "You boys need to learn to listen and hear. Expand. Learn something. It's good for you to be exposed to all kinds of people in the world and all kinds of new situations. You can learn a lot if you open your minds."

We slumped in our seats and looked at each other again. And then several of the other kids talked about how their periods made them depressed. Which I really didn't think was the same thing boys who were depressed go through at all. You know? But what bothered me was that I was fairly sure the therapists believed it *was* the same thing. It was like arguing with teachers and cops, though. Sometimes you gotta stop arguing if you don't wanna get wrecked.

So when I had a chance to jump in, I asked Melanie, "Do you have a background in something that makes you, you know, the right therapist to be here?" I wasn't sure if that was exactly what I'd wanted to ask, but it sort of was.

She said almost proudly, "I once smashed my brother's shoulder with a bat, *and* I have two PhDs." She straightened her back, looked down her nose at me. First of all, how was that a qualification to be here? Second of all, WTF?

"Uh, why do you look happy about that?" another drug guy asked.

She explained like she was talking to middle schoolers, "Because I did that awful thing, and look where I am now."

"Where are you?" the guy asked.

"I'm in charge of you, for one thing," she snapped. She quickly did the fake smile thing again.

One guy wrinkled his forehead, then tipped his head back and asked the ceiling, "Why am I here?" He lasted at that rehab about two days, and I lasted about two weeks, because it took that long for my mom to find someplace new that she thought seemed better. There were a lot of choices, because rehab therapy is a fucking industry. But the insurance company didn't approve the new place, and the holidays were coming up, so my parents couldn't decide what to do. Because even though my dad's business was doing well, he also had a lot more expenses now. And he didn't have as much time on account of wanting to be there for me. Mom and Dad were also only in their forties, so they didn't have that much saved for retirement. Some parents maxed out their credit cards or raided their retirement funds to pay for their kids' rehab. But Mom and Dad were against using credit cards for rehab except as a "last resort." Meaning, I guess, if I was addicted to fentanyl or heroin or something.

It seemed like the trick to maximize your money was to keep your kids off drugs for as much as you could, even if you never got to a hundred percent.

The director at the first place, Mr. Kevin, had said honestly when we'd started there, "You're just trying to keep them off drugs as much as you can for as long as you can. Then hope something clicks." Like I said, he was kinda my favorite of all these types of people I'd met, I guess because he was such a truth beast.

Anyway, the last day at the second place was the worst. I hated the way that same annoying therapist, Melanie, acted like she was having a great time telling stories around a campfire while some kids were talking about the time they tried to kill themselves or something. I wondered if the group for grown-ups down the hall was being treated the same as we were—this rehab was divided into two sections, one for minors and one for adults, separated by a locked door. So for them, who would listen to you at home when you were, like, forty-seven years old or something? What if your parents had already died? One thing I learned on the rehab treadmill is that there're a lot of fucked-up people in America, and most of them wanted to get better. But a lot of the time nobody actually helped them. Why is that? Just asking—I got no idea! God, I hoped I wouldn't still be going to these places ten years from now.

So, in the group with the parents that last afternoon, we were back on the topic of how parents should listen to their kids. Like, specifically. The other place emphasized that you should listen to your kids, but this place told the parents specifically how to do it. "I like to open my eyes a little wider," Wendy was saying. "Not too much, but just a little to express how attentive you are. Sometimes you don't have to say anything at all. You just need the right expression."

And this one mom—I wasn't sure of her name—opened

her eyes wide. Too wide, if you asked me. She said tentatively, "Like this?" She looked ridiculous.

"That's good!" the therapist exclaimed. "That's great!"

The woman's daughter said, "She says she'll listen, but she won't. She never does."

The mom looked stricken, then said bravely, "I'm trying so hard to listen to you. I'm trying so hard. *Please help me listen to you!*"

I mean, at these places kids sat in multiple groups for three hours a day, five days a week, with the therapists making a point of making sure everybody was listening to everybody else and that the therapists were listening to us and that the parents were listening to us. We were pretty much the most listened-to kids in the history of America. There had *never been* a bunch of kids so listened to. We could not possibly be listened to *more*. If the parents listened any harder, their heads would explode, bits of listening brains splattering all over. And these therapists had convinced the parents that if they just listened in exactly the right way, while opening their eyes wider, it would all get better. One therapist even suggested a parent tilt her head a bit as she listened. And say, "Mmmmm-hmmm." Which was batshit crazy.

I decided to repeat a thing I'd read just that day on the internet. "I have something to say." Everybody looked at me.

Wendy said enthusiastically, "Go, Elijah!" And she opened her eyes wide before I'd even said anything. She tilted her head slightly.

"I read that some Indian guy named Krishnamurchi said, 'It is no measure of health to be well adjusted to a profoundly sick society.'"

"Krishnamurti," she and the other therapist in the room

corrected me at the same time. Then Wendy continued, "So why are you telling us this now? I mean, it's great and interesting, but can you relate it to what we're discussing? I went through a period when I was quite interested in Indian philosophy myself, but I outgrew it when I matured. But tell us what you mean, honey."

"Well, because . . ." My face grew hot. "You're trying to make it seem like there's something wrong with us and the world is okay. And I think it's the opposite . . . honey."

If looks could kill. But then she took a deep breath and . . . opened her eyes wider and tilted her head. "Mmmm-hmmmm. Thank you, Elijah." She turned to another kid. "So what do you think, Bella? Do you feel listened to and heard?" And I kid you not, she widened her eyes at Bella before Bella even opened her mouth.

"I mean, the only thing that I think I sort of have to add is that I kind of agree with Elijah," Bella said. "I mean, even though my parents think I'm worse than the other girls at school, I know of at least three who are hurting themselves. They're cutting themselves mostly, but I know of another one who uses her nails to scratch the skin off her legs. Her entire legs below the knees are one big scab. And her parents don't even know. Like, I just don't think this could be normal. Like, why is this happening? Does anyone actually know why?"

"I think we're getting a little off-track here," Wendy said. "A lot of you have this tendency to not want to talk about yourselves, so you start talking about society or whatever. Or you talk in the third person, or about someone else. Remember, use the 'I' word."

"But you're not helping us," I said accusingly. "If you were, there wouldn't be kids going to five different rehabs, one after another."

"Well, we're really here to help you help yourselves, *Elijah*. Because we're not going to follow you throughout your lives. We want to give you the tools you need . . ."

And I was out. I'd heard the "blah blah tools" thing a million times. Tools to help your anger. Tools to help your cravings. Tools to get along with your parents. I just wanted to live; I didn't wanna be thinking about tools twenty-four/seven. Did people think about tools a thousand years ago? How did they get by? Huh? Someone tell me.

I'm listening. I'm all ears.

THIRTY-NINE

I still showed up for school, because there was really nothing else to do other than get high. I mean, sometimes I needed to do something else. I liked getting high, but just for variation, sometimes it was good to sit in class and only *think* about getting high.

Have I mentioned that Percocets are part oxycodone and part acetaminophen? So, you know, addictive. My grandpa's Vicodin had acetaminophen and hydrocodone, and it was a less strong than the Percs. Kinda similar high though. Lee loved Percs. He loved them. Lee and I had talked about how we were both getting headaches, but we weren't sure if it was the Percs or what.

So he and I were texting one day, and I mentioned a pressure on my temples.

Him: *Me too*

Then he added: *Dude I feel like I'm waiting for something it's bad but don't know what it is*

Me: *My grandpa says war is like that you're waiting for the THING, maybe the thing was getting your legs blown off maybe not*

Him: *That's exactly it write this all down dude write down our history*

Me: *I'll call it The History of Us*

One time it was just him and me at his house, sitting around with two controllers playing PS4, high on Percs. Lee was shaking his leg up and down really fast. His game character got killed, and I glanced at him. He was frowning, his head at a tilt as he looked into space.

"Yo, Lee, you just died."

He looked at me blankly, then turned to the TV. "I forgot we were playing." He frowned again. "I got an A-minus on a snap quiz today."

I paused. "Wow. Was that your first A-minus ever on anything?"

"Yeah."

"It's not that important. It's just one."

"Yeah, I know." But he looked worried.

"I got my first B on a test when I was twelve," I said. "It was kinda shocking, but once you get over it, you see it's not such a big deal. You've been taking AP classes for years. What's your GPA, anyway?"

"Five."

"Dude, you're gonna get into any school you want for undergrad, grad, and postgrad. Then you're gonna get a job at SpaceX and get Elon to Mars." I thought about that. "Hey, if you land a job at SpaceX and get to meet Elon, put in a good word for me if he wants a book written about the history of SpaceX."

His face brightened. "Sure thing."

Then he looked crestfallen. "There are Asians with four-nines who don't always get into their first-choice school. And did you know Stanford turns down the majority of applicants with perfect SAT scores?"

"Facts," I said. "But that won't be you."

"Yeah, I know. But it makes me feel less motivated." He tossed the game controller into the air and caught it. "Do you know where you want to go yet?"

"If I major in history, which I guess I will, then probably Stanford. They have a good master's history program."

"What's their acceptance rate?"

"I dunno, probably 5 or 6 percent. Are you still thinking you wanna go to Duke?"

He nodded, but he looked worried. He got that faraway look in his eyes again, and when I asked him what he was thinking about, he said, "A problem Mr. Hudson gave us in class today."

He kept thinking, I guess, because he was still staring into space. I didn't want to think about school. . . . Earlier that day my history teacher had told me that he knew the head of the Stanford history department. "I'm going to help you get in, but don't let me down. If you would just *focus. Elijah, if you would just focus.*" It was funny how adults thought that you didn't hear them or something, so they repeated stuff they said to you. The teacher was cool, though, I liked him. But I felt a little guilty at the moment. Because I didn't really feel like focusing.

Lee was looking down now, and he seemed sad. I studied him.

"So on the optimism scale, where are you right now?" I decided to ask. "Like, if you look out at the world, how do you feel?"

"Pretty low." I liked how I could always ask Lee something out of the blue and he would answer as if it was part of a conversation we were already having.

"How about on the hope scale?"

He thought that over. "Scale of one to ten, you mean?"

"Sure," I said.

"Ahhh, maybe four point three." He shook his head. "Maybe three point nine." He studied the controller in his hands. "If you factor in that I'm still pulling good grades, I was the only one in class who could figure out a problem the other day, I got a supportive family, I have you, minus I'm getting some brain fog so my brain is maybe only working at eight point seven . . . I'm losing some motivation—probably down to an eight point five on that, but that's weighted a lot as one of the most important factors."

"Wait, if you're still in the eights, that's still very positive. So how do you figure you're a three point nine?"

"Yeah, I know, let me explain it better." He was shaking a leg and idly studying the controller lever. "Uh, you need to be a ten on motivation, and it's one of the items weighted the most. So if I were, say, a seven in motivation—that would mean it's all over. There's also the trend line, which is down."

I studied his worried profile. He was taking the most advanced courses our school offered. He'd gotten a problem right that nobody else in one of those classes got right. As far as I was concerned, he was still at 9.5 in terms of how his life was going. But I could see how worried he was. I could feel it too. So I said, "Dude, you're chillin', you're like nine point three at the lowest."

Lee gave me a look like he wanted to believe me. Then he suddenly asked, "I just got *Ghost of Tsushima*, wanna play?"

"Sure, I heard it's lit."

And then we were back to normal, just two buddies playing video games.

FORTY

Lee showed up a couple of nights later so that we could go to Banker's. Whenever he showed up like that, I felt like I couldn't say no. Plus, my parents loved Lee and thought I was only vaping because of other kids at school. That's another thing about parents. They all thought there were these other kids who were "a bad influence," but they never thought that their own kids might be a bad influence on someone else. Not that Lee and I were a bad influence on each other. But we weren't a good influence on each other either. I guess.

So we ended up sitting in Banker's room, which is on the opposite side of the house from where his parents were. Davis was already in his own world off in a corner, listening to AirPods and kind of swaying around. Lee and I had dropped two bars, which was what kids called Xannies.

Lee suddenly said, "Uhhhh."

I stood up. "You okay? You look green."

He suddenly threw up. After that he wiped his mouth and said, "I feel better now."

"Goddamn it, Lee, clean that barf up," Banker said.

"Ah . . . you were green, Lee," I said.

"I felt green."

"You gonna be okay?"

"Yeah." He went to the kitchen and came back with paper towels and a spray bottle.

I had to go to the window and open it to breathe some fresh air. After Lee cleaned up, he stood at the window too. We looked into the backyard. There were old lawn mowers out there and a couple of trees, and for no reason Lee said, "What the fuck?"

I looked at him expectantly, but he didn't add more. I said, "What do you mean?"

"Just what the fuck," he said.

But he looked relaxed breathing some real air. Banker's room felt like a tomb.

I checked my phone for the time. Lee had a test tomorrow, so I wanted to remind him before it got too late.

Banker didn't have to think about school at all. He didn't have a job either, but his parents thought he had some kind of online gig writing ad copy. They had no clue that he made money selling drugs. I mean, maybe they had a clue, but they didn't take it kinetic.

I wanted to leave. The room still smelled, and it seemed at that moment as if every single thing in the world sucked. Then out of nowhere Banker asked, "What do you think— Should I kill my parents? Alex and I could get the house and sell it, and I could use my half to start some kind of business."

Lee and I looked at each other. I remember thinking maybe I hadn't heard him right. Because even though his parents weren't the greatest, they were still—I mean, they were his *parents.* I was sure Banker's parents loved him, though—I mean, like I said, they were his parents.

"Banker, that's fucked up," I said. I couldn't really think of much else. Though that pretty much was exactly the thing to say. Like, what else was there to say?

But then Lee, who was now sitting on the floor next to the window, went, "I know. Sometimes I get so mad at my parents I want to kill them."

"You're just like me!" Banker exclaimed. He walked over to Lee and held out his hand, and after hesitating, Lee high-fived him.

"Dude," I said to Lee. "Dude, you're not just like him, you know that, right? Lee?"

I was feeling woozy—the bars were hitting me hard. I thought I might barf myself.

Banker shoved me, but not so hard that I fell over. I thought about my dad telling me to stick up for myself, and even though I felt like crap, I gave Banker a hard shove back—harder than I meant to. He fell over, and I swear to God, when he got up, he was looking like he'd just added me to his kill list, whether before or after his parents, I didn't know. I felt a surge of adrenaline, because no way was anybody gonna kill me. . . . Although, wait, what was I thinking? Nobody was going to kill anybody, right? I tried to clear my head.

Davis piped up. "Guys, chill. What the fuck?"

And then *pop*. Banker relaxed. He put up his fist, and I bumped it, because I just really wanted to move on from this moment. "We're good, bro, aren't we?" he asked. "You're not gonna tell your parents about this conversation?"

Davis started crying right about then. Most teenage guys

didn't cry much. In general, what's to cry about? Life's crappy sometimes, but did you really want to start crying about that?

Right then, though, I knew exactly why he was crying: because he was scared. I think we all were. Even Banker.

FORTY-ONE

Then Banker said, "In their hearts our parents kind of hate us. Like yours." He said that to me. "That's why they drag you to rehab. Those places don't even work—I been there, done that."

And my jaw actually dropped. I could not believe what he'd just said. Because I'd always thought of my parents as loving me a lot. A real lot. In fact, I always figured I could do anything and they would still love me, except for a little bit of wondering, like when I threw the shoes and yelled at Joshie. But I replayed Banker's words in my mind. *Our parents hate us.* It made sense to me at that moment. All of a sudden, it seemed like, *Yeah, yeah, they do hate me.* I mean, why wouldn't they—I was a terrible son!

"You know what? You're right!" I agreed. Of course they hated me! And it seemed like I'd had some kind of incredible insight. I believed it with everything I had.

And then I felt doubt. I took out my phone to look at myself. I looked pretty normal. Every so often lately I'd look at myself during this descent into madness and feel surprised at how normal-looking the person staring back at me was.

Banker pounced over to Lee to give him a little shake. "Dude, if we killed your parents, think how much money we'd have!"

Lee looked surprised, but not that much. That is, he looked very surprised, but not as much as he *should have*. Then he seemed to be thinking. "I got an idea!" he said. "My sister told me she saved most of the money she's made working at the mall. She hid it somewhere, because, I dunno, she doesn't trust banks or whatever. Uh, so we don't have to kill my parents!" He looked at me, like he was excited about some other idea he'd just had. "She thinks you're hot, Elijah. You could get her to tell us where the money is."

"What happened to the basketball player?" I asked.

"Someone dumped someone, not sure which way it went. I heard her crying one day, and a few days later she started asking me about you."

I was trying to keep up with this conversation. It was going faster than my mind could work. "Dude, my brain feels like it's made of bacon bits," I said to nobody in particular. I concentrated on what Banker had said a little while ago and also on what Lee had just said. Then I was thinking about how his sister was really not my type . . . even though she kind of was. But like I said, she had that thin thing going. I liked girls a little thick. But Lee was looking at me pleading-like, so I said, "Okay, cool. I mean, great, actually. Let's not kill your parents, okay?" Geez, what was even going on here?

Now Banker was looking at me, evaluating. People in demonworld were always evaluating each other.

Finally, he nodded. "How much money does your sister have?" he asked Lee.

"Uh . . ." Lee chiefed on his vape pen. "Su-Bee's been working weekends for three months. So, uh, twelve weeks times sixteen hours times seventeen twenty—three thousand three hundred two and forty cents, minus taxes. She bought a bunch of new clothes the other day. Looked pricey, but she gets a discount. Eh—I'd say maybe sixteen hundred. Give or take. I don't know everything she buys."

Banker said, "Fuck taxes." Then he evaluated me again. "I'm counting on you to get that money for us."

"She's really not my type, though," I said. At least, I didn't think so, but I also did. Which, if we were gonna steal her money, it was probably better if she wasn't my type, and I didn't like her, and she wasn't Lee's sister. I felt confused. I knew we weren't talking about me banging her or something. I'd gone out on dates, but like I said, I'd only had that one girlfriend, for a whole month. Real life was like that. You're chugging along with your first girlfriend, and then a year and a half later you're sitting in some future demon's room getting high and talking about stealing money from a girl who's your friend's sister.

Banker and Lee were now discussing what Lee should say to his sister.

"I got this. Lemme call her. Everyone be quiet," Lee replied. He glanced at me and pulled her number up on his cell phone. "Hey, Su-Bee, 'sup?" he said in a really nice, friendly way. He listened a moment. "What kind of homework? . . . Oh, yeah, I heard he's a bad teacher . . . Anyway—sooo, hey, did you know that Elijah has the hots for you?"

Suddenly, Banker was giggling, as quietly as he could, and so was Davis. Davis's mouth opened wide, about as wide as a mouth can get, and his eyes were all lit up, and he started shaking with silent laughter. I started laughing as well. It seemed really hilarious. *Has the hots for you!* I couldn't stop laughing!

FORTY-TWO

Five minutes later we were all headed over to Lee's house, Banker driving—it was like he had taken partial ownership of Lee's car. We picked up Su-Bee, and it was unbelievably awkward, because the guys just dropped her and me at the beach and took off somewhere.

We walked down the steps, then onto the rocks. She tripped like three times, first small trips, then a larger one. I had to catch her!

"You okay?" I asked, still holding her elbow.

"Yes!" she said cheerfully. Then tripped again.

"It's pretty rocky."

"Wrong shoes," she replied.

We sat down just out of reach of the waves. It was a really nice night—beautiful, actually—and the waves were sparkling. Not gonna lie, it was magical. I felt like I had to comment on how absolutely stunningly beautiful the night was. So I said, "Nice night."

"It is!" she agreed.

I thought about that—did that mean she really thought it was a nice night, or was she just making small talk? I took a big breath. "So, like, Lee says you have a job at the mall."

"Yes, at The Grove."

Which was a fancy mall in Los Angeles. I had a weird dizzy feeling, didn't know what that was about. Maybe I was nervous? Or the bars were hitting me again?

"At Nordstrom," she continued. "I was working there during both times all those people came in and stole a bunch of expensive merchandise—it was on the news."

I didn't watch "the news," and neither did anyone I knew. We all got our news from Instagram and TikTok. But I said, "There's hella robberies. I was getting chips at the drugstore once, and a bunch of kids ran in to steal all the cough medicine on the shelves."

"Oh, right, Lee was there with you!"

Then I noticed she had on running shoes, which were the exact right shoes for walking on rocks.

She started taking them off. I'm not one of those guys into feet, but if I were, man, her feet were something else. "Your feet . . . you could be a foot model."

And she was so skinny, and seemed so trusting, it did make me feel bad. Like I had to really concentrate on my mission.

"My mom has good feet too," she said, but shyly. She tapped her big toes together and announced, "I work in handbags!"

I nodded, trying to think of something I could say about handbags. "My mom says handbags all weigh too much, and it's annoying . . . I mean, not to insult handbags or anything."

"I hate handbags!" she said passionately.

"Oh. You mean because you work with them?"

"No, I love handbags. I mean, people come in and buy

handbags that cost three thousand dollars, sometimes more, and they don't even think about it. I hate how they're so expensive, and some people like that. They just look around and point at a handbag and don't even ask the price. I used to think they're going to stop being interested when I tell them the price, but they just go, 'Okay, I'll take it. And that one too.' There're regulars who probably have fifty handbags."

"Wow," I said. "But I guess—I mean, I have a Trek bicycle that was pretty pricey. It was about three thousand. I only have one, though, and it has to last me for the rest of time or until I can get a new one myself. I wouldn't mind a second one, but I don't know what I'd need fifty for." I wasn't sure I was even making sense—bicycles didn't really have anything to do with handbags. And I guess it didn't make sense, because she didn't seem to be able to come up with a response. "The waves are . . . like, they're alive," I blurted out. If that made sense.

"They are!"

I drummed my fingers on my knee. "So what classes are you taking this year at your school? Do you have trig?"

"No, I took trig over the summer to avoid the teacher I would've had in the fall."

"Sure, absolutely!" I said. Even though I had never said "sure, absolutely" in my life. I thought I should say more. "I like my trig teacher. Sometimes he says weird stuff. Like, one time out of nowhere he said, 'Humans are not the most successful mammal on the planet. That's rats!'"

Which had nothing to do with trig. Or handbags for that matter.

"Hmm, rats" was all Su-Bee said. She held out her hands and

looked at them. Her hands were really pretty—so pretty, they didn't seem real. "I have a flaw," she said. "Do you see how my pinky on my right hand is bent?"

"Yeah, what happened?"

She turned, flashed a smile. "I was born that way!" She paused. "Do you have a flaw?"

"Nah, I'm perfect," I said.

She nodded seriously.

"I'm kidding."

She looked shy at that.

My phone dinged, and I glanced at it. *Did you ask her yet,* Banker had texted. I quickly put the phone down, but she wasn't looking anyway. She was examining a rock.

My phone dinged again. This time I didn't look at it, turned instead to Su-Bee.

I said, "Do you like working at the mall, except for the expensive handbags? I guess it's good to be making regular money?" That wasn't very slick, but she answered anyway.

"I need the experience." Her face got all bright. "I want to have my own store someday. My friends and I are going to design handbags, and they're going to be beautiful, and we'll sell them for under a hundred dollars!" She looked all starry-eyed at the thought of this store full of handbags under a hundred dollars. To be honest, that still seemed pretty pricey to me. I didn't understand women and handbags. It seemed like a secret society. When I overheard the Asian moms discussing handbags sometimes, it made no sense.

And I didn't understand getting all starry-eyed over a store full of handbags. You know? At the same time, I hadn't seen anybody this upbeat who wasn't a little kid in . . . in maybe forever. I slanted my face toward hers, and I mean, we were suddenly *vibing*. I mean, I *liked* her.

I reached my arm around Su-Bee's shoulder, and she lay her head on mine. We just sat and watched the waves as my phone kept dinging.

"Your phone's dinging," she said.

"It is?" I said. She looked at me funny. *Damn*. I was not a very good spy. I leaned over suddenly and kissed her. She wrapped her arms around my neck as we kissed.

But suddenly, Banker and Davis were calling out behind us, and we turned to them as they made their way over. Lee lurked on the dirt path behind them. There's nothing more annoying than someone bothering you when you're vibing with a girl. Then I remembered my mission. But I couldn't bring myself to ask about the money.

She put on her shoes and socks while Banker stood there mouthing words at me, probably asking where the money was. I shrugged at him, then stood and reached out my hand to help Su-Bee get up. Even though she was for sure too thin, there was something delicate about her, like a spiderweb, but in a good way. *Very* pretty girl. Silky girl.

"Dude, come on!" Banker was yelling. He was just a few feet away.

There was really no way I could've asked her where her money was. I could tell, though, that she would've told me. I could tell by the way we were vibing actually that she would tell me just about anything.

She checked her phone. "I still have a ton of homework. If I get a B in physics, my mom's going to make me study with a tutor."

She probably had a minimum 4.0 GPA like many of the Asian kids. Because some of the moms would have a heart attack if you ever fell to 3.9 in *high school*—you'd have tutors at your house twenty-four/seven. Tutors would wake you up in the morning, talk to you while you ate Cheerios, ride a bicycle alongside you, and put you to bed at night after homework.

We walked past Banker and Lee, and I could hear their shoes crunching in the rocks behind us. I felt a little protective and put an arm around Su-Bee as we climbed up the steps. At the car I opened the door for her, and she got in between Davis and me. Davis announced, "I hate the smell of fish!"

Su-Bee looked at him like she was thinking about that, then said, "I like it. It's real. It makes you really know you're in real life." She smiled a little like she was happy she'd said that, and then she grabbed my hand and said, "I study so much, I like to feel like I'm in real life sometimes."

"I got ya, homie," I said. Although I hadn't been studying so hard lately, I for sure knew what it felt like. I suddenly realized something about myself. I wasn't like Lee, who could study for four hours and then be surprised by how much time had passed. I knew exactly how much time was passing. Sometimes I just wished it would end. Maybe if I could read only whatever I wanted, it would be different.

At the Fang house Su-Bee sprinted up the walkway, stopping at the door to call out, "Bye, Elijah! Bye, guys!" We all waved and called out, "Bye, Su-Bee!"

Then I listened to the guys discuss if we should steal the money now or later. "Elijah, where's her money?" Banker asked.

And I dunno, but I was still vibing with that girl. She had nice skin. It glowed.

I was listening kind of in a daze, just trying, I guess, to separate myself from this discussion. I thought about how good it had felt protecting her at the stairs.

I didn't answer.

"He didn't find out," Davis said.

"Shit," Banker replied.

I stared straight ahead, through the windshield at the house. It was like a million other houses in SoCal, for people who were rich but not super-duper rich. My trig teacher said California had crappy income inequality—we had hella rich people and hella poor people. Which again had nothing to do with trig, but anyway, it was interesting.

Lee's house was stucco, two-story, beige. An Olympic-sized pool that overlooked the homes down below. It was pretty lit at his pool at night. But now hardly anybody I knew ever swam in their pools. The pools just sat there, looking blue and cool. There was also a putting green for Lee's dad in back. Lots of art on the walls inside. Nice house that they'd spent a lot of time on. Because Mr. and Mrs. Fang were all about their kids and making them a perfect home. Mr. Fang always asked Lee and Su-Bee if they liked something before he got it. He would send them a picture of an item and text, *If I got this chair, would you sit in it? Don't say yes unless you really would.*

And if I was there, Lee and I would discuss the chair. Or the wall art.

But now Banker turned around, reached out, and shoved me. "Why the fuck didn't you ask her?"

I felt my right hand ball up, in case he shoved me again. But he didn't. He said, "Get out."

I didn't answer, just got out. Lee got out too, and Banker drove the car off. "He took your car, dude," I pointed out.

"Yeah." He looked up at the stars, said, "When you're camping, you can see the Milky Way." Then he fist-bumped me. "He'll bring the car back. He always does. Later, Elijah."

"Later, Lee."

He took a couple steps up his walkway, then turned and asked, "Did she tell you where the money is?"

"Nah."

"Did you ask her?"

"Nah."

He looked at me quietly for a moment, then said, "Cool."

I paused, then said something honest. "You look bad. You need to get away or something, you know?"

"Bro . . . where would I go?" Then he kind of laughed, and I did too, and everything seemed okay.

I set off to walk home. That was the problem, really: Where would you even go?

FORTY-THREE

November's kind of a good month in Southern California. The holidays coming up, no hot days—you can wear your hoodies all the time. One night Lee was going to pick me up to hang out, but not until eight. So I wandered into my brother's room. The door to his room was always open, because he didn't care about privacy. There was a deck of Uno cards on his bureau. "Hey, Joshie, I bet you can't beat me five games in a row."

He whipped around, his eyes lit up. "Bet I can!"

He'd been playing *Mario Kart*. Lately he was into cars, and all he did was page through auto magazines and play *Mario Kart*. Literally, my dad got him every auto magazine that existed on the planet. He loved to look at cars, especially old ones. I didn't know if he liked them because he liked them or because I did. I liked old cars because new ones mostly looked like toasters or sideways refrigerators—like appliances. I said that all the time. So right then Joshie said, "First let me show you this picture of a car I saw. It looks just like a toaster!"

So he showed me the car, and I said, "Wow, such a toaster!" And we fist-bumped. It was an SUV, which I knew a lot of people loved, but, I mean: toaster.

Sometimes, if nobody would play *Mario Kart* with Joshie, he'd play alone. He could beat everybody in the house, so we'd all gotten tired of playing with him. He always put a dish towel over his hands, so you couldn't see what he was doing. He said he had "special fingers."

"Hold on, Elijah, I'm almost finished," he said—he'd paused his game. He quickly finished it off, his cart swerving and screeching on the screen. He yelled at the top of his lungs, "GET OUT OF MY WAY, DUDE!"

He liked to win for different reasons from me. I liked to win because I thought it felt really cool to beat the crap out of people. No mercy. It wasn't exactly happiness that I felt, it was more satisfaction. But for him, it was happiness. He needed these shots of happiness on the regular. Otherwise, he got sad or lonely or something.

But I was worried about how fucked up I was getting, because I didn't know if Joshie would be okay in the future. I thought I might need to keep an eye on him throughout life. I knew that didn't make sense, because how could I know that now? But Joshie was a responsibility I had, so I needed to make sure that eventually I could get back to normal. So, like, maybe party through college and then get my head straight again?

We played a few hands of Uno, which, if you've never played, is about the most boring game in the world for anyone over twelve. And for some reason nearly *everyone* cheats in Uno. Like, it's part of the game. When I was little, I played with kids who never cheated at anything, but they cheated at Uno. It was just like it was in the instructions or something that this was the one game you should absolutely cheat in, or you were a chump. I let my brother win every game—I noticed he cheated a couple of times, grabbing extra cards, trying to see my cards. Every time he won, he got up and did a happy dance. That made me smile. God, I wanted him to have a good future. The happiness, man. I just wished he could be like this forever. I did have a moment of doubt, because of the Buddhist concept of idiot compassion, which could be different things, including when you give people what they want, even though it might not be the best thing for them. Maybe it would be better to beat Joshie once in a while, make him a stronger person. Or not. Geez, I had no idea how parents ever made decisions.

Kiiro was there too, and every time Joshie got up and danced, Kiiro looked at me like he was in on it and knew I was losing on purpose.

We'd just started the sixth game when I heard the doorbell ring. A moment later my dad peered in and said, "Lee's here."

"All right," I said.

Josh slumped down, dejected.

And, like, I kind of felt the same. I was having fun in here playing this ridiculous game. Most boring game ever invented, but somehow I was having fun. But it was Lee, and I could tell sometimes that he *needed* me. So I said to Joshie, "Dude, I gotta get going."

In his high little voice Joshie said, "Go ahead, dude, I got things to do." Which I knew he didn't, and he still looked dejected. But I pushed myself up. Kiiro followed me to where Lee stood at the front door, and I kneeled in front of him and let him lick my face. "Everything's gonna be okay," I told Kiiro, not sure what I even meant by that or why I needed to say it.

I stood up. Lee shook his head and said, "Dude. Dude."

When we got into his car, Lee got behind the wheel for

once. Banker was in the passenger seat, and Davis was in back. There was a tense feeling in the car, and nobody said a word as Lee drove. I had a feeling there'd been an argument.

By the time we got to Banker's place, though, the tension had disspiated, because we'd just gotten high. So we sat in the driveway for a few minutes and just laughed and laughed.

Inside, we played some PS4. But then at one point I glanced over and saw Banker glaring at Lee. I mean, he looked like he was about to stab Lee in the brain or something. I tried to clear my own brain, but it was so foggy. Anyway . . . that didn't seem right—that glare. Then Banker's face went blank as it so often did. Maybe I had imagined that glare? Maybe?

Banker had two TVs and two PS4s, because his mom got him stuff he asked for every Christmas. Mr. and Mrs. Bank had thrown him into a residential drug rehab two or three years ago, and he had to stay there for ninety days. But now they let him do whatever.

Do any of those places even work? Because, like I said, there's more than one hundred thousand overdose deaths a year in America and fifteen thousand "recovery centers"—I'd looked it up. Didn't that make anybody ever stop and think that maybe, just maybe, something's, you know, going wrong?

Anyway, there was a shy knock at the door—I almost didn't hear it. That would be Mrs. Bank. And sure enough, she peeked half her head in. "You boys want some mac 'n' cheese?"

"Sure," we all said.

She nodded happily. "Ready in a jiff!" She pulled back her head and closed the door softly. The only place I ever ate mac 'n' cheese was in the cafeteria at school. My mom didn't make stuff like that, because it was usually in a box, and she didn't make meals from a box. Dad, on the other hand, ate frozen dinners for snacks in between meals. My mom practically thought that should be illegal. It was a running joke between them.

Anyway, we returned to PS4. We were playing this game called Hitman, which was the story of a genetically enhanced assassin. My favorite part was when they had him thinking for a moment about his childhood, before his life of crime, and a tear falls down his cheek. We could all relate to that, right?

Banker's phone dinged. He glanced down at it and said, "Food's ready."

We all got up pretty quick for a bunch of guys who were totally wasted, and then at the door we all laughed when we tried to get through at the same time. So there we were in the dining room, with Mr. Bank watching a football game on TV in the adjoining living room. He looked over. "Rams looking great this year. What do you guys think?"

We all stood there high out of our minds, trying to process what he'd just said.

But Lee rose to the occasion, because that was Lee for you. "Well, Mr. Bank, I only watch baseball, because I like all the statistics and because it's kind of boring, so there's a lot of time to think. But the Rams have potential this season, for sure." He spoke in that quiet, sincere way he had.

Mr. Bank paused. "Football has stats galore!"

"Yes, sir." Mr. Bank was frowning now, so Lee added. "You're right, maybe I should take a closer look someday."

Banker spit on the floor, for no reason. I mean, what reason could there possibly be? Mr. Bank stared at him for a moment, then said, "Clean that up," and turned back to his TV.

I just stood there looking at the glob of spit. Like I said, the

Banks' house was nice inside. The wooden floor looked brand new. Banker just pulled out his phone and started scrolling, ignoring his glob. And, I mean, I didn't want to be his bitch, but I couldn't stand that spit being there on that floor. So I went into the kitchen myself and grabbed a paper towel to wipe it off the floor.

I heard him say, "Fuck you, bitch," but I didn't look at him at all, just threw the paper towel into the kitchen garbage when I was done. One thing about when you're an addict, you get mad about ridiculous stuff. Like someone cleaning up your stupid spit.

I wondered if Banker's family ever ate together, even on holidays. That was one of the things they taught the parents in rehab, that families who ate together were less likely to have kids who became addicts. On the other hand, here were Lee and I, high out of our minds, and we ate with our families almost every night.

We stood there awkwardly—I thought the mac 'n' cheese was ready? But Mrs. Bank had her hands on her hips, looking at nothing that I could see. The refrigerator was in front of her, but it was closed. She was a super-nice lady, in a demented kind of way. She kept staring.

"Mom, is the mac 'n' cheese ready or not?" Banker asked.

"Hold on, honey. I'm thinking. The package didn't come with enough cheese. I'm wondering, should I mix in more?"

She gazed at the fridge for a few more seconds, then shrugged and said, "Yes, it's ready!"

I wondered what Mr. and Mrs. Bank would've done if they knew Banker had mentioned killing them. It actually didn't even make sense to kill them. Because they gave him whatever he wanted anyway. I mean, I didn't think anybody should kill anyone. I'm just saying that even by Banker's own "standards," it didn't make any sense.

Anyway, while we were waiting for Mrs. Bank, we stood around looking at our phones. Su-Bee sent me a Snap: ♥

I pondered, then sent her a "me too." I felt furtive, but the other guys weren't paying attention. I mean, I didn't want to encourage her if we were just going to steal her money. I was in fact a little worried that I'd accidentally find out where her money was and then tell the guys. At the same time, I couldn't not respond. Because like I said, we were really vibing on the beach. And I got that feeling I got a lot, that Hitman feeling with a tear falling down his cheek. Like maybe I should just join the army or something when I was eighteen and let them send me to whatever stupid war they might have that year. At least then I'd get away from Banker. But I'd promised my dad I would never join the military, except to defend what he called the dirt and rocks I lived on.

Mrs. Bank said, "Sit down, boys! Dinner is served!"

Davis said, "Thank you very much, Mrs. Bank. We appreciate it. We love your food. It's honestly just so good. You could be a pro chef." Davis could be so weird around adults. He went too far.

Chill bro, I texted him.

He texted back, *What?*

Mrs. Bank brought over four bowls on a tray. The food was bright orange. I mean, it was up there with Joshie's bike in the orange department.

She stroked the back of Banker's head. "Do you want anything else?"

"Don't touch me, please," he said.

"Sorry, hon."

The table was round. I knew a little about marble since my dad was a contractor and kind of a marble expert. This table-top was pale blue marble. It looked really cool, for a table. As I reached for a bowl, Banker spit on the table. He was looking right at me. I felt like I couldn't wipe it up this time, because he was challenging me. His mother froze there, and I realized she was scared. Of Banker? Of making a scene? She wiped it away with a paper towel.

Crap, what was I even doing there? I closed my eyes. I could feel my brain sailing. It relaxed me.

So I dug into my food. And it tasted delicious, I swear it. I could just feel the tangy cheese drawing saliva out of my cheeks. I muttered, "This is really good." I glanced up at Mrs. Bank, and she looked pleased. I stopped chewing for a second. Mrs. Bank had puffy cheeks and a slightly desperate look to her eyes. She was one of those Asian women who bleached their hair blond. But it looked dry. She wore a lot of black eyeliner around her desperate eyes. I didn't know what she was desperate for: appro-bation, maybe. (Yeah, I know that word.)

Not to be outdone, Davis added, "This is really very extraordinary-tasting." Now she beamed. He added, "It reminds me of meals I had when I was little. Thank you. Thank you very much, Mrs. Bank!"

So phony. But she loved it.

Then Banker said, "Mom, did you know Lee is the smartest kid in California? He's a lot smarter than Alex. Like, a *lot*. Aren't you, Lee?"

Lee froze, a forkful of macaroni in front of his face. "Um."

"I mean, they're both smart," Davis said.

"Yeah, but Lee is smarter," Banker snapped.

Mrs. Bank's mouth fell open. She looked like Banker had just hit her across the face. She even raised her hand to her right cheek, as if he *had* hit her. But then her expression turned bright. "At a certain level of intelligence, you can't really say one person is smarter than another . . . honey."

She didn't say "honey" sarcastically either.

Banker shrugged. "Lee is more like, you know, Richard Feynman or someone like that. He was a famous physicist who won the Nobel Prize. Lee was on the national physics team."

Lee put down his fork. "I heard Alex is pretty smart."

"He's not as smart as you is all I'm saying."

Mrs. Bank perked up and said half-jokingly to Davis, "What about you, are you smart, Davis?"

"I don't know, ma'am," Davis said. "I get some A's but not all A's, ma'am."

The next bite I took tasted like cardboard. I had a brief sensation like maybe I was back in reality, not high anymore, and this is what the mac 'n' cheese really tasted like. I wanted to get out of that reality, though. I wished I could've taken my vape pen out of my pocket and had a hit, but Mrs. Bank thought Banker and his friends were some kind of angels. Which, when you think about it, was tragic.

Banker turned his bowl upside down, even though there was some food left in it. Then he turned it right side up, with the leftover food now on the table.

"You're tripping, bro," I said.

Mrs. Bank was scribbling on a piece of paper. "I need to remember to get more mac 'n' cheese."

I dunno. Just so depressing at that house. Banker was talking about killing her, and meanwhile she was worried about whether she might run out of mac 'n' cheese.

What a great and terrible mom she was! She was great because it was kind of innocent to be worried about mac 'n' cheese when she had a son like Banker. But she was terrible because she didn't have the fight in her that a parent needed to have. Same with his dad. Even I could see that. When I'm a dad someday, if I live that long, I'm gonna fight like hell for my kid. It ain't about getting a B, it ain't about college, it ain't about a car after you break your leg; it's about how much fight you got in you. These parents today, the world's falling to pieces for their kids, and they're like, "Did you do your homework?" They ain't got no fight. They're just reading a script.

And then Mr. Bank even said it, "Did all you kids do your homework?"

FORTY-FOUR

Like I said, I was supposed to visit my grandparents every weekend, which I actually enjoyed. My grandparents are great. At this point in their lives they basically just wanted to sit around listening to Simon and Garfunkel and telling you how tall you were getting. You'd think I was the tallest kid they'd ever seen. I'm not making fun of them, they're very cool. But I saw the way they looked at me lately: they were worried.

At the same time, like I also said, I did steal Grandpa's Vicodin sometimes. He had back pain from a car accident a couple of years ago. One day he might need surgery to insert a little electronic device into his back to kill the pain, but for now he was on pain pills.

My grandparents lived in a townhome in San Luis. I rode my bike there. I had to admit that since I'd started vaping a lot, I didn't have as much stamina as I used to. Riding there was more of a chore than it used to be.

My grandparents' townhome had that old-people smell. It was weird, because they didn't smell, but their house did. And I wasn't sure where the smell came from. Maybe just from all the old stuff around. They had actual books on the shelves. I looked through some of them once, and the pages were yellow, some even taped together. And there were a million of them, plus old clothes and old furniture and old curtains. So if you added all that old stuff together, maybe that was where the smell came from.

My dad said that he remembered the curtains hanging in his parents' living room from when he was a young kid. He remembered when they were brand-new, when the family was poor, and how proud he was of those new curtains then. Because of those curtains, he said, he felt like he could hold his head higher when he had friends over to the apartment they used to live in. I wondered if Grandpa and Grandma knew how happy those curtains had made my dad. They had *value*, as Grandpa liked to say.

So there I was one day at my grandparents' place while they took a nap, and I was kicking back to some Vicodin I'd stolen from the bathroom, and I walked over and looked at those curtains, the ones that had made my dad so proud, the ones with all that value. They were slightly shiny and beige-white, and they were pretty much normal—nothing at all special about them. They seemed completely standard, like you could get them at Target. But for whatever reason, touching those curtains that were maybe forty years old, I felt like my whole brain got flooded with *wishing*—I just wished so bad that I could be that kid who could be made happy by a bunch of curtains. And I didn't wish that even for me, but for my parents. If I could be that person, maybe my parents' lives wouldn't be so crappy at that moment. Because all the kids in rehab, their parents' lives were crappy. Their lives would be even worse if they knew the whole story of what their kids were up to, but that wasn't the point. The point was, how could you possibly get back to where you could maybe appreciate stuff like my dad used to appreciate? If you figure it out, sign me up.

So then Grandpa came downstairs. He walked extremely slowly. He must have been having a painful day—some days were better than others. Eventually, Dad and I were going to set up the downstairs office to be their bedroom. But for now he and Grandma walked up and down the stairs very slowly. Grandpa's right pant leg was at his knee, and the bottom of his leg was skinny and wrinkly. I said, "Hey, Grandpa" but he didn't hear me, just went into the bathroom, where he made that throat noise that I guess guys start making around their forties—that was when my dad started, anyway.

However, I was vibing so hard from the painkiller that all those noises seemed like the most super-cool thing in the world. I suddenly thought it was just outstanding that Grandpa had made enough money at some point to buy some decent curtains for his family. They'd saved up a good amount of money, apparently, but didn't spend much. I guess when me, Joshie, and my cousins were all born, my grandparents knew they wanted something to leave us. No way I would ever tell that to Banker, because he would want to kill my grandparents or something!

Grandpa came out and sat down on the couch the way he sits down—kind of slowly at first and then lets gravity do the rest. He said, "Elijah, get me some, uh, what do you call it?"

"Water?" I asked, because that was all he ever drank these days.

"That's right. Oh, and thank you. You know even when I don't say thank you, I'm thinking it. If I could give you some advice, don't ever forget to say thank you. All right?"

"All good, Grandpa." If my mom said that to me, my entire head would explode, because lately everything she said made me mad. But old people were cool. I went to get him some tap water, because he only drank tap, so as to avoid the microplastics from bottles and because "you don't know what they put in those filters they make water with." Which didn't really make sense, because you don't really "make" water, and also I was sure they must use filters to "make" tap water. I put exactly three cubes of ice into his cup. He liked his water cold but not too cold: "Being old is like being an elite athlete," he told me. "You like everything just right if you're going to put it into your body."

Comparing being old to being an elite athlete seemed like just about the most nonsensical thing he'd ever said, but I let it go, because like I said, old people were cool. Like, no matter what my grandpa said, it was cool. I came here for the pills, and that stuff was killing me because I just loved it so much. But at the same time, it was like my grandparents were keeping me alive. Joshie was keeping me alive. Kiiro was keeping me alive. I couldn't think about my parents, though. That was tough.

So it was like death and life all rolled into one at their little home there.

When I set the water in front of Grandpa, his eyes were closed. But he must have heard the cup clink on the table because he said through his closed eyes, "Is that my cup?"

"Yes, Grandpa." His favorite cup, at least whenever I was there, was the coffee mug I'd made for him when I was eight, when some girl had a birthday party at a ceramics place. The cup said PA on it. Sometimes I saw him just studying that word on the cup, and he seemed really satisfied.

I sat down next to him. "Did I ever tell you something?" Grandpa asked.

"Um, maybe, about what, though?" I answered politely.

"About how my brother died?"

"I didn't know you had a brother."

"Yes, I had a brother, and then I didn't."

"Wow . . . ," I said. Grandpa was staring into space. "How did he die? If it's okay to ask."

"Cancer. Vietnam. Suicide."

"Oh . . . I mean, which was it?"

"He was drafted and went to Vietnam. He got exposed to this chemical the army used in Vietnam called Agent Orange. And he got cancer from that, or I believe he did, and then when he knew he was going to die, he committed suicide."

"Well . . . wow. That sucks. I always thought . . ."

"Thought what?" He looked at me with watery eyes.

"Um. I guess I thought you kinda had an easy, or easier . . . or I guess I didn't realize bad things happened to you. I mean, I knew some things did . . . You lived in Oklahoma back then, right?"

"Yeah. Yeah. That's where he died. Afterward I got into his old car and drove all over the country for three months. Quit my job. It was the best time of my life up to that point. I always say he gave me that trip. He gave me the best time of my life. Up to that point. I was driving along in a storm, and lightning kept hitting close to my car. I didn't stop driving because I knew the lightning wouldn't hit me. It wouldn't hit me because it was him, just trying to say 'hi.' And also 'bye.'"

Grandpa slapped his thigh several times: *whack whack whack.*

"So do you think he went to heaven?"

"Oh, sure. Sure he did. He was a good man."

"Cool."

"I saw the lightning hit a tree, and then the storm was over. That was just him telling me he had to get going. I guess it's busy after you die. You got things to do. That's why I figure he doesn't come to me in dreams or anything like that. He had things to do, so after he hit that tree, he moved along."

I nodded, but he wasn't looking at me. He was looking at those lightning bolts. He was looking at that tree. He was looking at his brother.

But then after he'd stared with watery eyes into space for another few moments, he said, "Sorry to bother you young man but can you get some water for your grandmother too she's already awake I just heard her." He said it just like that— sometimes lately his brain stopped using commas when he talked, like he was going to fall asleep at any minute and just had to say this one last thing before he passed out. His body was even drifting back and forth right then.

I hadn't heard my grandma, but my grandparents can read each other's minds. I figured that happened when you got married. So I went for the water. Grandma didn't have a favorite cup, and she didn't like ice, because "I wouldn't want to choke."

When I came back with the water, she was sitting next to Grandpa, and he said, "Is there ice in it? She doesn't want to choke."

"No, Grandpa."

"Okay, good."

Grandma's pant legs were both pushed up, one all the way to the knee and the other halfway up her calf. Her ankles looked exactly like Grandpa's. Like, if you couldn't see the tops of the people, you would think it was one person with four ankles. I just stared at that. It seemed like a miracle, the way their ankles all looked the same.

They didn't say anything for such a long time, I asked, "Want me to make you a sandwich?"

They looked at each other, kept looking without saying anything. Then Grandpa turned to me and said, "Sure, peanut butter for her and ham with provolone for me."

I went to make the sandwiches. When I brought them back, I placed them on the coffee table. My grandparents didn't notice, because they were actually holding hands and looking at each other like they were still in love. And it was the first time in a long time that I had one of those perfect moments that used to hit me sometimes . . . in the Before Times. I mean, I was outside of the perfect moment, but I could feel it in the same room as me.

Do you ever wonder: What was life like in your grand-parents' time? And where did things go wrong? Like, why are there now drug addicts in tents all over the streets, and why do so many kids my age know somebody who overdosed or killed themselves? At school or rehab or just among people you knew, when somebody overdosed or committed suicide, the girls all cried and told each other, "I love you," and the guys all told each other, "Hey, homie, I got your back."

And then: *zap!*

Suddenly, I felt good again!

Grandma and Grandpa were now holding their sand-wiches as if somebody might steal them, leaning over their plates so no crumbs fell on the carpet. Ha ha, if my parents ate like that, it would make me want to rip their heads off. But I dunno, my grandparents were cute. My grandpa used to work at a big plumbing company where Grandma answered phones. I would never want to be a plumber, because of all that dirty water. But at the same time, if I could change places with him—like, if I could go back to the 1980s and be a plumber and he could have my life today—I would. Well, actually, I wouldn't, because then he'd have to be me, and that would suck for him.

God, I just suddenly loved my grandparents! I *loved* their townhome. The Land Time Forgot. I was sitting there with two old people chewing the crap out of their sandwiches, with forty-year-old curtains hanging on the windows, with old-people smell all around me, and I just felt like life was perfect. I felt like I wasn't even me, like I never had to go anywhere or do anything.

FORTY-FIVE

So not long after visiting my grandparents, we were all over at Lee's house one afternoon, on account of his parents and Su-Bee being gone for a few hours. And we were sitting around vaping and listening to rap when Lee suddenly got up and went outside. We peeked out the window and saw him lift the lid to the garbage can and throw something away.

He came back in and announced, "I'm done with Percocet. I just threw some away."

"Why didn't you give it to me?" Banker asked, all pissed off.

Lee didn't answer, just hit on a vape. Then in about fifteen minutes he suddenly jumped up and left the room again. On a hunch, I pulled aside his curtains and looked outside, and there he was digging through the garbage can. Outside on the street.

"Bruh," I said.

Then I closed the curtains and lay with my face in his rug so that I could hardly breathe. What were we becoming?

But, you know, addiction isn't always like you're burning inside because you want some drug so bad. Sometimes it's more like an itch. Other times it's more like being an automaton, and you just go through the motions like you're not really alive. And then you get the vape and you inhale the THC, or you get the pill and you swallow it, and it sends this signal through your head like, *Yeahhhhhh. Yeah!*

It was like all was right with the world—every single thing—and all was wrong with the world, at the EXACT SAME TIME. It was enough to tear you in half.

FORTY-SIX

I was getting pretty tired of the world. It seemed like a lot of work, even though I wasn't doing much actual work. So when Su-Bee called all cheerful and suggested we go see a movie at the mall in Torrance, I was kinda like sure, but inside I was thinking about all those holiday decorations that would be at the mall, and I wasn't really feeling it. Still, I thought about those moments on the beach with her and decided to go anyway.

She had her parents' second car when she picked me up. We found parking at the far end of one of the lots and stepped out into the windy night. Even though it wasn't even Thanksgiving yet, colored Christmas lights were wrapped around the trunks of palm trees, and reindeer hung across the parking aisles. We strolled toward a big Nordstrom sign. Halfway there a car cruised by, and then two guys jumped out of the passenger side. One guy jacked up the car and stood guard, and the other crawled underneath. A passerby yelled at them, and a third guy got out with a blowtorch yelling, "Back off!" There was a buzzing noise, and then the guy under the car came out with a catalytic converter. They all hopped back into their own car, which sped off. I think the whole thing took a little longer than sixty seconds.

"Ohhh," Su-Bee said. "That happened to my mom's car. You have to buy a lock now so nobody can steal your catalytic converter."

"Yeah, it happened to my neighbor in his own driveway," I said. "They had a lock, but someone got it off anyway. The garage told him they get fifteen people a week who that happens to."

Which, what were you gonna do? You had to park your car somewhere. Annoying for sure, and kinda sad. But it was everywhere, every day, and it was also the holiday season, and suddenly, I was feeling it. I was going to see a movie with a cool, pretty girl. So, like, you move on from the existential battle sometimes, you know?

I was about to take her hand, but before I could, she wrapped an arm around mine and was saying, "What's the best Christmas present you ever got?"

I tried to think back. "The first time I got a gift card when I was ten, I thought I'd struck it rich. Then it got so bad with everybody buying everybody else gift cards for every occasion that we banned them for Christmas presents."

"My first gift card was fun too! It was for Forever 21."

"What's that?"

"Really, you don't know? I used to think they had such cute clothes." She leaned back and looked at me, her fingers still lightly touching my arm. "That's a cool hoodie. Did you pick it out?"

"No, I get all my clothes for my birthday and Christmas, and then that's all I wear all year." I paused. "Unless I get crappy stuff, in which case I can also wear last year's clothes that still fit."

She laughed with what I can only call "delight." Then she leaned against my arm and said, "I like you!"

Wasn't sure what she meant by that. I suddenly wasn't even sure which hoodie I'd put on, so I glanced down and saw that it said REAL TIME, REAL FUN. Whatever that meant. But I liked the design—kind of psychedelic lettering.

It was a cool night, so I put my arm around her as we walked. Lee had this idea that optimism was not much different from pessimism—both unearned. Hope, he said, was earned—you suffer, you fall, you fail, and then you hope. And I guess I couldn't say I'd really suffered a lot yet, or maybe not fallen all that much, or completely failed. But life had gotten pretty grim, and I figured maybe I'd earned a little hope. Anyway, at that moment I had what I hoped was hope. Su-Bee and I slipped through the Nordstrom doors, and I saw her eyes roaming and halt at the handbags. She pulled me along. "I can't stop myself," she said.

In the bag department I randomly looked at a price tag: $500. "The expensive ones are in the case," Su-Bee said.

"Five hundred for a handbag isn't expensive?" Like, why? Why not just get pants with pockets and put your five hundred bucks in there?

"Not to some of these people."

I leaned over, studied a bag in the case. It had tan strips of leather woven through each other. These two little, uh . . . strappy loop things stuck up on the sides like ears. And there was a longer strap to carry the purse with. But the loops were not long enough to use to carry it. They were just kind of stuck there. "Why does it have ears?"

"I know!" she exclaimed.

I didn't know what she "knew," but I went with it, because she was so sincere.

Her face was full of excitement. She looked around like she had a secret, then said with a lowered voice, "See, there are women who would buy a thousand-dollar bag with ears, as you call them. And it looks stupid, and they wear it proudly because it cost so much money. I feel sorry for them."

"It's Italian," I added, reading the tag. I was trying to remember conversations I'd overheard of the Asian moms. "Aren't handbags better from Italy?"

Su-Bee squinted at the bag. "It does look like nice leather." She whipped around. "I could make a bag like this without the ears and sell it for two hundred dollars tops!" She paused. "It might not be the top *top* leather, though."

"But why do you feel sorry for the women?"

"Because they're paying a thousand dollars for a purse with ears."

We moved to the next bag. It was dirty yellow with what looked like cheap, shiny rocks embedded in the leather. And a giant logo covering almost the whole front.

"Wow," we both said at the same time. A saleswoman came up assessing us: Were we rich kids seriously looking, or not?

"Just looking," I said.

"Take your time, take your time!" she said cheerfully. Before she moved on, she added, "That bag is one of my favorites!"

Maybe if I were high, that would've seemed cool, but seeing that I wasn't, I just stood there in that store and seriously wondered WTF. Because I suddenly saw every single thing at the same time: Martin dying; all the studying; mountain biking;

the thousands of missing catalytic converters; the addicts on the streets; these stupid purses; getting sent to Costa Rica; a homeless guy I saw walking along the sidewalk, so bent over he couldn't see where he was going; the genius of Lee; Attila the Hun; beautiful Su-Bee; my grandparents; the Iraq War my dad fought in; all of it; everything. I saw it all.

All I could think to say, though, was, "Oh, shit."

Su-Bee asked, "What?" But then she took my hand and said, "Oh, we're going to be late for the movie!"

We had to jog through the mall. She had on these clunky boots that went *clop-clop* as we ran. And I felt a little like I did that time at my sixteenth birthday party: all of us against the world. Now, though, it was her and me running through it all—all of it I mentioned above, just the two of us vibing as we ran through a world of thousand-dollar purses and people overdosing on the streets, trying to get to a movie on time.

We were both panting when we got our tickets and stepped into the theater.

We had time to buy popcorn, and we sat down. There was an ad playing about a local glasses shop. She nudged me and said, "Why did you say 'Oh, shit' before?"

"I was just, uh . . . I'm not sure."

She looked at me curiously.

"Costa Rica," I said. "I was thinking about, uh . . . addicts on the street and just a lot of stuff all at once."

"You make no sense. My brother does that too. It's the smart-guy syndrome, I think. One day at dinner he started giving us all a lecture about Flight 370—remember that Malaysia Airlines flight that disappeared when we were little kids? I didn't even know he was interested in that."

"Yeah, he definitely has smart-guy syndrome. I don't even know what he's talking about sometimes."

She pulled two bottles of water out of her handbag and handed me one.

"Thanks," I said. She had one of those big handbags that I guess made sense for carrying water. And it was true that when I was little, it seemed like I could ask my mom for just about anything, and she would have it in her big purse.

Su-Bee also pulled out one of those ceramic Asian good luck cats, a small one. "I carry my luck in here." Then she looked really, really shy and handed it to me. "You take it for now."

"I don't want to take your luck!"

"Please?"

So I took it. "I'll give it back if you need it," I said. I stuck the cat in my pocket.

Quirky girl, but in a fairy princess not-quite-real kind of way, not like a goofy kind of way. Trusting, real, and quirky. I felt like I'd gotten a glimmer of seeing some stuff about Su-Bee. Like I said, I had a girlfriend for a little while, but it never felt like this. I mean, I liked this other girl, I guess, but she was kind of just a girl . . . not sure how to explain. She was cute. I got no idea what was inside of that one, is what I mean.

It was a small movie and just about the weirdest film I ever watched. The story was about a woman who foresaw stuff about her daughter in her dreams, but it turned out it was repressed memories of her own childhood. So it ended with the woman, her mom, and her daughter all hugging. Su-Bee was sniffling at the end, which I admit was kinda cute, but including snacks, it was hella money to pay just for a little bit of crying. Still, it was a lot of fun. Because we were just really *there* together. I could feel her there the whole time, which was honestly a lot more interesting than the movie.

We walked around the closing mall afterward. Stores were lowering metal doors in front of their glass windows.

Then we sat quietly among all the closing, and then closed, stores. A few people meandered around, some carrying shopping bags. I inhaled the smell from the giant Christmas tree rising up in the center of the mall. I felt hope flood through me.

We sat there like that for nearly an hour, not even talking, not even kissing. Just sitting together, surrounded by Christmas in November.

FORTY-SEVEN

So I'd been thinking maybe I could be like Priscus, who was supposedly a big deal during the Byzantine Empire. Remember, the guy who wrote about Attila the Hun? The Byzantine Empire formed in the eastern part of the Roman Empire after Rome's collapse. Those were some wild times back then, and people were moving around a lot. But the Byzantine Empire ended up lasting a long time. Also, some of these historian guys wrote about their present times, not the past. I started thinking I should be writing the history of me and my homies. I really thought I oughta do it, instead of writing about all this old stuff like I usually did.

But back in September, in AP history, I did end up writing a paper on the past history of indoor plumbing. It made me wonder now, though, who was going to write about the *present* history of plumbing? About the plumbers of *today*? See what I mean? The olden guys like Priscus wrote about their today.

Anyhow, there's been plumbing since thousands of years ago, because ancient people figured out that you get sick from sewage. They had copper pipes in ancient Egypt. I know from my dad and grandpa that copper pipes are the best. And then in Crete they had a whole indoor plumbing system. The Athenians even had pressurized showers! The Mayans had pressurized showers a little later. Ancient people were hella smart. I guess I'd written that paper to respect my grandpa. I asked my teacher to enter it in a California essay contest. Entries didn't have to be history essays, so I added a lot of details about my grandpa. If I won, I planned to give him the plaque or ribbon or whatever prize they gave me for his Christmas present this year. And I did win—the contest sent me an email saying I won and to expect a manila envelope in the mail. But somehow I didn't get that excited. For some reason. Things just didn't feel right. I didn't even tell anyone I won. It was like whatever.

Because it was nearly the end of the first semester of my junior year, I started taking practice SATs. I got a 1450, which I mean, KMS. I know that's high for some kids, but seven of the Asian kids I knew got perfect scores. So basically that meant if I didn't improve my grades, I wouldn't be going to a really top school, if I even decided to go to college.

I was starting to wonder if the University of Chicago was the best place for me. They had a top history department. Also, Lee and I kept track of the free speech thing, and they were a good school for that. Because the teachers at our school were always tripping over what we could or couldn't say, and who knows—I might want to say whatever I wanted in college.

But it was crazy because I was taking tests, writing all these essays, and working out which schools to apply to, and meanwhile me and the guys were doing all this stuff and acting like idiots. And then the biggest idiot thing was that Lee got Su-Bee to tell him where her money was, and a few days after that he stole it.

He randomly came over one night without warning me. We got in the car, and he said, "I stole my sister's money. Not all of it. I'm going to tell Banker it was all of it, though."

I started to say, *Dude*, but instead I said, "Goddamn, Lee, it's your sister."

"Yeah, I know, it's bad. But I did it." He glanced at me. "You're not gonna snitch to her, are you?"

"Of course not." I mean, I would never do an anti-bro move like snitch. "But she seems like a really nice girl is all."

"She's my sister. So, no, she's not always nice. But I get what you're saying . . . she's a good person. But not always. I have a baseball signed by five of the Angels, and she threw it into the pool. I still have it, but a little of the ink ran."

"Really? Okay, that sucks," I said. I was eager to not feel bad about the money, so I added, "That really sucks. She might not be that good a person." But I was pretty sure she was.

"Yeah . . . I mean, she was going through a lot that year. Nobody knows why."

"Dude . . ."

At a stoplight he rubbed his temples and groaned. "Should I put the money back? She'd never know. We could turn around right now."

"I just—I can't tell if Banker wants the money or wants to, you know, fuck you up."

He looked at me in total surprise. "What do you mean?" He just sat there even though the light had turned green. He looked mad, maybe at *me*.

Someone honked behind us, and he started driving again.

"I dunno, it just popped into my head," I said.

"Here's the thing," he said. "I . . . have to do it, because I need the money. I owe Banker some money, and . . . and I also just, I need some money. Otherwise, it's bad. It'll be bad."

I was going to ask what was bad, but we'd just arrived at Banker's place.

Lee brought the cash inside. It made no sense, but then as I sat at Banker's, I started to feel really mad at my *parents*, who had nothing to do with any of this. I guess it was the shame—you don't really want to feel it, so you kind of displace it onto someone else. I just sat there in Banker's room feeling like I hated my parents, which please don't tell me was irrational. Precisely none of us was worried about being rational.

"I hate my parents!" I blurted out.

"Me too!" the other three said.

I paused. "You hate my parents or your parents?"

"My parents," they all said.

Lee turned to Banker. "I got the money."

"Lee! You didn't let me down!" Banker grinned. "You're the master of finesse!"

Lee seemed like maybe he was pleased to hear he was "the master of finesse," but at the same time, maybe he wasn't. "So are we going to divide it or what?" he asked, kind of like he was suddenly tired. "It's six hundred dollars."

"Why only six hundred?"

"That was all she had in her hiding place."

"Well, let's think about that later, like where she might keep the rest," Banker said. "But first let's think about what we want to get with all this."

And already I could see Banker was putting himself in charge of the money, like he had with Lee's car.

There was some change mixed up in the cash, even pennies. For some reason that made me feel terrible.

Banker was fingering the bills. "I'll count it again," he said. "And I'll hold on to the money until we figure out what to do with it, since it was my idea." I glanced at Lee to see if that was okay with him, since it kind of seemed like he should be in charge of the money. But he looked relieved and even rubbed his palms on his pants, as if rubbing off what he'd done.

I tried to get it straight in my head: there were some bad people in this new world we'd entered, but the drugs themselves also brought out that side of you that was bad—that part of you that maybe you didn't realize you had in you a few years earlier, and now you knew that you did have. I thought about that guy who was in the Omarska camp, how he talked about the thin line between the perps and the righteous. Anyone could become either one—that was half of history. Nobody knew what they were capable of until the moment arrived. Like for instance, Banker being such an asshole, but also being the only person I'd ever met who was willing to run in front of a bus and get wrecked, to save somebody he didn't even know. People thought they had that in them, but when the moment came, who actually did it? Banker, that's who.

It also made me realize that being a leader like Banker had nothing to do with anything. You just had to want it, and you had to be one of those people who happened to have the knack for making people follow you. In Banker's case, somehow he'd been born a spellbinder and an asshole at the same time. I looked at Banker, eagerly counting money, and could see how much he wanted to be the one in charge. That was the other half of history—the wrong people wanting to be in charge.

Then Banker put the money in a drawer. "I'm gonna figure out something for us to do to make a profit, you know? Or maybe just get some good stuff."

I actually felt kinda relieved to see the money go into a drawer. I wanted to forget about it and maybe not ever think about it again, if that was possible. My mind drifted back to earlier. What did Lee mean by "it's bad"?

Davis had an idea. "I can get some bars. I know a guy who's selling them cheap." He seemed proud to have said that.

"How cheap?" Banker asked.

Myself, I liked Xanax okay. I liked Percocet a lot more, though. It depended on my mood. I liked vaping the most. It relaxed me, and it was cool that it was just steam. Also, you couldn't overdose from vaping, so you were safe—you just had to quit before your lungs got ruined.

Once in a while, and admittedly more and more often, I just felt like going somewhere else, and that was what the pills were for.

Davis said, "I'm not sure. I'll make some calls."

Banker's face filled with rage. But he said calmly, almost *sweetly*, while doing the thing with his fingers, "I can get better stuff than you, Davis. Plus, I want to take Lee around and show him how it's done. Elijah and you need to learn some things too."

That caught my interest, to be honest. "Learning some things" was always interesting, right? At the same time, it made me really uncomfortable. Because it made me wonder if Banker was training us to operate more expertly in the upper demonic levels, you know? I wondered suddenly if he went to even lower levels sometimes. He put an arm around Lee and pulled him close. "I think of you as my true brother."

"Yeah, thanks."

Lee was kind of swaying around, looking dizzy as he sat there. "You okay, Lee?" I asked.

"Yo, man, I think I'm gonna barf. I took some bars." Bars really did not agree with Lee. He rushed to Banker's garbage can and threw up. He looked green. Not bright green, but just really off.

"You good? Yo! Lee!" I said.

He threw up again, then at last looked like normal color was filling his face again.

"Yeah, geez," he said. "Don't know what was in that."

"What did you take?"

"I gave him something good the other day," Banker answered for him.

"It must not have been that good," I commented.

Banker didn't even look at me. He arched his back in a stretch, and it was like I hadn't even said anything.

But Su-Bee was texting me. *Can you talk?* she asked. Shit!

"Uh-oh, it's Su-Bee," I said. *What is it I'm with the guys,* I texted back.

It's important.

"Ask her what she wants," Banker said. He pointed at Lee. "She's got you now. She's gonna bust your ass." Banker laughed. "She's probably already called the police on you, bro."

"She doesn't know," Lee said, looking paranoid that she *did* know. "No way she knows. Just call her, Elijah, make her happy."

I really, really did not want to talk to her right then. On the other hand, I really, really did. So I stepped outside, into the backyard.

It was one of those otherworldly California nights when

the Santa Ana winds were blowing hard and you could hear the air whirling through the branches and it was like you were experiencing every other night you'd ever felt the Santa Anas, all at the same time. I saw a palm frond fall into the next yard. The rusted lawn mowers in the Banks' yard had been sitting there since the first time I came here. It seemed like three or four years ago, but it was maybe three or four months. Banker had told us that he'd collected the lawn mowers to fix them up and sell them for drug money. But instead he just stole the money from one of his mom's friends. Banker always said that working was a waste of time. The way he saw it, there was all this money out there for the taking. For instance, in people's wallets. All you had to do was get it somehow with the least amount of effort. What I was learning was that there were different ways to make money, and they all involved moving money from one wallet into another. You could do this by being a hard worker like my dad or by being an asshole or by being an actual demon.

I took out my vape and inhaled deeply, but I didn't feel the rush of confidence I expected. Instead I felt dull. Then I took out my phone and called Su-Bee.

"Oh, Elijah," she sobbed out. "Someone stole some of my money from the garage! I only told three people where it was! I think it was my so-called friend Julie's boyfriend. He's such a douchebag!"

"You told Julie's boyfriend?" I asked.

"No, but I told *her*, and she tells him everything. He's such a jerk. And he doesn't even treat her right." We were quiet for a minute while she cried.

It was weird how I could see and hear and feel the wind,

but I now felt separated from it. It blew lukewarm air against my face, and while I knew this was happening, it still didn't feel real.

"Maybe . . . I guess you shouldn't just assume it was Julie."

"Who else could it be?"

"I mean, I don't know." But I didn't want her to suspect Lee. Maybe I could change her thinking—you know, what the kids studying business called "nudge theory." "It's hard to save money. I tried once, and I couldn't save anything. I really tried too. But . . . I mean, if you're a person who can save money, then you can save it again. If you're like me, you can't save. But you can do it, I know you can. Just don't tell anyone about it next time. Don't tell me or anyone, okay? Promise? Did you hear me?"

"Yes. But how can I get the money back?"

She needed more nudging. "If you can't prove anything, then you really can't get it back. But promise me you won't tell anyone where you put the money next time. That includes me. Don't tell anyone at all. Okay?"

"Okay. But why can't I tell you?"

"Because you need to get into the habit of not telling anyone. You can't trust anyone in this world. Just start saving again, and this time hide your money better and don't tell anyone where."

"I *can* do it again," she said firmly. "I can save it again. I have an idea where I could hide it where nobody would ever find it. Can I tell you?"

"No, I just said *no*." Geez, I just said no! "Su-Bee, NO."

She paused. "Okay." She paused again. "Thank you for your advice. I knew I could count on you. His name is Peter. The jerk boyfriend."

"Yeah, what a jerk. I hate that name." I paused. *"Don't trust anyone,"* I added urgently.

"Okay . . . Are we going to get together again soon?"

"Sure. Yeah. Of course." There was a silence, and then I felt it again: we were vibing. I didn't have a car yet, but I could Uber when I had to. A lot of parents got their kids onto Uber so they'd never get stranded anywhere. "I can come by, and we can go catch another movie." I laughed. "Can I choose the movie this time?"

"Of course! Okay, good, let me know when! I gotta go, bye!"

"Bye, Su-Bee."

I stood there for a minute, then texted her, *Ever hear of banks??*

She texted me back a laughing emoji.

I went to sit across the yard, in the farthest corner from the house. The yard was big, but it was dried and yellow. There was something I didn't understand. Like, with Martin: Why did someone want to go after a kid? Even with Banker, why Lee? There must be older and bad people he could take advantage of. But why go after people who were more, you know, *innocent* than you were? Like Su-Bee. Why were we doing this to her? Why couldn't we rip off somebody bad? See, of course if you stepped outside our situation, you would ask, why rip off anybody at all? But from *within* our situation, using our own stupid logic, why target the innocent when there were so many other people to rip off?

But can you even tell for sure who's good and who's bad? For instance, I didn't really have *that* bad of a feeling about Banker early on. You just can't tell with people—that's the tough thing. Yes, there are some obvious assholes, but there are also some people who, you just can't tell what they are inside. You can't even tell who *you* are inside. If you listened to the Omarska guy, you don't know for sure who you'll be in a certain situation until you're in the situation.

And then, for the second time, I had the thought that maybe Lee was becoming like Martin. With a perv? It just popped into my head. For a second I *knew* that was it. Then I *didn't* know it anymore. That couldn't be it. Right?

The wind was picking up, blowing a couple of shirts off the clothesline. And out of nowhere, something the pastor had said at church years ago popped into my head: "What if you did something good for someone bad? What would happen?" So I went to pick the shirts off the ground. I had some doubts as I did it. Because I mean, fuck Banker's shirts.

But I picked them up from the overgrown grass. There were no clothespins, though, so I figured the shirts would just fall off again. I hung them up anyway. Then I noticed that one of them was Lee's. It was a Versace thing—pricey. But Lee gave Banker stuff sometimes, and I guess Banker supplied him with whatever. And now here it was, hanging on the line in Banker's backyard. I felt bad for Lee's mom; she had bought him that shirt for his birthday. But as soon as I had the thought that I felt bad for Lee's mom, I felt bad for Banker, too. Because his dad bought him nothing but sports shirts. And Banker didn't even like sports. And all of a sudden, that made me sad for him. Lee's parents would've bought Lee a thousand shirts if he wanted, the exact shirts that he wanted, if he cared about shirts. They would've taken out a *loan* to get him shirts, if he wanted.

That's why I felt sorry for Banker. He was friends with a guy whose parents would take out a goddamn loan to get him a shirt, and here he was walking around every day in Dodgers shirts. He probably couldn't even name a single Dodger. It was kind of humiliating if you thought about it.

Most of our parents were parents *specifically* to us. Even if they got you a stupid T-shirt, when they bought it, they walked around the mall for an hour and picked one out *specifically* for you. It might seem like a small thing, but I dunno. If they didn't do that, if they just got you random Dodgers shirts, it might break your brain, especially if you didn't even give a crap about the Dodgers.

FORTY-EIGHT

Then it was the Wednesday before Thanksgiving weekend. I got home from school, and nobody was there—a note from my mom said she was food shopping with Joshie. So I decided to call Su-Bee, and it turned out she was free. She drove over.

She was wearing a tie-dye dress with a jean jacket and her wire-rimmed glasses. She looked like she stepped out of the sixties.

I gave her a soft kiss on the lips at the door, then couldn't think what to say. I came up with, "Wanna play GTA?"

Her face brightened—a lot. "Okay!"

So I took her hand and led her to my bedroom. There was an extra chair at my desk from one day when I was watching *Madagascar* with Joshie—he liked to watch it on different screens sometimes. To me, it was the same movie whatever screen you watched it on. But to him, it was different; go figure.

I turned on the console and TV and handed Su-Bee the extra controller, warning her, "You don't mind torture and stuff like that, do you?"

"Torture like . . ."

"Teeth extraction, electrocution."

She laughed. "Well, let's try it, I guess!"

So we careened through the game, stealing cars and beating the crap out of people, and she screamed the whole time. "I can't believe the character said that!" "OHHHHH MY GOD." GTA is the greatest, most demented game ever. Basically, you just go around stealing cars and doing things to put people in a world of pain.

My mom came home without me hearing, because she peeked in and said, "Eli—oh, sorry!" Then she closed the door.

I put one of the chairs against the door. Then we made out for a while on my bed. Su-Bee always seemed super clean, like she just showered an hour ago, and she smelled slightly perfumey. Not a lot, but a little. Her hair was super clean too; I could tell when I ran my hand through it.

And I did wonder for a minute what this super-clean, super-soft girl was doing with a guy like me—a guy who now knew where part of her stolen money was. I tried to make it work out in my head: Banker was an asshole, and I needed to unload him as a friend at some point; and Su-Bee was this girl who made you feel you'd rediscovered hope, and I would be happy to lie here all day with her. So, then, how did it make sense that I knew where her money was? It seemed like a tragedy. My grandma made me take a Shakespeare class once, because she never read him and thought it would "help round you out as a person." And now my life was turning into some Romeo and Juliet–level stuff. Because, I mean, Su-Bee was such a cool girl, and Lee was such a cool guy, and I just didn't know how we were all going to get through this. I mean, the only way out is through. This exact moment was maybe the first time when I really got what my grandpa meant by that. It was when everything was maximum fucked up, and you had to keep going forward anyway.

Then Su-Bee and I were just kind of lying there, and I could hear the wind blowing the bushes in the backyard. The windows were open, because I had them that way at all times, just to hear the outside sounds.

She sat up, put on her glasses that she'd taken off. "I've done some bad stuff. I used to be really jealous of my brother, and I did some very bad stuff." She looked like she thought she was saying something urgent. So I sat up too.

"Bad stuff like what?"

"I hid Lee's homework once, and he had to stay up late and do it over."

"Wow. Did you confess?"

"No, I got found out. And then it still took me three months to apologize. I refused to apologize."

"Damn," I said. "I thought you were perfect."

She laughed shyly, then hung her head. "I threw his signed baseball into the pool while we were fighting. It was special because I guess someone hit a home run that won a big game, and then some players signed it."

"Well . . . did you feel bad?"

"No, I felt good when I did it. I did other things too that I never confessed to. I can't even tell you until I know you better."

"Damn." Like, I was sure she'd never done anything as bad as we'd now done, but then I suddenly wondered: Had she? And just like that, I saw more of what was inside this girl. It was complicated with dark spots, and she'd gotten through it.

She was doing a little thing where she lifted her feet a few inches up and tapped her big toes together. "I guess I'm going to major in psychology or business in college. I love my psych class a lot." She put her feet down. "I'm trying to figure some stuff out."

"Like why you did bad things?"

"That too! We're studying mass psychogenic illness. It's more of a girl thing, because we're more empathetic than boys, but that makes us relate a little too much to each other, I guess. My teacher thinks MPI is what happened during the Salem witch trials, and maybe during the dancing manias in the Middle Ages. It happens today too, where a bunch of girls might start twitching and hitting their own faces and fainting."

I searched the files in my brain for anything about any of that. "Did you know back in Salem they squished a guy to death who was accused of being a witch?"

"What!?"

"Yeah, some historians think a plank or something was put on him, and then they piled on rocks until he was squished."

"Wow . . . I didn't know that. That's screwed up! I mean, I feel bad for everyone. It kind of wasn't the girls' fault, because they were barking and fainting and acting crazy, and that's why they thought someone was putting a spell on them. When MPI happened at a school in New York, everybody in the town got really upset and suspicious and paranoid."

"Sometimes I look at history and think there's this *thing* that rises out of the earth every so often, and it's like smoke," I said. "It floats around and surrounds people, and a lot of the people go crazy. Then it floats away, and everybody is okay again. And they don't even realize they went crazy."

"That's MPI!" she said. "It starts when there's a lot of psychological stress." Suddenly, she was crying. "Maybe that's what's going on with my brother!" She put a pillow over her face and started crying like that.

And I mean, my old girlfriend's mom used to cry a lot at the end, at the kitchen table, when she was getting divorced. But damn, I didn't know what to do then either. It was an education, because I knew that people got their hearts broken, but I'd never seen it before. It filled the whole kitchen. I could feel that mom's heartbreak like warm air when I stood in their kitchen.

And I felt that same warm air now.

"What do you mean?" I asked her.

"I mean I know he's getting high. Honestly, I get high sometimes too. But I don't know, would that change him as much as it has? He seems like he's changed. Sometimes I—sometimes I feel scared of him. He gets so mad."

"Really?" I thought about the time I threw my shoes in Joshie's room. But Lee had always been kind of mild-mannered. I wouldn't say he was weak, but he was kind of gentle. The way Su-Bee was, actually. And, I mean, he was still pulling all A's, even though he was high all the time. And he worked at some recreation center, selling Gatorade and snacks and stuff behind a counter. I honestly had no idea how he got any sleep.

"Yeah," Su-Bee was saying. "I hear banging in his room when our parents aren't home, like he's throwing stuff or hitting things. He hit me on the head with a deodorant stick."

"Deodorant? What for?"

"Because I caught him going through my parents' medicine cabinet. I heard him in their room, so I went in, and then I heard him in their bathroom. When I asked him what he was doing, he got in my face, screaming. At first I just stood there yelling back. That was when he grabbed the deodorant and threw it at my head. I almost fell down. So I got scared and went into the kitchen looking for our dog. I thought maybe she would protect me. But he kept following me."

I tried to think what to say. A day ago I wouldn't have been able to picture Lee doing that. But now the picture was taking shape in my brain. Lee screaming. Lee hitting his sister in the head with deodorant. I could almost see it until I *could* see it.

Su-Bee gave me the most intense look! "Will you talk to him?" she asked.

"Sure," I said. "But I'm not sure I can understand him. He's kind of, you know, he's Lee. I don't get him sometimes. I'll talk to him, though."

Su-Bee leaned her head on my arm until my arm fell asleep. But I didn't say anything. And then she fell asleep, so I knew I couldn't move. And I felt like I should try to get her money back for her. I fell asleep, and when I woke up, she was gone and my arm hurt.

I took out my vape pen and inhaled a few times. And I felt good, but it was different from the kind of good I felt with Su-Bee. It was not hope-good. It was stupor-good.

But as dusk set in, I drifted farther and farther away from Su-Bee, from my parents, from everything and everybody. I wished I could be alone all night. I wished they would die and I could live here by myself for a while, and then when I ran out of whatever money they left me, I could sell our fancy house and use the money to buy a million vape dabs. I wouldn't care if I were homeless; I would just lie in a ditch somewhere high until I died. Why not?

I hated myself.

FORTY-NINE

My phone dinged a little later: my mom saying my paint therapist had just arrived.

Yeah, paint therapist. Once a week for the past few weeks, I did two hours of paint therapy with some guy my mom had found. Apparently, one of the other Asian moms had made her daughter do paint therapy, and that kid supposedly enjoyed it, or at least told her mom she enjoyed it. Then this mom told Lee's mom about it, because Lee's mom could tell Lee was stressed. So then he had to do the paint therapy too. And then my mom found out, and she made me do paint therapy with a different person—one who specialized in addicts. This was my third week. Did I mention that there were a bunch of different tutor types who specialized in kid addicts? So you could take music or drumming or painting or writing, taught by teachers who worked with kids who had drug problems. This one was a white guy, because even though I had Asian or hapa everything, there really weren't that many Asians involved in addict stuff.

Me and the therapist did the painting in the kitchen, where the paint was easy to clean up. Usually everybody left me alone.

But my mom was cooking pumpkin cream cheese cupcakes for tomorrow, which was Thanksgiving. Yes, somehow all the usual things went on, like Thanksgiving and school and TV shows and the wind and the stars and the rain. Joshie was helping her, measuring out all the ingredients.

The teacher, Andrei, said, "Let's do orange, for Thanksgiving."

"Yo, you mean *only* orange today?"

"Yeah, let's try that."

He poured an entire can of orange paint into a pot he'd brought. "Try swishing your hands around in there."

I scratched my head. "Dude . . ."

"Just try it!"

So I stuck my hands in and swished them around.

"Squeeze your hands into fists and open them!"

As I was doing that, he set up a portable Bluetooth speaker and started playing music. He was Russian, so he put on a compilation of Russian composers. Some of it was really dramatic. "Many of these composers' talents were recognized at a very young age, younger than you are. So I want you to think about that for a minute, then find who you are and have been from a very young age." He laid out a blank stretched canvas and shouted, "Now paint!"

I took my hands out of the pot and put two handprints on the canvas. I hesitated—I'd forgotten to think a minute. So I closed my eyes.

"Find who you have been forever!" he demanded.

I closed my mind, and what I thought about was this: Did you know that between 32,000 and 40,000 years ago, humans started to put handprints and hand stencils on caves all around the world? Indonesia, Spain, France, Australia. And then they kept doing it throughout the centuries. There's a place in Argentina called Cueva de las Manos, or Cave of Hands, where humans made like 2,000 handprints and hand outlines in surges between 9,500 and 1,500 years ago. It would happen all over the world, and then it wouldn't happen as much for a while before it happened again. For some reason they're mostly left hands, some with missing fingers—and this was true all over the world too. Some are the hands of children. Nobody knows what the reason was, for the hands or the children or the missing fingers. Were the children sacrificed, or what? Did people cut off the fingers on purpose, or what? I liked to think it was a message to us, the people of the future. Maybe it was just a message to say "hey."

Some Neanderthals made kinda different ones too, way, way before that. The Neanderthals were dope. I never understood why "Neanderthal" was an insult. They were around a lot longer than we humans have been, in much harsher conditions than we've lived in. They took care of each other too, when they got hurt—which was all the time. A real success story, if you actually think about it.

Now I closed my eyes, tried to imagine myself as a Neanderthal. Why would I put my prints on a cave wall? Maybe because I was one of the last of the Neanderthals? In that case, I wouldn't be saying "hey." I would be saying "bye." I held up my pinky, so that it seemed like it might have been missing.

"What are you thinking about?" Andrei asked.

"About my finger being missing."

"And why would it be missing?"

I thought about that. "Uh, I'm a caveman, and I had a battle with . . . some animal I needed to kill for my clan to eat. I guess."

Andrei was nodding as if I'd just said something important. "Isn't that the truth? Cavemen probably had to battle for meat."

I don't know why that should've made me feel good that he said that, but it did.

At the end of the lesson I stood there with orange hands and said, "Thanks, Andrei. Have a good holiday, seriously."

He reached out and shook my orange hand, and then we high-fived.

Later as I washed my hands, my mom handed Andrei a check and said, "I've never listened in before! That was amazing!"

I cleaned up the table and went to my room, where I taped my canvas to a wall. I gotta say, Andrei was a pretty good therapist. Mom also sent me to the one Japanese therapist she'd somehow discovered, and I mean, he was okay, but I had to kind of LOL at my mom thinking that just because he was Japanese, he would be a good therapist. A lot of Asian parents were like that. Like, I had an Asian guy who cut my hair, and an Asian chiropractor I went to for a while when I hurt my back, and an Asian optometrist, and so on. Everybody else had Hispanic gardeners, but we had an old Japanese guy who was like seventy-three years old.

Lee got sent to a psychiatrist who was five hundred dollars an hour, which is not that pricey for these guys. Some of them charge twelve hundred for the first session. But a lot of psychiatrists liked to put you on meds. In fact, they'd wanted me to go on meds at both rehabs I went to. But eventually, my mom found the paint therapist instead.

• • • •

So anyway, for Thanksgiving my grandparents came over. My cousins' family always had Thanksgiving at the home of Auntie Pam's good friend. And for no reason my mom asked me to say grace.

"Really?" I said. "Um." I looked down and thought about the Cave of Hands. "So about nine thousand five hundred years ago, a bunch of humans in Argentina started making stencils and prints of their hands in some caves in Argentina. And nobody knows why. I kind of wish I knew why. See, humans had been doing it all over the world for tens of thousands of years. Some years they did it more, and some years they did it less. How come they all did it at the same time? I just think that's really cool. Uh. Thank you, God, for the handprints and for this food. Amen."

I looked up at everybody. They were all looking at *me*.

Nobody said anything for a few seconds.

Then Grandma chuckled and said proudly, "He's such an original young man!" She placed her hand on her heart and shook her head like I'd just said the most genius prayer in the history of prayers.

Then we ate, but I hardly said another word.

Later that night I thought about all the civilizations that had lived and died. I thought about Lee and Martin and Joshie and Su-Bee and my parents and about how in America we had fifty times more overdose deaths per capita than Japan. And probably more than any country in the world. We had hella suicides and hella car accidents, too. We were a short-lived people, compared to every other rich country. So, a very stressful country. A good time for MPI.

I fell asleep and dreamed I was in a cave with Kiiro the Wolf Dog sitting next to me, waiting patiently, ready to kill my enemies. And me putting handprints all over the walls, so people of the future would know someone had been there.

FIFTY

I didn't have much to do during the times my parents were full of messianic energy about me getting sober; they made me come home right after school. One night at dinner my mom was sitting next to me, chatting, and I really wasn't in the mood. I was *bored*. With life. The whole world was boring. The *design* was boring.

"I was thinking of making carrot cake tomorrow—what do you think?" Mom asked. "Do you feel like it, hon?"

Sometimes all of us, with our moms, were just like, *What is she even talking about?* We're thinking about where we can get money for pills or nic or THC or even harder stuff—or in this case thinking about *boredom*—and our moms are talking about carrot cake. I felt that rage I was starting to feel more and more suddenly building up in me, but I concentrated really hard on keeping it under control.

"Cool," I said. "Carrot cake."

But the rage. It was a high all by itself. I could have gone to that rage right there at the table, but instead I said, "Love carrot cake!"

I could see that pleased my mom. Like I said before, she

was such a—such a mom. The devotion of the addicts' parents was kind of nuts. You could hijack a bus while high out of your mind, and your mom would bring you carrot cake in jail. Your dad would bring you car magazines.

And I think it was just . . . you hated everyone because they didn't get it. They were trying to get you back to happyland, and that place just didn't exist for you anymore. It was like if your dog just died and someone asked you if you wanted carrot cake. It made no sense! Do you see? Do you?

Also, it wasn't personal. You wanted money for drugs so bad that you just looked at other people and saw right through them. And, I mean, some therapist was talking like, "What are you feeling?" and meanwhile you were dying inside and think-ing about the money in their pockets.

My parents were letting me go out for walks with Kiiro in the evenings. So I had no money, and I could go for walks. I figured I should do something I thought I would never, ever do: sell my Shimano shoes.

One thing about my parents is, they'd never gotten me expensive clothes. Like I said before, I asked for a collector's Supreme shirt all the time, but I never got it. My dad said, "What do you need a collector's shirt for? What if you get ink on it?" He thought it was pretty funny that I even asked. But he didn't mind me having the shoes, maybe because I paid for them myself.

Then I sold the shoes to a girl from Snapchat for a hundred twenty-five bucks, even though they'd cost me three hundred. But the cash was great! I felt pretty smart with cash in my pocket. Felt like I had *earned* it. I took Kiiro to a vape shop, and a homeless guy got me a disposable vape that I planned to use in school the next day. But I felt dumb, too. Because those shoes were dope.

School: boring. Some kids got high even in the classroom. Mostly guys. Show me even one teacher who's not clueless about what's going on with half the boys. I'll wait.

FIFTY-ONE

One Saturday in December, Joshie wanted to prep for next spring, when there would be a race for kids his age in Oregon that Mom and Dad had decided we should go to for a family vacation. I was a little worried about that, because one of the dads in rehab had told everyone about a vacation to Singapore his family took, and his son was wigging out the whole time because he couldn't get any drugs, and the dad felt like it was the worst vacation any family ever went on.

But anyhow. This Saturday was overcast with very light drizzle. I was high, kind of pleasantly out of it. Totally worth it to sell those shoes after all!

Dad had put together a couple of plastic ramps to make a small hill. So I set the hill in the middle of the street. I meant to put the cones up, but I'd never once since we'd lived there seen a car drive too fast down the road. So I didn't bother.

I kind of wanted to sit on the curb and look at the sky. When I turned my face upward, the raindrops felt like little pops of coolness on my skin. It might even be nice to lie on the grass.

"Bro! Bro! Are you ready to watch me?" Joshie was asking.

I felt a little annoyed but smiled at him and said, "Sure thing."

I tried to find the hype inside me, so this would be fun the way it used to be. But I wasn't feeling it, unfortunately. "Remember, don't go too fast up the hill," I said.

"I got ya, homie," Joshie called out. He'd had a growth spurt, so the bike was already getting a little small for him. He made a sound like revving up, then pushed off. He was going too fast.

"Slow down at the hill!" I called out. He did. I looked toward my house, then turned away from it and took out my vape and inhaled as Joshie pushed up the hill slowly, then glided down.

"I did it! I did it!" he cried out.

"Yeah!" I called out. But like I said, I still wasn't feeling it.

He powered forward for about ten feet, then turned to go over the hill again. I turned my face to the sky again to feel those little pops. Next thing I knew, there was honking and a screech, and a car was swerving out of the way a few feet from where my brother was atop the hill. Time was moving in slow jerks—like every second was broken down into sixty mini-seconds. Joshie frozen with his hands raised, like he was protecting himself; me moving through time in little bursts as I ran toward him. The car bumped over the curb, the driver yelled "ASSHOLE" at me, and then the car was gone around a corner. As soon as it was gone, time returned to normal.

Joshie had fallen over, his legs still astride the bike, stiff and unmoving like he was frozen in time.

"Joshie!" I shouted, running over.

He looked confused.

"Joshie," I repeated when I arrived.

Then he looked outraged. "Did that car break the law?"

"I dunno. You okay?"

He looked at his right elbow, which was bleeding, but not badly. "Just this," he said.

I took a big breath, held Joshie's head to my chest. I felt something, but it was a faraway feeling. Then it got closer, and it was that pain I mentioned earlier, like somebody was stabbing my gut. But from the inside, not from the outside. Sounds wack, I know, but that's what it felt like.

"Sure you're okay?" I repeated.

"Yeah, I'm good. That just surprised me, is all. Maybe we should quit for now. I don't like my bike today."

When he said that, I knew he was shook. God, I was a fuckup.

I started gathering up the parts of the ramp.

I paused. "Say, Joshie?"

"Yeah?"

"Uh, don't tell Mom or Dad that I didn't have the cones up, okay?"

He looked confused again, then said, "I won't if you don't want me to."

"Thanks," I said.

"Thanks for helping me win the next race!" he said cheerfully.

Which was good, I guess. I mean, it was great. I did feel a little pathetic asking a five-year-old for a favor. But I was glad he wasn't going to snitch. I was ashamed and glad and a little pathetic. Joshie closed his eyes and suddenly pressed his head into my chest. "I would never snitch on you for a billion dollars." And for a moment I just thought it was too much responsibility, for me, right then. It was too much responsibility how much he loved me. How much everybody loved me!

FIFTY-TWO

I dunno . . . Lee and I were getting depressed. We were sad, which made us mad. It was the holidays, and our families were all cheerful. Even Su-Bee was excited, because she'd gotten a paycheck, and she felt she had enough to buy everybody nice presents. "Everybody" meant her family, plus me. I'd never gotten a girl a Christmas present before. What could you really get a girl when you knew where her stolen money was? I wondered sometimes what would happen if we dropped out of school and biked across the country. Her and me. Or Lee and me. Or me alone. It was a thought that just hung there in my head all the time now.

Banker had been blowing up our phones, but we were feeling so lethargic, we didn't even answer sometimes. Maybe we were getting a little exhausted by everything. This seemed to make Banker really tense—he was super addicted to the new pain pills that his dad had gotten for his back, which apparently got sore from sitting on the couch so much. But Mr. Bank didn't get enough of them for Banker to keep stealing without getting caught. I didn't mention to him that my grandpa had the same prescription.

Anyway, one night when my parents thought Lee and I were going to the mall, we went to Banker's and started to get blazed on vodka and THC, and Banker said to Lee, "How much are your parents worth altogether?"

Lee was lying on the carpet with his mouth hanging open. Whenever he did anything besides THC, he looked like he was getting ready to barf. If you want to know the truth, I didn't think he enjoyed getting high anymore. I had no idea why he even did it.

And Lee said, "You mean, like, money?"

"Yeah, dude, money," Banker answered impatiently.

"I don't know. Eight million? Ten?"

"Including their house?"

"Yeah, they own two houses, and then they got—have—investments. They showed me some stuff once, 'cause I'm their oldest. They have stocks and investments."

So I mean, *damn*, I wished Lee hadn't told Banker that. I could see Banker thinking, *Hmmm, is there some way I can get money off Lee's parents?*

"You said once that you hated your parents?" Banker said.

Lee paused, like he was unsure what the point was. I didn't see it either. But then I did. I said the only thing I could think to say: "For fuck's sake."

Banker said, "Let's kill 'em."

"Kill who?" Lee said.

"Get a grip, Banker," I said. I wanted to sound firm but heard fear in my voice. I was scared of whatever it was that was happening.

And then Lee sat up, still looking like he was gonna barf, and said uncertainly, "What the fuck?"

"There's only two of you," Banker said. "You and your sister.

You'd be worth five million apiece. We could buy drugs whole-sale and sell it for twice as much as we paid for it. Three times as much! And we wouldn't have to pay taxes on the money we earned." He was talking eagerly, excitedly.

And there was Davis crying again. We ignored him.

Suddenly, I had a headache, a big one. I don't think I'd ever had a headache this bad besides when I had a concussion. Now it seemed like my head was filled with pus and about to explode. "Ahhh," I groaned, holding my head and sinking to the floor. "Shit, my head hurts. Holy fuck!" I couldn't hear what they were saying, because I thought I might actually be having a brain aneurysm. "Aw, shit," I said as I realized they were still discussing killing Lee's parents. *Aw, shit.* It was one of those crazy moments when you can see your whole past, your whole future, and everybody in the whole world at the same time. I saw *all* of it. And yet in terms of where I was, I was sitting in a filthy room with a bunch of idiots with my head about to blow into a million pieces.

"Dude, you're not dying or something, are you?" That was Banker, giving me a hard shake.

"No, I got a bad headache," I said. "I mean, maybe I'm dying. That wouldn't be a bad thing. *Awwww.*" I clutched my head, trying to hold my brains together.

After lying in a ball on the floor for a minute, I opened my eyes, saw the three of them staring down at me. As my head-ache started to subside, I couldn't see the past or the future or the rest of the world anymore. I said, "Let's not. Let's fucking *not* kill anyone."

"No," Banker said quickly. "Of course not." But I could see him evaluating me, like I was a moron and he might even want to kill *me*. "You know, we're your only friends. You know that, right?"

"So?"

When I was a kid, it was easy for me to make friends. Every year it was easy, and then suddenly this year, these three morons in fact had become my only friends. Because Banker controlled who your friends were. I don't know how he did it, but he did.

And then he just grabbed the PS4 controller from Davis, put in a new game, and played a long time while vaping and then dropping a bar and finally passing out right in front of the screen.

FIFTY-THREE

When I got home, my mom and dad were sitting in the living room. No TV or anything, just waiting for me. They both stood up when I walked in.

My mom looked at me closely, and then she and Dad glanced at each other. "He doesn't seem like he's been vaping," she said with relief. I was pretty sure Banker had sobered me up with his talk about killing Lee's parents.

"I'm proud of you, son," my dad said.

"Thanks, Dad. Good night."

I went to my room. There was a big manila envelope on my desk. I knew immediately it was the manila envelope the writing contest had told me I'd be getting. I opened it, and it was like I entered another world for a minute—the world from the Before Times. It was a nice letter, telling me I'd won five hundred dollars for first place for my essay on plumbing. *The judges were impressed with the originality of the subject matter as well as your approach.* There was an invitation to Sacramento to read my piece to an audience of historians and teachers. I got a certificate. I remembered how I'd planned to give my grandpa whatever prize if I won. There was no plaque or trophy, but I knew Grandpa would be just as happy with the certificate. And even though deep inside myself, I felt proud I'd won, another part of me felt kinda sad. I wondered if I'd ever win anything again. I mean, maybe I would.

I also felt sad because I wanted to buy Grandpa a Christmas gift with some of the money, but on the other hand, I already knew I wanted to spend it all on drugs.

I felt like the old me was dying or maybe dead. The next day I deposited my check. I tried to stay sober for a few days, and mostly succeeded. Then when my check cleared, I told my mom I was going to Lee's but instead took an Uber to the mall before I could change my mind, and I bought my grandpa a present. I walked through maybe fifty stores, and I actually found a kind of plumbing-related gift. It was a gold-plated necktie clip in the shape of a pipe wrench. I decided I would give it to Grandpa for Christmas. I also bought Christmas gifts for everybody while I was sober. It was interesting, being sober and walking around the mall. The mall sometimes gave me an empty feeling, but at the same time, it felt good buying things for my family. And I got Su-Bee an ankle bracelet, because she wore one every day. The one I got had a real pearl.

There was a shirt at the sporting goods store with a bicycle on it. The extra-small would be a little big for Joshie, but not that big. I couldn't decide between the orange one with a blue bike on the front or the blue one with an orange bike on the front. Because Joshie's bike was orange, he might like the orange shirt. But he might also think it was cool that the blue one had an orange bike. I stood there so long that a guy who worked there asked me, "Can I help you decide on something?"

He looked really *human* and *normal*, and frankly, I hadn't felt as normal as he looked for months. So I explained my issue to him, and he said decisively, "The blue one with the orange bike."

Wow. Did I ever used to be that decisive when things were normal? I honestly couldn't remember.

I got my dad board shorts and my mom a hat for gardening. For Grandma, I bought the hand cream that I got her every year, because she didn't want anything else. Like, literally, we all got her the same hand cream. You'd think she'd have a whole closet full of that stuff by now, but every year she wanted more. Not sure why anyone would want forty-buck hand cream, but then I wasn't a grandma.

I thought about the two hundred dollars I had left. I decided to hold on to it, in case Lee ever confessed and we needed money to pay back Su-Bee.

And I didn't really get high that much before Christmas. I guess I was kinda shook by Banker suggesting that Lee kill his parents. I mean, I knew Lee would never do it. He'd jump off a mountain before he'd do that. I felt I knew him well enough to say that. But . . . would *Banker* do it? He for sure wouldn't, but would he?

We always had a little party for Christmas. Mom made Christmas cupcakes, which—yes—were carrot cakes, with a little Christmas tree in the middle instead of a carrot. I ate mine on the front porch, sitting by myself with Kiiro. Every so often I gave him a piece. He never begged, though—I'd taught him that much.

My cousin Matt had been wait-listed for some kind of exchange thing with high schoolers in Prague, and he announced that someone had dropped out at the last minute. So he'd be leaving in a few weeks. Our dads were part Czech (from Grandma) and part Nordic (from Grandpa), so we had some relatives we'd never met in Prague. Matt and Mike's school had all kinds of programs to design their lives better, and this exchange thing for seniors was one of them. They called it "excursion education."

Anyway, later we were eating KFC, because in Japan they'd been eating chicken on Christmas for years. Then KFC did an intense advertising campaign to get everybody to eat *their* chicken on Christmas. So I guess Mom felt it was kind of a cultural thing. Which was weird, because KFC is an American company, and then it traveled to Japan and the Japanese did their own thing with it, and now that thing was being done in our home.

I sat on the floor at the coffee table with my cousins and Joshie while the grown-ups ate in the dining room and talked about some earthquake from before I was born and how we hadn't had a big one in a long time. Lots of little ones, though.

Matt said, "Yo, Elijah, you should come visit Prague for spring vacation."

"Wow, that would be lit!" I said. And it would! But I did worry about two things: (1) What were their drug laws? And (2) would Kiiro be sad? It would definitely be lit, though. The thought of getting out of California for a week and going to a totally new place made me *yearn* for it. Right then, sitting on the floor, I was yearning so hard, I thought for a moment I was gonna shout, *I wanna go!* Maybe Lee could come too. It would be good for us!

Matt bit into a drumstick and said, "Yeah, I'm staying with a family, but you could stay at a hotel."

Then my mom, who'd overheard us, said, "That's it! That's it! I was thinking you need to go somewhere! Prague is it!"

Everybody looked at her surprised at how loud she'd said

that. So then the grown-ups got into a big conversation about Prague and how beautiful it was. After a while my cousins, aunt, and uncle had to get home to open presents.

So we all walked out with them to their car. The adults were talking, but me, Matt, and Mike hung back a little. "Damn, so you're going to Prague," I said.

"Yeah, I'm excited. Then I guess I'll be back for the summer, then on to Princeton." Which he'd gotten into.

"Matt, my man . . . I guess I won't be seeing so much of you," I said. I felt pretty sad suddenly. I mean, we'd been fighting and hanging around since we were toddlers.

"Yeah, I got a lot to do, but I'll be over to say bye. Think about visiting, buddy." He studied his feet, then said, "Who knows? Maybe we'll hang in Costa Rica later too, you know? Sometimes I think we will."

The three of us gripped one another's hands and lifted them into the air like champions. "Here's to Costa Rica," I said.

I watched them drive off, thought about all the years of camping and playing video games and arguing and going to family parties. I gave Mike a black eye once when we were seven and got in hella trouble for that. After all that growing up together, it was crazy to think that "conscription" was a thing that we would now be thinking about, and that our parents would be thinking about. It was pretty trippy that in America, every time a guy grew up, there was always a war or invasion or some kind of crap we were doing overseas. I wondered if historians someday would think we were a warlike country. Which we totally are.

I felt that tug inside me, like I wanted to get high. But I didn't, because I felt something else more. I felt really good about my gift for Grandpa.

So when it came time for presents, Grandpa opened his, and it was my essay printed out, plus the certificate and the tie clip, with a note saying that the essay was about plumbing and that I'd written it for him.

Everybody got really quiet. Then Mom said, "Oh, Elijah, you're so wonderful!" She hugged me hard, which was a total mom move. But it was Christmas, so I hugged her back.

Grandpa nodded his head up and down. "I did the pipes for entire houses when I was younger." I swear, his chest expanded with pride. He patted me on the shoulder. "I always felt good after a big job. There was one job that took five months . . . biggest job I ever did. I needed four extra guys." His eyes got that faraway look, probably remembering that five-month job. "Thank you, Elijah. It's the best present I ever got."

Then everybody was making noise and opening presents again. We always used cheap paper, because when we used to use nicer paper, Mom and Dad got all neurotic about saving it for next year. Joshie ripped his presents open like he was part animal. I half expected him to start using his teeth.

I was opening a present when Grandpa smiled at me for no reason. I felt pretty good about myself, for the first time in forever. I thought maybe I could possibly be becoming a good person again. I thought there might be an escape from demon-world, since I hadn't gotten too deep in yet.

Also during Christmas break I took Su-Bee to another movie— she drove us to the mall, and we exchanged late Christmas presents in the car in the parking structure. She opened her present carefully, like she might be planning to save the paper.

When she pulled out her ankle bracelet, her mouth fell open. "I love it!" She immediately took off the one she had on and put on the one I'd given her. "Now open yours!" she said excitedly.

So I ripped into mine and opened the box and pulled out . . . a scarf, a very soft plaid scarf. Which was kind of like a sweater. Did guys actually wear scarves in Southern California? Like, why would you?

"Wow, I needed one of these!" I said. "I've wanted a plaid scarf for a long time! It's soft too!" Then I thought that was overdoing it, because no self-respecting high school guy in Southern California had been wanting a soft plaid scarf for Christmas. But I wrapped it around the neck of my hoodie, and she seemed to think that was the greatest thing ever.

"Scarves and hoodies are so cool together!"

I wondered if she felt the same about her ankle bracelet that I felt about the scarf, and we were both just pretending. I decided to ask her.

"So do you like your ankle bracelet for real?"

"I love it!" she said. She looked completely sincere and threw her arms around me. Her mouth was close to my ear. "Do you like your scarf for real?"

"I love it!" I said. "I'd been thinking I needed one for when my neck gets cold." I wondered if I was overdoing it again, but she pulled back and started arranging the scarf around my neck, so I put my hands on her face and pulled her close and kissed her.

Pretty much, it ended up being the best Christmas in a long time. I didn't get a Supreme collector's shirt, but there was nothing new about that. I'd ask again next year.

FIFTY-FOUR

But you know what? Christmas ended.

New Year's passed.

And as the weeks wore on, Lee was calling me a few times a day. While I'd mostly been staying sober over winter break from school, he'd been going over to Banker's, and now he really wanted me to start going with him again. It was during this time that we all went to the house of the demon who looked like a normal guy in a normal neighborhood in Playa del Sol. The guy who put his finger on my arm. We spent some of Su-Bee's money there.

Banker texted me one day: *Nobody ever leaves the life believe me*

Me: *What life*

Banker: *The life I'm showing you*

I thought about the five, six, seven rehabs some kids ended up going to and the ten, twelve rehabs some adults ended up going to. And the people on the streets. And Martin and Noah. And now the four of us. The life called you. It was a living thing, and it called you.

FIFTY-FIVE

Think of something really empty—say, outer outer space, where there are no planets, no stars, no comets. Just a big nothing. Picture it—that was Banker's eyes. There was nothing behind them. But one time he said, "You know, my dad never bought me a single shirt that wasn't related to sports. Not one." There was a flash of something—sadness?—in his eyes. But it was gone fast. I had seen other dads like his, actually. I didn't really understand it. My dad loved to watch sports, but he liked doing other stuff, too. He didn't buy only sports T-shirts. But some dads were like that. Sports was all they could talk about. I didn't know why. There were dads even in rehab like that. Their kid was dying inside, and it took a massive effort just to get their minds to think about something that didn't have to do with sports. They made the effort, but you could see how hard it was for them.

The new year already felt old. I kept thinking about how at the beginning of all this, when he was sort of *chasing* Lee, it was like Banker admired him more than anybody on the planet. Like Banker just felt so flattered that Lee would be his friend. He was always trying to please Lee. "Lee, do you want this drug or that?" "Lee, do you want a Coke or a Pepsi or plain water?" "Lee, should I grab you a burger?" Like Lee was *above* him.

But he wasn't chasing Lee anymore. He hadn't been for a long time.

I was walking Kiiro one morning and thinking about all this. Then suddenly, I had a thought. I walked my dog over to Lee's house. Before I rang the doorbell, I wondered if Su-Bee might answer. But Lee answered, looking tired.

"Yo! Lee!" He waited for me to say more. "'Sup?"

"'Sup," he replied.

He looked like I'd woken him up after a long night of studying. Or a long night of not studying. So I just blurted out my thought. "Lee, why do we hang around so much with Banker? Wanna go biking today instead? Why not?"

He seemed to be thinking about it. He stood there kind of frowning in the doorway. I saw him concentrating. He looked like he was concentrating so hard, his brain would explode. He even held his head with his hands, like he was trying to keep it from exploding. "I don't understand what's happening. At first it was fun, because I felt like he was showing me the real world. I mean, I guess."

I realized he was answering my question.

"So let's go biking like we used to," I prodded. "We'll dig a pit somewhere! We'll use real spikes!"

He scratched at an eyebrow. "What time is it, anyway?"

I checked my phone. "Nine a.m."

"Nine a.m.?" He looked at me like I was crazy. "Lemme sleep more, and I'll call you later. Maybe. Maybe we can go biking."

But he didn't call me back, even when I called him a few

hours later. So around seven that evening I rode my bicycle over there. Banker's car was outside. I rang the bell.

Nobody answered. But the door was ajar, so I pushed it open. I heard talking from the back, so I walked in.

Banker and Davis were there with Lee. I saw this look in Banker's eyes when he spotted me. I mean, he looked like he'd just turned into a hyena or something—that's how bizarre the look was.

"We're busy," Banker said coldly. "Why don't you go *biking*?"

"Hey, come with us," Lee said eagerly. "Come on, we're going to the beach." He had a kind of desperate look in his eyes.

"Um, I mean, I have to get back soon. Where's your family?"

"Su-Bee's at her friend's. My parents went out to eat with my uncle and aunt. It won't take long," Lee said. "Come on."

I felt like he was sending me thought rays or something. So I said, "Yeah, cool. Okay."

And it turned out that Banker had brought the rest of Su-Bee's money that we hadn't spent at the psycho's house in Playa del Sol, and we were going to buy some "really good shit" at the beach. And it's hard to explain, but it felt like Lee and I didn't have free will anymore, and for some reason Banker did.

Banker kept saying this dealer at the beach was amazing. He drove Lee's car as usual and started talking about how this dealer had a phenomenal reputation. "It's just like buying a desk lamp or something and getting a warranty. It's really hard to get in with him. He gets his stuff straight from a medical clinic."

"Cool," I said. A desk lamp and a pill you bought at the beach were two different things, obviously. Part of the problem out there today was that a lot of people were addicted to fentanyl—they *loved* it. So it was all over the place, not necessarily because anyone was *trying* to kill you, but because there was a big demand for a drug that one person might love but that might kill *you*. I figured at some point a while back the dealers had weighed it in their heads: What was more important—you being alive or them making money? And then once they had their answer, they didn't think about it again. But if Banker said this guy got his stuff from a medical clinic, then, well, we chose to believe him.

At the beach we got out of the car, the Asian posse. I couldn't help it—I felt a kind of thrill: I was seeing the *world*! Like, there's something about doing something *wrong* that just felt exciting, kind of like jumping over a pit with a bike, except in the grown-up world. And doing all this outside somehow made it even better.

The moon was skipping off the surface of the water. It was super evocative. (Yeah, I know that word too.) Sometimes there were little things like that, stuff that pulled me back into the world, almost back to before this whole mess started.

Some big black guys walked by us, going in the opposite direction. I met eyes with one of them, and he said, "'Sup, G?"

"'Sup," I said back.

Banker walked confidently ahead with Davis, and I stayed with Lee. The other two got way ahead of us.

"Elijah?" Lee said once they were way ahead.

"Yeah?"

"I mean . . . do you think Banker is losing it a little? All he thinks about is drugs and money."

"Yeah. I mean, no. I mean, I think about that stuff a lot too."

"I do too, but it's not the only thing I think about. Like, I need to go to college. My parents would kill themselves if I don't go to college. I gotta go to Duke. That's what I've been aiming for." He paused, then added, "I already got in."

"Really? Congratulations!"

"Yeah, it's cool. They got the most amazing oak trees around the campus. I was thinking I could sit out there in the forest with my laptop sometimes."

"Dude, if you gotta go to Duke to sit in the forest, then you gotta go to Duke." I thought for a second. "Did you know that in ancient Rome they used oak leaves to heal you?"

He looked super interested. "Really? I want to go so bad." We took a few quiet steps. "But Banker keeps talking about wanting to kill my parents. Is he even serious? Because I know I complain about them and they're annoying, but I can't, you know, kill them. I shouldn't even be listening to him talk like that."

"I'm pretty sure all parents are annoying sometimes," I said. "I mean, that's kind of their job. And, uh . . . why are you even saying that, like that has anything to do with, you know, killing somebody?" I stopped and looked at him, and we just stared at each other for a couple of seconds.

"God," Lee said. "God, everything's so messed up. I'm getting confused." He actually fell to his knees and seemed to be praying. When he stood up, he looked at me lost-like, like he was a little boy.

"Dude, nobody's really going to kill your parents, if that's what you're worried about."

"Nah, I know," he said quickly, like he was embarrassed.

But I could see in his face that he didn't know that. He

didn't know that at all. Although, how could he possibly not know that?

It was a cool night, almost cold for Southern California. I could see the waves cresting in the distance. I pulled my hoodie over my head. A comet flashed in the sky, and that seemed like good luck. I made a quick wish: that Lee would go to Duke.

But Lee was crying! Slobbering even. He wiped snot from his nose. I mean . . . like—I had no idea what to do.

So I laid my palm on his shoulder. "Hey, bud, *nobody's* going to kill your parents. You know that, right? Don't just say you know it, I'm asking if you really know it."

He looked at me like he was a madman. "I'm afraid *I* might."

Before I could stop myself, I reared back, like I was avoiding a punch. "Dude, bro, what are you talking about? I mean, you're—you're *you*. If you don't want to kill them, all you have to do is not kill them." What was I even saying?

"But what if I do?" He looked at me full-on, his face wet and shining in the moonlight.

"Lee. I—I don't get it. You're *you*. You don't want to kill them, so don't kill them. I mean, don't kill them even if you do want to kill them, okay? But you don't even want to. So why would you? You're not making sense, Lee."

His face was so full of despair, I felt like I was looking into the face of someone who in fact had just killed his parents.

"Banker's gonna make me."

I just stared at him. I was honestly stupefied. "Lee, what you're talking about is impossible. You know that, right? You're not gonna kill your parents because you're you and you wouldn't do that. Dude, this whole conversation makes no sense."

"He berated me for an hour about it."

"Berated you?"

Lee nodded.

"Well, Lee. I mean, Lee. Just don't do it. Why are you acting like he's making you? He can't make you do anything you don't want to do."

"But will you still be my friend?" he asked suddenly. "Will you?"

"Of course I will!" But I felt like we were third-grade schoolgirls or something. *Will you still be my friend?*

I squinted forward. Banker and Davis were so far ahead that I couldn't even see them anymore. I took Lee by the shoulders and turned him toward the waves. "Look at that, Lee. The waves. They're great. They're beautiful. That's out there. I mean, if that's out there, it's all gonna be okay, okay? Because that wouldn't be out there if it wasn't going to be okay."

"What about wars?"

"What?"

"The ocean is out there, and there're still wars. There've still been lots of wars no matter if the waves are beautiful. There've been battles *on* the waves."

Then I thought about a film I saw in history class once, with soldiers landing in boats at Normandy during World War II. Saving the world and shit. And the waves. I could imagine how the waves would have kept rolling in, over and over, until the battle was done, and thousands of those guys were dead. Some of them were older, but some of them were just a few years older than us. Than the age we were right at that moment.

Banker's age. Lee's and Davis's. But people didn't get it when they lectured us, when they said, "Look what *these* men did when they were young." They didn't get that we would give everything to care that much about *anything*. Just to have that feeling of caring that much—that there would be something worth dying for.

FIFTY-SIX

Banker and Davis were waiting for us now. When we reached them, Banker said, like we were idiots, "What the *hell* are you guys doing? We got important business."

We walked on silently until we reached a couple of guys vaping in the wind on the path. One was a tall guy, a *really* tall guy. I had to bend my neck back to look into his face. The other guy was tall too, but more like six three. The tall guy was actually the tallest guy I'd ever seen in person. Maybe more than seven feet.

"Banker?" the tall guy said.

"Hey," Banker said.

"You're late."

"Sorry, we didn't realize how long the walk would be and—"

The tall guy cut Banker off. "You got the money?" He had a strangely high voice. Not like a girl's. But you would have thought a guy that size would have a deep voice, is all.

"Yeah, sure. What you got for me? It better be good," Banker added accusingly.

The tall guy laughed pleasantly. Then, like an animal, he stepped quickly and threateningly toward Banker, and Banker stepped back, almost stumbling in fear.

Tall Guy laughed again. He nodded at me. "I'll deal with this one."

"Me?" I said. "I never— Sure."

He took out a baggie of pills. "Try a couple of Oxy. They're twenty milligram, that's all I got right now," he said. "Since you're a first-time customer, I want you to trust me that they're good."

"Uh, sure. Um. I only need one, though. I'm not, uh, a professional." Which was a dumb thing to say. I tried to call up enough saliva to wash the pill down, then swallowed. It was true that there was always the thought in the back of your mind these days that anything you took might have fentanyl in it. But what were you going to do? You wanted to get high.

"Go on, take a walk. I got another customer on the way. Come back when you're satisfied."

So the four of us kept walking down the path. It got really dark, and we had to use our phones to light the way. We tripped along until we couldn't see the tall guy anymore. Then we sat down on some rocks and waited in the dark. The other three scrolled through their phones. I just stared into the night. Something scampered across the way. Banker was inhaling on a pen as he looked at his screen. "This girl keeps sending me crotch shots, and I never even met her. She says she'll send me a video for five bucks. Should I do it?" he asked, still studying his screen.

"Hell, no," Davis said.

"Stop being cheap," Banker retorted.

"A thousand other guys will have seen that same video."

"She's cute. Here's her face."

Banker showed Davis her picture, and Davis said, "God*damn!*"

Lee got up to look at her picture and said, "Wow. Imagine how much money she's making."

"Elijah, look," Banker said. He showed me the girl's picture. Super cute and sexy. But the picture kind of made me sad. There were all these girls selling pictures and videos of themselves. A lot of girls. Those were facts.

I thought for an uncomfortable moment about Su-Bee. She wasn't like that. She was different. And we were sitting there at that moment with her money.

But then my body started to feel warm. And a minute later I just felt like the *perfection* of the wind and the rustling of the bushes were things that nobody in the world but me had ever experienced in the same way. I had no idea why everybody was always so depressed all the time. The sky was not just amazing, it was a miracle. Goddamn, I felt good! The breeze on my face was supernatural. "The world is awesome!" I shouted. "The world is amazing!" I mean, if hot girls wanted to sell pictures of their bodies on the internet, what was wrong with that? Every single thing was fine with me!

"You moron," Banker said, glancing at the others. "He's a moron. The world's not awesome, that's the OxyContin. The world sucks. All right, come on, let's go back."

When we arrived, Banker nodded at me. I looked up at the tall guy.

"The world is beautiful," was what I heard come out of my mouth. "We've got four hundred dollars." Banker shoved me and gave me a look. Did he want to negotiate? But I just told him, "Fuck you." Once again, if looks could kill, etc.

Still, he took out Su-Bee's cash and handed it over to the guy. "I got some change too." He dropped it in Tall Guy's other palm.

Tall Guy looked at the change in his hand and tossed it over his shoulder. But he counted the bills eagerly while his partner shone his phone light on them. Tall Guy handed me the baggie—maybe twenty pills?—and I stuffed it into my backpack. I hesitated, then walked over and started searching for the change. I mean, it wasn't a small amount of change. This sounds ridiculous, since we were using Su-Bee's stolen money and all, but she had gone to the trouble to save that change, so it seemed wasteful to throw it away like that. I felt like I was picking it up for her sake. Which was dumb, I know.

"For fuck's sake," Banker called out. "*Fuck.*"

But I picked up all the change I could find and dropped it into my pocket. Then we left, Tall Guy calling out to me, "Come back when you need more. You know how to find me!"

"All good, homie. I'll give you a holler," I answered.

As soon as we were out of sight, Banker and Davis and Lee all surrounded me saying, "Hand it over" and "Come on" and "Gimme." So I handed the bag to Banker, and the three of them eagerly grabbed a couple of pills each. Lee downed both his pills. And I mean, *damn*. How was it that Lee could handle forty milligrams? But then that miraculous wind hit my face. Life was perfect! Like, who even invented something as perfect as the wind? And the stars? And the waves?

What else did I know about waves? I knew that centuries ago men rode the waves on crappy boats. That was just what they did back then. I was into that in fifth grade—I read everything I could find about that stuff. Magellan set off from Spain in 1519 with five ships and two hundred and seventy men. Three years later, only one of the ships returned to Spain with just eighteen of the original men. Magellan was not one of the eighteen. He'd been killed with a poisoned arrow on an island. And you know who one of the eighteen was? The guy who was writing a chronicle of the journey. That coulda been me if I'd lived in those days.

Now, I wondered how many suicides there were back then. Did they even have drugs you could OD on? And murders— how many? Did people drink themselves to death? What was it all about back then? Did they feel like I felt at that moment, full of the clarity of the night, of the clarity of being outside in the wind and under the stars? If they did, they felt that way without Oxys. Right? And I suddenly realized that's exactly what the past was. Pain and suffering and hardship like now, plus laughing and love like now, but somehow also the clarity of being alive. I didn't imagine the old buildings or the old ways of life or the old clothes. I imagined people felt the clarity of the moment I felt with Oxy, but that they felt it just because. Because that was the way life was supposed to feel.

FIFTY-SEVEN

When Lee dropped me off at home, Kiiro met me at the door, and I just held him. I suddenly remembered Lee's desperate face on the beach. Fear washed over me. Lee's face scared me. Kiiro sat very still while I pressed my face into his fur. I felt him doing that thing that was in a song my grandparents liked: "Like a bridge over troubled water, I will ease your mind."

That was dogs for you. Maybe I should lend my dog to Lee! But I knew it wouldn't be the same for him. Not to mention, his family already had a dog, and Lee didn't pay much attention to her. Also, I realized that I might actually die without my dog. It was possible. That made me feel like we were all of us on the edge, and it was only because I'd gotten Kiiro years ago that I was still hanging on today. I pressed my face deeper into his fur. He didn't move. He always stayed perfectly still when I hugged him. Like he was soaking it in. Like he was trying to absorb the badness. Like he would poison himself if he could just take away whatever was poisoning me.

FIFTY-EIGHT

On Monday, I'd taken half an Oxy before school, but had the other half in my pocket. I rode my bike, jumping on and off the curb, swerving around through the streets.

I had a moment of that old feeling, like from when Lee and I were still hanging out with Logan and Ben. When I got to school on my bicycle, I spotted the low wall on the far side of the teacher parking lot, and I rode toward it and hopped my bike onto the top, rode for about five seconds, hopped down, then rode the wall, which is when you do a horizontal semicircle on the wall. I stopped quickly and looked back, reliving the last thirty seconds and thinking about how satisfying that had been.

Then all of a sudden, a man was shouting at me. I turned around, and it was Principal Manson. First of all, in what alternate universe would someone with that name not change it? Second of all, he goes, "Do you know how dangerous that was?"

"Well . . . it wasn't, Mr. Manson," I said, kind of rebellious but kind of polite at the same time. But maybe more rebellious than polite. Because WTF? There were guys who sailed thirty feet into the air on their bikes!

"You can ride your bike home and leave it there, even if you miss part of first period, and then I don't want to see you with that bicycle again for two weeks." And he walked away, lifting his hand in a wave at a teacher who was waiting for him.

That made me remember one time my dudes Ben and Logan and I went to skateboard in the skate park. Covid had hit, and the city had filled the skate park with sand. Someone actually got paid to make decisions like filling a skate park with sand. Please don't even have the thought, *They were trying to save lives*. You don't save lives by filling a skate park with sand. You fill a skate park with sand because you're power-tripping. *It sucks.*

All right?

FIFTY-NINE

So I got home and took the other half of my pill and never returned to school that day.

Nobody was home but me and Kiiro. I lay on the grass in back with him, pretended we were floating. I had to admit that going to the beach that weekend was in some ways pretty cool. Because I saw the underworld there, outside by the water, in the wind. Under the moon. It was an adventure. And, like, there are no adventures left. You can't even say "Fuck you" while playing PS4 without some snitch reporting you. And the thing about the underworld—people were *free* there.

Like, once on a road trip, my family pulled over at a rest stop that was the most under-under-underbelly place I'd ever seen. I was about thirteen. There was a guy wearing a jacket stamped with SECURITY, and he looked like he'd just murdered a security guard and stolen his jacket. He was super jumpy, his head shaking backward and forward in little jerks. There were probably thirty people in the small store, and they all looked like they had just escaped from hell. A woman and man who looked like they hadn't slept for two weeks were arguing about which shampoo to buy, the cheap one or the one that smelled good. I could smell the restrooms throughout the whole store. And there was an ATM there—but who would use it? You'd get robbed the second you took out your money! The cashiers looked like they'd beat your ass up if you even made eye contact with them in a way they didn't like.

One thing about my mom that's cool and uncool at the same time is that she kind of lives in her own little bubble. So on the one hand, she doesn't really notice her surroundings, and that's kind of annoying. But on the other hand, she's only five foot one and 105 pounds, but she was standing there in that crazy place and didn't even seem to notice that it was crazy. She even started giving shampoo advice to the arguing couple. All while holding baby Joshie.

And you know what I felt like? I felt *free*. I just felt like I was soaking in freedom and a little bit of adventure. This was the kind of place that a lot of people probably avoided and that some didn't even know existed. But it was a free place. It filled me, a thirteen-year-old kid, with a yearning to be free. Like, I could totally scream out the word "retard," and nobody would send me to detention. In the under-under-underbelly of America, you could say whatever you wanted.

So later I think that was part of it, part of the adventure of being an addict. You're living in the underbelly, where it feels like nobody can screw with you.

But the problem was, after a while the freedom part runs out, and the addict part remains. And then there was Lee becoming more and more tense and anxious. I guess I didn't realize until the beach just how upset and anxious he was getting. Lee *liked* to worry, it was part of his personality. It hadn't seemed so different until that night.

So there I was at home having all these thoughts.

I didn't know where Joshie was—probably at my grand-parents? He'd gone to kindergarten for a week in September and hadn't liked it, so since kindergarten wasn't mandatory in California, he stayed with Mom most days. But I knew Mom was stepping in for the guy who did all the office work for my dad's business. It felt good to be alone. I called up Lee, and when he answered, I said, "Lee! Are you at school? I figured it all out!"

"Huh? I'm, no, I didn't feel so good today."

"Listen," I said. "I figured everything out. The actual secrets of the universe."

"What do you mean?" he asked. And he sounded a little like the old Lee, the curious Lee, the genius Lee.

"All our teachers and parents and all the grown-ups. They're messing with our heads. They're screwing with us. The universe won't even let us say 'fuck you' during a video game anymore. You know what I mean? They won't leave us alone! They're designing our lives, and it's *our* lives."

And Lee said, "Video game?"

"Yeah, I'm talking about, uh, the universe. We have to take back our universe, you know what I mean?" And I suddenly had an absolutely brilliant thought. "Banker is one of the bad guys! He's not one of us! He's—he's like a secret agent who's really on their side. You know what I mean? Do you? There's something out there besides Banker and the design. We gotta figure out what."

"Dude, I was just going to call you. It's important. I can't talk on the phone. Can I come by and talk to you? It's some-thing I gotta tell somebody. You free?"

"What? I mean, sure. Yeah, I'm at home by myself."

"Thanks, Elijah."

A few minutes later I was perched on the front steps. When Lee pulled up, I walked toward his car. I noticed it had a dent on the back bumper, and I wondered if it was him or Banker who'd done that.

"Hey."

"Hey." He was getting out of the car. He looked like shit. He glanced around furtively. "Banker really, really wants me to kill my parents."

"Lee," I said. "Come sit down. You need to relax." And I dunno, I was suddenly thinking about how lindy Shakespeare was, you know? Like, here we were living through a play he totally could've written if he'd been around today. I just wanted to stand up and shout, *Stop the play!* What I said instead was, "We gotta stop this thing, man."

"What thing?" Lee asked.

"I—I'm not sure."

We sat on the front porch. Our Japanese gardener had done this cool rock arrangement on a patch of dirt. There were also some purple flowers my mom had put in a planter. It was one of those great, clear-skied late-January days—right at the edge between cool and warm. I tried to concentrate on that, because Lee's vibe was so bad.

He took a couple of deep breaths. "I'm scared," he said at last.

I looked at him full-on. "You don't have to do something just because he wants it. You know that, right?"

He got that desperate look on his face again like at the beach and said, "He's pressuring me. I'm afraid I'm going to break down and do it. I can't stop thinking about it."

"But, Lee . . . That's crazy. You can just . . . not do it." Lee didn't say anything. And instantly, it hit me like an avalanche that things had gone way beyond where I thought they had gone. I tried to find my bearings, felt almost like there was ringing in my ears. "Lee?" He honestly looked like he was having some kind of nervous breakdown. "Lee?" I put my arm around him and said, "Buddy?" Then I said something stupid. "Wanna hit a vape?"

I asked softly because my parents had security cameras all over the place. Lee said, "Did I tell you I'm supposedly going to Duke in the fall?"

"Yeah, you did, and wow, that's great. You're gonna be a superstar there. And the amazing trees. Your laptop . . ."

"Thanks. I wasn't even sure I'd get in because I'm Asian and everything. I mean, we need to be exactly right to get into good schools."

"It's amazing . . . Lee, *you're amazing*." I paused. For some reason I took his shoulders in my hands and turned him toward me. "You're amazing, dude. You know that, right?"

"I took months to write my application essay." He looked away, then back at me. "But I know it's not going to work out."

"What do you mean?"

"I don't know. I just don't see it out there. Duke. I don't see it out there."

"I know what you mean! It's like I look out there into the future, and I don't see anything . . . if that's what you mean, I mean."

"Yeah!" He sounded surprised. "The future is finite *and* it's bounded. That's what I mean. I don't think I'm going." He pressed one hand against his eyes, then pressed his lips together and started crying. "I want to go, though. I want to start over."

"You can! You're gonna do that! You are going to do it! It'll be great! Duke has oak trees! You never have to see a palm tree again if you don't want! Fuck palm trees!"

He smiled a little at that, and I felt relief. "Palm trees suck!" I continued, encouraged by his smile.

"Yeah, oaks. And they have a whole forest."

"Lee, that's cool. You can take your laptop into the forest, right? And you can hang with guys like you, except you'll be even smarter, because you're amazing." But his smile had faded, and he seemed to have this smoke of sadness around him.

"But it's too far! There's no way I can get there."

I didn't understand that at all. I ruffled his hair. "Uh, can't you fly? You know, airplanes?" I said it like I was teasing him, but he didn't smile this time.

I saw him mouth the word "fly" quizzically, like he wasn't following.

"I mean . . . you and your family could take a road trip out there?"

"Banker calls me five times a day," he suddenly said. "He Snaps me about twenty-five times a day."

"Lee . . ?" But I felt something slipping away. What was happening? For a moment I thought I should punch him, like to snap him out of it. "*Lee*. Just don't answer him. You're outta here; you're practically in North Carolina *now*."

"He's blackmailing me!" Lee blurted out.

"What?" How could anybody blackmail Lee? "You mean because you're doing drugs?"

He stared blankly at me like he didn't understand the question, like the question made no sense. He grabbed my arm. "A lot of things you don't know about."

I frowned, then did something weird, instinctively, I guess. I reached out and placed my fingers on his temples like it would help me read his mind. Then I started pressing his temples. "Dude . . . I mean, *Lee*, what's he gonna do?" I asked. I lowered my hands. I was genuinely perplexed. "You could blackmail him right back!"

Lee shook his head. "Elijah, I did some stuff. It's bad." He groaned softly. "It's gross. I just wish I could start over. But he won't let me."

"There's nothing, there's nothing that bad . . ." I hesitated. "You didn't kill anyone, did you?" I paused. *"Did you?"* Wait, what was I even saying?

"You know," he said. "I did some stuff to get drugs, from that guy in the apartment."

"The one . . . oh." Oh. Well, *shit*.

"Yeah, him. More than once. And another guy you don't know about. I mean, Banker told me it was a cheap way to get drugs. I was so high . . . Banker was like my agent or something for the deals." The emotion drained from his face. He didn't look desperate anymore. His eyes scared me, the way they now had the same empty look that Banker had all the time.

"But why? You coulda sold something for money."

"My parents got me all my possessions. It would hurt their feelings if they found out."

"DUDE. Hurt their feelings versus . . . you're not making sense."

I got really scared then, like I was in farther over my head than I even knew was possible. How can you just suddenly realize that you're ten feet underwater? What exactly was happening? *I wasn't sure.* I wondered if I should go get a grown-up.

I even turned to our security camera above the porch, as if I could talk to *that*. I almost wanted to say "help" to the camera. I thought about our neighbors, wondered if they were home.

Lee's phone dinged. He glanced at it—must have been from Banker, because he quickly hid the phone from me before saying, "I gotta go, man."

"Well, wait." I didn't know what to say. But I didn't want him to go. Because, where was he going? "We have carrot cake my mom made!" Geez, I sounded just like her. "Hey, let's go to In-N-Out and get some burgers!"

"Actually, I just ate." He stood up. "I have a hard physics problem today, I'm gonna dip. I'm gonna ignore Banker today and, uh, do my physics."

Physics? Who thinks of physics when you've just been talking about killing your parents? But he looked better, actually—maybe physics brought him back to his real self. He looked almost *normal*, like Lee.

"All right, that's a good idea!" I said. "Physics!"

"There's a note in my car." He got up and walked off.

"What?"

"I gotta go, homie," he called back.

I sat there while he walked to his car parked at the curb. A hummingbird hovered near our flowers.

All of a sudden, something occurred to me . . . a note. "Lee!" I shouted. I leaped up screaming, "LEE!"

An image flashed in my mind, an old photo I'd seen. Robert Kennedy lying on the floor after he'd been assassinated in 1968. I broke into a run.

And just like that, a *pop*. It wasn't even very loud.

I felt like I was running in a soundless tunnel toward the

car. "Lee!" I stopped as soon as I saw him slumped over. I took a few big breaths and flung open the passenger side door, saw blood dripping onto Lee's lap.

"Fuck! FUCK!"

I dropped my phone as I tried to call 911, then picked it up and called.

"911," a woman's voice said. "What is your emergency?"

"Can you—can you . . . ? 3400 La Cantina in Rocosa Beach. I think my friend is dead. I think he might be! Can you send an ambulance right now, please, PLEASE?"

I spotted the note and didn't even know what the dispatcher was saying. "I gotta go. If he's still alive, you need to get someone here immediately to save him."

I clicked off, and I guess I picked up the note. Because all of a sudden, it was in my hands. It said this: *I really love my family. Bye, Su-Bee, sorry I stole your money. Bye, Mom and Dad. I'm sorry. I guess I'm not going to college. I'm sorry.*

Like . . . like he thought they would care more that he wasn't going to Duke than that he was dead.

"We all stole the money together!" I shouted. "It was all of our fault!"

Lee was gone. I could tell. The ambulance didn't matter. Then I noticed how bright Lee's blood was. It was like redder than red. It was the reddest thing I ever saw. FUCK. I didn't know what to do, but I wanted to do *something*. I wondered what my dad and uncle and granddad had done when one of their buddies died. I remembered Grandpa saying he once touched his dead buddy's bloody chest, because he wanted to remember forever what wars did.

I got into the car, sat in the passenger seat, then reached

over and lay my hand on Lee's chest. I wanted to remember this forever. Then I looked at the blood on my fingers. "Hey, bud," I said to Lee. "I'm sorry you never got to Duke. But I'm sure there are oak trees in heaven." I pressed my lips together. "Bring your laptop. It's gonna be dope up there."

I got out and glanced up, squinted at the sky, and said, "I see you, bud." I kind of did too, like a little wavering heat thing in the sky. But the heat went away. Then I heard the ambulance.

SIXTY

And I don't know why, but I Ubered down to Venice Beach the next day, walked among the homeless people—among the people shooting up and zombied out, among the people begging for money. This is the world we kids belonged to that our parents didn't fully comprehend that we belonged to. They knew, but they didn't know. These homeless, these drug addicts, they were part of our future, part of our world. Not our parents' future, not their world.

I said "Hey" to some people by their tents as I passed. There was an Asian guy with a beard—he looked like Logan's dad. I even said it to him. "Yo, you look like my friend Logan's dad."

"Oh, I know, I know," he said. "I know!"

As I walked toward the sand, I thought of what Lee must've been going through in those last days. We took only one class together ever, advanced philosophy. I didn't get Nietzsche when we read him. But now I remembered what Nietzsche said about how just *thinking* of suicide could console you: "By means of it one gets successfully through many a bad night." That was probably what Lee's last week was like, getting through those bad nights by thinking about—about what he eventually did.

But I just wanted to get down to the water. I took off my shoes and stood in the ocean by myself—no dog, no little brother, no friends. Did I even have friends anymore? I remembered Logan saying that I could still call him. God, he was a great person. They were all great. Logan. Ben. Lee. And even Anthony. My old posse.

I took a few steps back and reached down to press my hand-print into the wet sand. My left hand, because maybe that had some special meaning I didn't know about, but that people thousands of years ago did know. I know this sounds crazy, but for a minute there I felt like I was at one with them, those people from so long ago, all of us pressing our hands into time. Except I wasn't, because a wave came and took my handprint away.

The water looked like it went on forever, like there was nothing out there except the beach I was standing on and all that water. I saw a drone video once, of one of those sad whales going around and around its theme park, dying a little more with each circuit. Which was crazy when you thought about how much water was out there in the ocean.

"Do you got money?"

I spun around. It was one of the homeless women I'd walked past. She was wearing mismatched sneakers. I reached into my pocket and pulled out my wallet, gave her all my money. For some reason. She stood there counting it like she was making sure I'd given her the correct amount. Then she nodded like I'd gotten it exactly right. "Seventeen dollars, that's right," she said. She hesitated. "Did you want . . . something? I have a tent." I mean, how do you end up in a place where you'll do anything to anybody for money? For drugs. For seventeen dollars. For a few pills—was that what Lee had gotten?

"Uh, no thanks," I said.

"Thank you, mister." She walked a couple of steps, stopped, and turned around. "Come back to the beach anytime!" Then she rushed off like I might change my mind and "want something."

I turned back to the waves. I suddenly felt like my insides were burning, and I thought about how way more American guys had killed themselves or overdosed or been murdered in the last five years than had died in World War II. We'd been in a war these last few years, but nobody had bothered to tell us.

SIXTY-ONE

Over the next few days I called Su-Bee probably twenty times. She never called back, and I knew she never would. Which I totally got: the spell had been broken and couldn't be fixed. Lee's parents had told mine that Lee had already been cremated and that there was going to be a memorial for him at their home later in the week. They wanted me to be one of the people who said a few words. I sat on the front steps the night before trying to figure out what I should say. A lot of bugs out there! Mosquitoes, moths, crickets. Spiders. The moon was just a crescent. I imagined my dad out in the night in Iraq under the crescent moon, wondering what came next.

Couldn't figure out what I should say at the memorial—was I speaking to Lee, or was I speaking to his parents? I pushed words around in my head while Kiiro slept on the welcome mat. Trying to think of what Lee would want me to say, I came up with nothing and ended up sleeping only a couple of hours before showering.

In the morning my grandparents came over to babysit Joshie. My parents and I and Kiiro walked through a light drizzle to Lee's house. I felt like I needed Kiiro with me. It was raining pretty hard by the time we arrived, our dress clothes wet.

Mrs. Fang was sitting in the big back den clutching the urn, bent over like her back hurt. Even when my mom went to hug her, she held on to the urn with one arm. Mr. Fang's brow was furrowed as he watched his wife seemingly without understanding anything at all. Like he was confused, thinking, *What are we doing here?* Su-Bee was staring into nothingness.

There was a little microphone, and there was a pastor who was a friend of the family. He talked for a while about heaven and love. And moving on after someone so young dies and how to move on and what happens after you move on. He quoted from the Greek poet Aeschylus: "In our sleep, pain which cannot forget falls drop by drop upon the heart until, in our own despair, against our will, comes wisdom through the awful grace of God."

Then we turned down the lights and watched slides of Lee on a screen. There was a soundtrack of music—I knew only one of the songs: "These are the days of miracle and wonder . . . and don't cry, baby, don't cry." Grandma used to sing that to me when I was sad, and after Joshie was born, I sometimes heard her singing it to him.

We saw Lee as a baby on a blue quilt. Lee playing baseball while wearing glasses held to his head with a black band. Lee opening Christmas presents. I closed my eyes but saw the bright red blood dribbling down his face—I quickly opened my eyes again and saw a picture of Lee jumping on the diving board out back. Then him and me in suits for a school dance. Su-Bee was photobombing us from the side.

Mrs. Fang wailed in the background. The music got low, and the pastor asked for speakers.

Su-Bee went to the microphone, looking frightened. Then her eyes touched mine, but she quickly looked away. She was wearing her glasses, and her eyes were swollen. She glanced at her parents before speaking softly to the urn. "Lee, everybody could have done better. We're going to start all over, because it's what you would want. I'm sorry I wasn't there for you. I—I should've realized that if I was scared of you, then something was very, very wrong. I could've done more." She glanced away, then back to the urn. "I just wanted to say that sometimes I was jealous of you, because you were smarter than me. I remember exactly all the times. I kept a diary. I was jealous all during seventh grade. And again for a few months in ninth grade. And even for a while in tenth. I did some really mean things that I've never told anybody about. I'm the one who dented the top of your laptop. And other stuff. I guess I just wanted to get that off my chest, because I never told anyone except . . ." Her eyes lowered, then raised again. "And now I miss you so bad. So, so bad." She closed her eyes tightly and kind of staggered back to her seat, sobbing.

Like I said, she had dark parts inside her but had gotten through it. I felt a pang, felt like we coulda had a real thing that would've gone on and on. But the spell: broken now and forever. I understood that.

A few more relatives spoke. Then Mrs. Fang turned to me and said, "Elijah? You were the last to see him . . ." Alive.

Kiiro followed me to the microphone, barked once, and lay down at my feet. I tried to think what to say.

I'd already lied to the police. That is, I didn't lie, I omitted. But now I looked at the eager eyes of Lee's parents. At Su-Bee, who was weeping. At my parents, who I'd been such a disappointment to. I think everybody in the world except Joshie and my dog thought I'd been a disappointment.

I searched my brain for words, then spoke directly to Mr. and Mrs. Fang. "He . . . He didn't want to hurt you. I know you're thinking he hurt you the most a parent can be hurt. But there was another way he could have hurt you more." I said that last sentence uncertainly, because I could see it wasn't true. I could see his parents would rather be dead themselves than know their son was dead.

I tried again: "That last day he talked about going to Duke. He was the smartest guy I knew. But, you know, he got caught up in stupid shit, uh, stupid stuff, because, like, he got knocked off the road. He got knocked off the road so hard. And . . . all I can tell you is that you have a beautiful daughter, and she's *beautiful*. So . . . you still have that. And you got those pictures of him as a kid, and those are really cool. And I know he loved being a kid. He loved his swimming pool. He said it was a lot of fun having that pool. He had a perfect childhood. But he got a little older and got knocked off the road, all right? He didn't fall off, he got knocked off. I mean, the world just swatted him off the road. And he was a good guy. He was fucking heroic, pardon me for saying it that way. He was heroic, because he fell off the road, and he was lying there by the side of the road, and the last thing he thought of before he died was everything you'd both done for him. That was the exact last thing he thought of, because it was everything to him."

I could see everybody's blank faces. But I was satisfied that I'd said my piece.

And then I felt exhausted, like I had to get out. But to be

polite I stayed until the snacks started—is there a more official name for them?

Su-Bee had disappeared, and I headed to her room to see if she was there. At her door I knocked softly. I could hear music and opened the door. She was dancing maniacally to music, like she wanted to sweat out the sadness. She was right there, but I could feel that she was in her own world, which was now very far away from mine. I hesitated, said, "Su-Bee?"

She turned suddenly, gaped at me for a moment before turning down the music. "I can't" was all she said.

I reached into my pocket, took out what I'd brought for her: my leftover prize money and all her change I'd picked up. "This is yours," I said, setting it on her bureau. I'd also brought the little good luck cat to return, but right then I decided to hold on to it.

I left, trudging out the front door and to the beach with Kiiro. He ran happily ahead. His old name had been Cooper, but I changed it when I got him. I remembered with pride how he'd learned his new name the very first time I used it.

I sat on the rocks depressed out of my mind. Because I saw the thing. Your teachers aren't gonna help you. Your therapists aren't gonna help you. The recovery centers aren't gonna help you. Your parents would help you, but they don't know how. My parents couldn't help me through my life any more than I would ever be able to help Joshie through his. I would be there for him, for sure, I would fight for him forever. But I couldn't get him through his worst days. I could try, but ultimately, he would have to do it himself. Like I had to.

Because like I said, when you fuck up, it's all yours.

I remembered something my grandpa had said. I asked

him if being in the Vietnam War had made him a better man. He said no, but that later, thinking about the things he had seen made him make himself a better man. In other words, yes.

And then as I sat there, I realized someone was nearby. I turned around—it was my dad at the top of the stairs leading to the beach. Had he followed me? He yelled out, "You okay, Elijah?"

"I'm good," I yelled back. He nodded and started to walk away but stopped.

He waved almost shyly and called out, "If you need to talk about things, I'm always here." He hesitated, started to walk off again.

I closed my eyes, assuming he'd left, but then I heard noise and turned around, and it was him, but right next to me.

He sat down for a moment, not talking. Then he took out his phone and said, "I've been meaning to show you this. I guess you could say it's a historical photograph." And he opened up a photo album on his screen, and the first picture was a guy sitting on the ground. He had a few bloody shreds where his right arm should have been. And his face was kinda gone. "This is my buddy Russ. We called him Rusty. We had a pact that if either of us got hurt so bad that he wanted to die, we would shoot the other one dead. Our other buddy had a camera and took this picture of him. Rusty couldn't talk that well, because his lips were gone, but he said, 'Do it to me, Pal. Like we promised.'" I knew Pal had been my dad's nickname in Iraq.

We both paused. Then I asked, "Did you?"

"Of course not. I didn't even lift up my rifle."

"But you promised. What if he had a shitty life after that?"

"Yeah . . . I thought about it as I stood there. Maybe if he'd been injured even worse, I would have. Like legs and arms all gone. Maybe I would have. If it was worse, for sure I would've at least lifted up my rifle."

It felt like the realest conversation I'd ever had with my dad. I totally wouldn't have understood a week ago, but I felt like I was a different person now. So I suddenly got it: You had to make brutal decisions in war. Depending on circumstances, you had to kill men and sometimes women and kids, and maybe even your good friend. It made me think I should've beat the crap out of Banker. Maybe I should've even tried to beat some sense into Lee! I should've told Lee's parents to take him somewhere far away. I never even got around to telling Lee we oughta go to Prague in the spring. I'd learned that was how some people got clean, just moved away from where the battle was.

"How come you never talk about him? Is he still your friend?"

"Yeah, he called me one day after we'd been stateside for a year and asked me to come to South Dakota and help him build up a business running an adult ice hockey league—he loved hockey. And I did. I stayed in his apartment for a year, and we built up his hockey business. It's doing really well. And he has three kids now." He paused, his eyes glazed over. "I'd been dating your mom, and she waited for me to get back. That's how I knew she was the one."

I bit back tears. Then I kind of laughed. "Did she make carrot cake back then?"

He laughed. "Nah, that started when you were about three." Dad's eyes were far away, maybe in another country in another time. "He fought for it," Dad said urgently. "He fought for his life harder than anyone I've ever known." He paused. *"He inspired me.* I woulda stayed there five years to help him. I woulda spent the rest of my life in that cold, dirty-ass apartment to help him, as long as he wanted to fight for it."

He pinched his lips together, and then my dad started crying. I'd never seen him cry. I hadn't even known he *could* cry. "Sometimes life sucks, bud. And then you make it better. And then you make it good. I guess I was trying to protect you from the parts that suck. That's what I worked so hard for, to protect you and Joshie. But maybe I shoulda been around more. Maybe that would've been better. But the house, the better schools . . . It's hard to know what's right."

"Dad, you—you're the best dad!" Now I started crying. "I let everyone down."

He didn't deny it. "Next time you'll know better. Don't forget that. There might be a next time, and you'll have to do better if there is. I believe you will do better."

I nodded yes. "I *will* do better," I said. I paused, then blurted out, "But there's demons. I'm kind of scared of them." I was still crying, snot running down my face.

"I know, Elijah," he said. "I promise you I know. Shit's scary. You wouldn't believe how scared I got sometimes when the shooting started. But you keep going. In these moments you gotta be all in. You gotta want dominion over everything in your path." He added, "*You're* going to keep going too"—as if he thought maybe I was thinking of doing what Lee did.

I was really slobbering now. I felt grateful that I hadn't screwed up my life so bad that nobody at all loved me anymore. There was always that. Then I had the thought that people had loved Lee too, and look how he ended up. I had too—loved him, that is. The great and powerful Fang, boy genius, my buddy.

SIXTY-TWO

I sat in our backyard one cold February night with Kiiro, a couple of weeks after Lee died. I never had gotten around to telling Obaachan that I didn't wear sweaters, so she'd sent me three. I had one on. She really loved me and Joshie. That was why I wanted to wear the sweater. It felt good. I might even have worn it during the day if it didn't have FLAME FLAVOR written on it in ice-cream cones, with flames where the ice cream should be. WTF?

I thought about Kiiro and Joshie. Joshie's kind of—he's kind of high-energy and kind of oversensitive. He was gonna grow up someday. I guess I needed to turn myself into a good big brother before he did that. In case he needed advice or something when he was out on his own maybe being oversensitive.

And Kiiro, he's pretty much perfection in a dog. He's got those beautiful wide eyes and hair that's still yellow and thick. He's intense about everything. If you throw a ball, it's the most important thing that ever happened to him. It's the clarity I was talking about before. I wanted that.

So how could I, Elijah, with everything I now knew, get the kind of clarity that they had and that I once had?

I thought about Priscus, the historian. Back in his day, more than fifteen hundred years ago, he was writing the history of now. *His* now. But first he had to go out and see what was out there.

The sky was overcast, so you couldn't really see the stars, like it used to be in Lombard at night. Do you know how it is if you live in the city? You can see a few stars, the moon, a couple of planets. But you don't really get the full effect of the sky. Somehow, though, that seemed just right—it seemed like, um, is it called a "metaphor"? Because that's where a lot of us guys are right now. We can't see the stars. And we want to play four square, and we like being better than you at it. Some of us like beating the *crap* out of you in four square. We want to be *all in*. And some of us want to design our own lives. So what?

There was a rustling in some bushes, and Kiiro took off, racing toward the noise. The most important thing in the world to him was to find out what that noise was. And there, under the faded night sky, I just suddenly really, really wanted to know: What else is out there? Besides the homeless and the addicts, besides the murders and the suburbs, besides the rich and the poor and the overdoses and the waves, *what's out there*?

Kiiro came and lay near me, and in that moment I knew that I was now the most important thing in the world to him. Like I said, that's dogs for you.

But this story is not dedicated to the dogs, and it's not even dedicated to my family. It's dedicated to my homies. I wish you happiness. You know? I didn't save Lee. I should have. But here's what I'm gonna do.

I'm gonna find what's out there and write the history of now—*our* history. It's my only life, and I'm gonna fight for it.

It's what guys have always done. We fight for things, and we figure things out. We build worlds. We bop each other in the head like me and my cousins, just because we feel like it.

You know who I'm gonna do all this for? For Lee. For Lee's parents. For my family. For my dog. For Martin's parents. For myself. For Su-Bee. And for you, boys, mostly I'm gonna do it for you. I'm gonna ride my bike across the country and tell you what's out there for us. I swear to God, I'm going to do just that.

And, guys: If you ever got any questions, hit me up.

Acknowledgments

Lately it's been feeling a little like the end of history, or like a line I remember someone saying about Chekhov's stories: nothing happens in some of these stories, except one world ends and another begins. So how do you thank people at such a time? Nonetheless one must try.

From Simon & Schuster, thank you to my great editor, Caitlyn Dlouhy. Who would've thought all those years ago in grad school (when we were young and the country still somehow felt young as well) that someday we'd be working on our eleventh book together? Surely this was our most difficult, but it strikes me as hopeful for the world, and our friendship, that we could get through that. Thank you always and forever to the sublime Justin Chanda; Jeannie Ng, who seems like she should be my sister or cousin or something; the glorious design department; and the salespeople who make it all happen in the real world. (The day after I won the Newbery, a salesman said something to me, like, "That's not bad, but what's next?" And I told Caitlyn later what a tough audience the salespeople were. I guess that's one reason I love them so much.)

Thank you as well to the generous Alex Tsuchiyama and the

always-wonderful Reiko Lee for advice and corrections for the chapter in Japan; the brilliant Luigi Warren for sharpening up some scenes and inspiring me to make further cuts; Markham for mountain bike advice; and the talented copyeditor Cindy Nixon. Also, thank you to the final, very thorough, very smart readers Alexandra Rakaczki, Kaitlyn San Miguel, and Miloni Vora.

About the Author

Cynthia Kadohata won the National Book Award for *The Thing About Luck* and the Newbery Medal for *Kira-Kira*. She's also the author of many more critically acclaimed teen and middle grade novels, including *Checked*, *A Million Shades of Gray*, *A Place to Belong*, *Weedflower*, *Half a World Away*, *Cracker!: Best Dog in Vietnam*, *Saucy*, and *Outside Beauty*. She lives in California. Visit her online at cynthiakadohata.com.